"SO DARNED GOOD YOU'RE GOING TO READ IT, ENJOY IT, TALK ABOUT IT!"
—Pittsburgh Post-Gazette

"Are you ready for a well-told story, about people you'd like to invite to your home? . . . This is a book to laugh over, a book to make you think the world really has nice people, a book to keep and to reread . . . the story, the characters, the writing is something to cherish and to remember for a long time."
—Fort Worth Press

"A sort of *Catcher in the Rye* out West."
—Library Journal

"A novel of consequence." —The New York Times

Red
Sky at
Morning

a novel by
Richard Bradford

PUBLISHED BY POCKET BOOKS NEW YORK

POCKET BOOKS, a Simon & Schuster division of
GULF & WESTERN CORPORATION
1230 Avenue of the Americas, New York, N.Y. 10020

Published by arrangement with J. B. Lippincott Company
Library of Congress Catalog Card Number: 68-11373

ISBN: 0-671-83695-1

First Pocket Books printing June, 1969

24   23   22   21   20   19

POCKET and colophon are trademarks of Simon & Schuster.

Printed in the U.S.A.

For Julie and Tom

Red
Sky at
Morning

WE WERE USING the old blue china and the stainless steel cutlery, with place mats on the big oval table and odd-sized jelly glasses for the wine. The good stuff was all packed and stored, and the Salvation Army was due the next day for the leftovers. My mother called this last dinner a picnic, but she didn't wear her overalls to it. She had on the blue hostess gown with the purple flowers.

Dad looked four sizes smaller in his newly delivered summer uniform, and the tight stock collar was giving him trouble. He kept swallowing and twisting his neck. The two and a half stripes looked good, though; they made a nice contrast with Jimbob Buel's civilian seersucker. He was holding a glass of my father's Tavel rosé, looking at the candlelight through the wine, the perfect Virginia connoisseur. He was probably thinking a seventeen-year-old snot like me was too young to know its virtues.

Well, I do know its virtues, Jimbob boy. Paul and I knocked off a bottle of it just last week, warm, a refined accompaniment to cornbread and beef cracklins.

Courtney Ann Conway squeezed my leg under the table. "Ah bet you'll be sorry, leavin' Mobile with all the pawties and all comin' up." I didn't answer right away. I was figuring how to get Jimbob into the Bankhead Tunnel, and pump a little mustard gas in there. If I could block the exits, and use two pumps, maybe. . . .

"Josh, are you listenin' to me?"

"I'm sorry, Corky. I know I'll miss a lot of parties, but I really have to leave town. You know: the war and everything."

"You're such a brave and manly chap," said Jimbob. "I think it's charming of you to defend your country off there in Utah, or Iowa, or wherever it is."

"Mr. Buel, I forgot you were wearing khaki. The candlelight makes your clothes look more like seersucker."

"Now, Joshua," said Mother, very sharp and offended. "That is enough of *that*. Quite enough. You've been terribly rude this evening. Mr. Buel's asthma is well-known."

"Sorry again," I said. "Sorry all around." Jesus H. Roosevelt Christ.

"Josh," said my father, "have some more ham-with-Coca-Cola-sauce. Probably the last time you'll have it for the duration." He picked up a thick slice of the nasty stuff with the serving knife and fork, and I passed my plate. Glup. Good salt-cured Tennessee smoked ham. Perfectly decent Coca-Cola from Atlanta. Put them all together, you've got Secrets from a Southern Kitchen.

Jimbob's helping himself to another glass of wine; I notice he's not eating the ham. Corky's burping, soft and low, an excellent thing in woman. I suppose the bubbles in the sauce got to her. And Amalie's sitting over there stoking it away, okra and ham on the fork at the same time, all stuck together with grits.

"I think the Navy's so romantic, Mr. Arnold. You look like a regulah ol' salt." Good for you, Cork. Even with your head full of cornpone you always say the right thing. I'll bet old Oscar Wilde is lying there in Paris right now, gnawing on his knuckles, wishing he could have made bright talk like that.

"Miss Courtney's absolutely right, Frank," said Jimbob. "You seem positively encrusted with salt. And to be a Commodore right off the. . . ."

"Commander."

". . . Commander, pardon me, right off the bat like that, why, the Navy Department must have great faith in

2

your seamanship. My family, of course, were usually Army, not nearly so fashionable."

"I'm considered a fair hand with a Dolphin-class sloop, I admit," Dad said, straightening up and looking a little keener. "It's a shame the Navy isn't using them this war. Last I heard, they'd converted to ironclads throughout."

"And rightly so, I maintain," Amalie said, poking her fork at Dad. She's been concentrating on the grits so hard she hasn't heard anything. Look at her sitting there like a big pale lady bullfrog; that concentration on the grits is paying off in fanny.

"Rightly so what, Amalie?" my father said, genuinely puzzled.

"That about the boats, with the iron on them. Much better. Didn't you say something about putting iron on boats? Well, I think it's a wonderful idea, and I'm only sorry they didn't think of it sooner. Frank, honey, would you pass me another slice of that delicious ham, and maybe a tee-ninecy spoonful of okra? Lord, Ann, I surely wish you'd give me the recipe for that delicious ham. Everytime I have it here I eat more than's good for me. Thank you, Frank. Little more grits? Thank you, honey."

"There's really nothing to it," said Mother. "The trick is, you're supposed to *warm* the Coca-Cola before you pour it over the ham. Then you just keep on basting. Lacey got it right the first time I showed her how." Yeah, she got it right, and she still cries every time she has to pour Coca-Cola over a country ham. You messed up the best cook anybody ever had, and I'm glad she's got a good job at the compass factory. They don't float that old needle in Coca-Cola.

"You do run a superlative kitchen, Miss Ann," Jimbob said. And you get a superlative amount of free victuals over here, too, don't you, Buel boy? When's the last time you missed a meal with us? Was it the time I had the mumps? Must have been. You wouldn't want to catch it and have that patrician Virginia jawline puff up. You wouldn't want somebody to safety-pin your pajama bottoms to the bed. If Grant's artillery had been a little sharper they might have hit your house and killed your

3

grandfather, and stopped the whole useless line of Buels right there. Worst mistake of the war.

We finished off the dinner with some pineapple and chopped marshmallow, a grand old recipe Mother had found in the *Girl Scout Cookbook,* while Dad explained that he wouldn't be put in full command of the Pacific Fleet until he got a few weeks of seasoning and some training in Care of the Uniform, How to Salute, and Spitting into the Wind.

Mother pressed the little button with her toe while we were having coffee, and Paul came in. "Call Lacey in, too, Paul," Mother said. This was Mother's big surprise, a $10 bill for each of them, token of the affection and loyalty, etc. etc. etc., and we certainly were going to miss them when we set up housekeeping in Sagrado, etc. etc. etc., and we'll be coming back to Mobile as soon as the war's over etc. etc. etc., and their old jobs will be waiting for them if the defense plants don't inflate the economy, etc. etc. etc., and be sure to write.

I don't know how Paul and Lacey faked those happy smiles and sounded so grateful. Dad had slipped them a $500 check that afternoon, and a letter with the lawyer's name and address so they could get more if something happened to their jobs. But they beamed and wailed and carried on, and said Mother was "a real lady," and all of that, on top of the ham, just about did it for me. One more minute and someone would have to help me from the room. We all clapped for Mother, with Dad clapping the fiercest of all, the hypocrite. He gave me a great wink when nobody was looking.

After dinner they settled down to a last bridge game at a fortieth-of-a-cent a point, which meant that on a really exciting night maybe a dollar and a quarter changed hands. I never learned the game. Paul taught me seven-card stud, and that was enough for me. Corky asked if she could watch because it mus' be fascinatin' to be able to play such a stimulatin' cawd game, and I went out to the kitchen.

Lacey was doing the dishes, and Paul was drying, packing them away in a box for the Salvation Army. She

4

had tear streaks on her dark face, as she always had when she'd been laughing hard.

"What are you two going to do with those big old ten-dollar bills?" I asked. "That's a lot of money for a couple of childish darkies."

Paul whooped and almost dropped a cup. Lacey turned on me and said that if I ever told my mother about the money Mr. Arnold gave them she, Lacey, would kick my butt clear to Pensacola.

"I'd like to be able to tell her something," I said. "I think she's afraid you're going to buy a two-dollar Iver-Johnson thirty-two-caliber Saturday Night Special and shoot a policeman with it. As a matter of fact, I think that's what she wants you to do."

"I'm going to give my ten dollars to Reverend Father Muzzo," said Lacey. "He's had his eye on a new pipe organ for a couple of years now."

"If it's all right with you, I'll tell her you're thinking of getting a half-dozen bottles of hair straightener and a pair of red high-heeled shoes. It would put her mind more at rest."

"Be better if she did," Paul said. "Every spare dime she gets she gives it to the mackerel-snappers. I should have married a nice Methodist girl when I had the chance. They save their money."

"I think Mother wants you to sing later, Lacey. Will you?"

"I might as well. It's the last time. You know, I have to tell about that singing every time I go to confession? Reverend Father says it's not a big sin, but I keep adding 'em up."

"You want a little drink of your father's wine?" Paul asked. "Me and Lacey popped the cork on a real good one, nice and sweet. Tastes kind of like muscat, but smoother. I'll get it out of the icebox."

Paul and I each had half a jelly glass of Château Yquem, 1934. As he said, it was nice and sweet, but a little too sticky for my taste. Lacey gave me a roasted coffee bean to chew on, for breath, and I went back to the living room.

"Two clubs," Dad was saying. "I personally give this

hand to Adolf Hitler, and if he can play it I'll cede the British Isles to the son of a bitch."

"Frank," said Mother, "the rules on bidding are clear, and that's illegal."

"As far as I'm concerned," Amalie said, "that's a plain little old two-club bid. If he's talking in code I don't know it."

I saw that Corky's blue eyes were beginning to mist over with boredom, so I invited her out to the arbor, the most romantic arbor in Mobile, full of gardenias and Russian olives and oleanders and azaleas. "Come on," I said to her. "I have something to show you."

"What?"

"A dead cat on the end of a string. Come on. I'll let you swing it yourself."

She shivered, but she came along.

"Lucky fellow," said Jimbob, with that nasty smirk.

It was hot and still in the garden. All the lights of Mobile were bouncing off the clouds and coming back orange. Corky took deep breaths as we walked toward the arbor, and said the gardenias smelled heavenly. To me, gardenias smell like a big pot of boiling sugar, or a hot cookie.

"They sure do," I said.

"Do they have gardenias out there in the mountains where you're going?"

"I don't think so," I said. I couldn't remember. "They have piñon trees, and aspens, but they don't smell like much of anything." What a dumb conversation.

"Will you miss me?"

"Sure I'll miss you." But will you miss me? You'll miss me for about ten minutes, until old Bubba Gagnier starts taking you out in that leaky catboat of his, and giving you that stuff about his old man's eighteen hundred acres of loblolly pine in Sumter County.

"You think I'm a good dancer?"

"You're a great dancer, Cork. I don't know how you stand dancing with me. How do your toes feel now, by the way?" I'd stomped on her that past Saturday.

"You didn't hurt me one little bit. Besides, it wasn't your fault. Somebody shoved you." I'd heard toe bones cracking, and she'd limped through two foxtrots, a waltz and the Conga.

We sat in the arbor swing. I said, "Corky, I'll really miss you," and put my arm over her shoulder. I knew right away it was a mistake, because she was wearing a skimpy sun dress and her shoulders were just as sticky as her hands. I took a deep breath and kissed her, and we held on without breathing for a count of forty-three, Alabama style. During the count, I waited for the earth to move, as Mr. Hemingway suggested it might, but there was no action, as usual.

We took deep breaths and kissed some more. Courtney Ann Conway always closed her eyes. Several other girls at Point Clear Day School closed their eyes, although I never mentioned that to Corky. I kept mine open and unfocused, and she appeared to have four closed eyes. Then I crossed mine, and her right eye seemed to drift across the bridge of her nose and land somewhere above her left eye.

She let me put one hand down the top of her sun dress. It was a tight fit, and very clammy work in all the heat. The swing was moving, all right, but the earth was just sitting there.

The screen door opened, and Paul stuck his head out. "You all better come in, Josh. Your mother says come on. Lacey's going to sing."

Courtney Ann said, "Shoot."

I worked my hand out of her dress. It was really sweaty, and I wanted to dry it off on my pants leg, but that wouldn't have been good manners.

Dad and Jimbob were sitting on the big sofa. Mother was playing chords, and Amalie was standing by the piano at her left, ready to turn pages if there were going to be any pages to turn. Lacey was standing in the curve of the piano, blushing through her dark skin and saying, as usual, that she sounded like a bullfrog. That wasn't true; Lacey had a high, strong sweet soprano. She just didn't like to sing Protestant songs.

This whole singing business had started about three years before, when a marine architect from Connecticut came to our house and mentioned that the only thing he liked better than a yar hull was listening to spirituals. Mother told him we had a colored woman working for us, and all colored women could sing, so she called Lacey out and asked her if she sang at church. Lacey said she sometimes hummed along with the choir, especially on "Stabat Mater." The Little Flower of Jesus Catholic Church had an all-white choir.

"Do you know 'Swing Low, Sweet Chariot'?" the man from Connecticut asked her.

"No, sir."

"You know 'Deep River'?"

"No, sir."

"Lacey, don't be silly," said Mother. "All of your . . . everybody knows those songs. They're traditional."

That night we taught Lacey two verses and the chorus of "Swing Low, Sweet Chariot," and the man from Connecticut said her heart might be with Rome, but she sang like a Baptist.

The next day I drew a month's allowance in advance and bought Lacey a copy of "One Hundred Twenty Negro Spirituals, arranged for Soprano, Alto, Tenor, Bass," and we picked out the tunes on the piano together. Lacey learned to sing "Hold On," and "Sweet Li'l Jesus Boy," and "Joshua Fit de Battle ob Jericho," and "Ain' Gwine Study War No Mo'," and "Dry Bones," and ten or twenty others, and every Saturday she went to confession and laid her soul bare about backsliding.

On this last night, we started off with "Swing Low," and Lacey sang it just the way Mother liked, with lots of sliding up to notes and putting blues catches in her voice, which she'd learned by listening to my Bessie Smith records, and Amalie helped her by squawking out what she thought were African Baptist exclamations during the dotted notes:

LACEY
Swing low, sweet chariot
Comin' for to carry me home

AMALIE
Sweet, Jee-eee-sus!

8

LACEY
Swing low. . . .

AMALIE
Ha' mercy!

LACEY
. . . sweet chariot
Comin' for to carry me home.

AMALIE
Hallelujah!

Every time Amalie let out a howl Dad winced, but Mother and Jimbob and Corky just beamed and congratulated themselves on their appreciation of the genuine, right-from-the-belly, folk music.

Lacey sang till eleven, and then she and Paul had to catch the last bus across town. We gave each other hugs, and I cried and Lacey cried, and Paul told me to stay out of the wine and to write to them if I could think of something to say that wasn't childish. When they left I walked Corky to her house around the corner, kissed her good-by, and went home.

2

IT WAS STILL HOT and damp when I went to bed, and the sheets were gummy. The usual lone mosquito whined around the room, waiting to pounce and drink a little blood. The room was empty and spooky, with nothing in it but my suitcase and the big tester bed.

I thought about Sagrado, and how cool it would be there, even in summer, but I was going to miss Mobile and the lumpy old house and Paul and Lacey and those

Swedes at the shipyard and sailing on the Bay and swimming on Santa Rosa and even old Corky, with those hands like a pair of warm oysters.

Someone knocked on my door, which startled me, because people usually just busted right in. I said, "Come in," and the big carved door swung open. In the light from the hall I could see it was Amalie Ledoux, carrying her bourbon and water and blinking her eyes.

Nobody had ever mentioned it right out to me, but I understood that twenty years before, when Dad first came down from Baltimore with his new degree in Marine Engineering, a couple of good ideas, and a chinchy bank loan, it had been a sort of tossup between Amalie and Mother, the acknowledged belles of the season. Even in those funny 1924 flat-chested dresses they had been knockouts. Amalie had looked fresh and rosy and jolly, then. Maybe Dad could read her bone structure the way he could read a marine blueprint, and prophesy that her stern would begin to draw more and more water, and her prow would thicken enough to impair her headway. I don't know. He married Ann Dabney Devereaux, anyway, the one the young men brought punch to and opened windows for, and Mother's lines were trim as ever while Amalie, as he put it, had become "beamy, deep and able."

"Where's your light switch, Josh?" Amalie said, groping around.

"It's on the other wall, on the other side of the door. The architect had a great sense of humor."

"It's just too much bother in all this heat." She closed the door and slid her feet over the floor until her knees bumped against the bed. "May I sit down here on the side of your bed?"

"Sure," I said. "Plenty of room. Me and the Dionne quintuplets could fit in here, with space left over for a couple of half-hounds."

"My," Amalie said, taking a pull at her bourbon, "that sounds like quite a scene." She sat on the edge of the bed and the mattress tipped way over to her side.

"You're going to miss your house, aren't you? This beautiful old place."

10

"I'll live through it, Amalie. We'll be back as soon as the war's over."

"Well, I promise I'll rent it to some real nice people who'll take care of it. When you all get back from the West it'll be just like it was. Everything will be just like it was."

"Amalie, can I have a sip of your drink?"

"Why, sure, honey. It's real weak anyway." She handed me the glass, and patted my knee through the sheet when I took it. "I didn't know you were a bourbon drinker."

"I'm not, really," I said, "but it's hot up here. The water out of the tap's warm." As I drank, I could taste her lipstick on the glass, like strawberries.

"That little Courtney's a cute girl," Amalie said. "Did you say good-by to her properly. Or, uh, improperly?"

"I kissed her, and told her to stay off Bubba Gagnier's catboat while I'm gone."

"That sounds terribly proper to me."

"Either way, she'll probably be crewing for Bubba inside a week, and sticking cleats in the wrong grommets."

"Doing what for Bubba?"

"Crewing. Aw, come on, Amalie, you know what I mean. Helping out on the boat."

She swallowed the last of her drink and stood up, smoothing down her dress. "May I kiss you good-by, Josh?"

"Okay," I said. "Sure." Always the continental lover. I knock the ladies over with my epigrams.

She leaned over and kissed me right on the mouth, and we breathed a little bourbon on each other. Then she patted my leg, and squeezed. "You take good care of your mama out there, hear? Maybe I'll come see you." She walked to the door and opened it. The light from the hall didn't do her a bit of good.

I lay in the hot dark and thought about the Bay, and how it smelled on an April day with a ten-knot breeze from the north. There wasn't any sailing water at all in Sagrado, not even a good-sized river. Dad didn't have to send us out there to the boondocks. That stuff about how

11

showy it was to keep two houses running in wartime made a little sense, but his other reason—that Grand Admiral Doenitz was probably going to order Admiral Raeder to sneak up the Bay in U-Boats and shell the Semmes Hotel—that was crazy. I think he just wanted us out of here, for private reasons.

It was just too hot to sleep, so I got out of bed, turned on the wall light and lay on the carpet to do push-ups, which sometimes help. There was a mark on the floor where my faithful, genuine horsehair rocking horse, Skipper, had stood for years. He belonged to the Orphans' Home now. As I did the push-ups I said, in rhythm: "Good-by, old Skip, I'm a-leavin' Cheyenne."

I didn't hear Dad come in, but when I'd done about thirty-five, and was about poohed out, he put his foot in the small of my back and like to scared me to death.

"Boy, you are really out of your head. I have raised me up a genuine imbecile, with documents to prove it."

"I was just doing some push-ups," I said. "You do push-ups sometimes."

"I don't very often do them at one o'clock in the morning, with a belly full of ham and a snootful of sauternes. And I don't recite poetry to myself."

"What sauternes?"

"That white wine you and Paul polished off was a sauternes. I gave it to Paul, but I don't recall making you any offers. Did you like it?"

"It was a little sweet."

"Well, that's good to hear. Maybe there'll be some left for Papa when he comes back from the wars. That stuff's expensive, and the French are shipping it all to Hermann Goering these days. Why don't you get up off the deck and get back in bed?"

"Can't I just lie here on the old rug?"

"What you really ought to do is take a shower. You have that locker-room smell."

So I went into the bathroom and took a shower, standing up in the high, old tub with lion's feet, that Paul had gilded for me. Nothing like gold claws under your tub to make you feel like the Emperor Solomon J. Nero.

Dad was smoking a cigar when I came out, dry from

12

the shower but starting to sweat some more from the heat. He wasn't sweating, and he was wearing a tie. He told me once that it wasn't in the nature of a Dane to sweat unless the going really got tough, and the going didn't get tough that often. I've seen him sweat twice. Once, in a Manta-class race in the Gulf, south of Dauphin Island, the wind changed sixty points to everyone's surprise and he had to fight a jibing boom with his bare hands. He had sweat all over his upper lip that time. The other time was when I got my scar. I was six, and horsing around by myself with a poker in the living room. I'd picked up a little swordplay from the movies, and I was giving the old thrust and parry to the coals in the fireplace. I'd gallop across the waxed floor, stick the poker in the coals, and say, "Die, Saracen pig!"

My last thrust was a little off balance. I skidded on the floor, got the poker jammed in the grate, and hit my head on the cinder guard. It was a good clonk, and they say I was out for an hour. But when I hit the floor, a loose coal was under my head, glowing. It was Lacey who smelled burning meat, and she knew something was wrong, because she was cooking redfish that day.

I woke up at the hospital, with a hole in my temple the size of a Franklin half-dollar. The first thing I saw was Dad, sweating on his upper lip, his forehead, and even under the arms of his shirt. After the graft took, and all I had to show was a round, discolored spot, he claimed I'd smelled like a very poor grade of hamburger, but he didn't fool me. He'd been sweating.

"You feeling better, Josh?"

"I didn't feel bad in the first place. I was just doing a few push-ups."

"So you told me. Well, you smell better, anyway. Here . . ." He offered me his cigar. "You want a smoke, too?"

"I don't smoke. Not even in secret. It's bad for my wind."

"I see. But they serve Château Yquem at the Point Clear training table, I suppose. When you do start smoking, and I give you two years, maybe three, you sure as

13

hell better lay off my Exquisitos. You start with corn silks, like everybody else."

"Yes, sir."

"Sit down and cool off. My God, you've got hair all over your legs. You're getting grown up everywhere but in the head."

This was just the kind of talk to make me squirm, and he knew it, so I sat there for a while and squirmed, and he puffed on the Havana and grinned. He took it out of his mouth, and looked at the tip, and then shot a left at me that caught me on the shoulder and stung down to my kneecaps.

"Hell, you'll be all right," he said. "A few more muscles and a lot more brains, and you can walk down a public street without a keeper and a shake-rag."

"Thanks."

"Don't thank me. Thank that eight-hundred-dollar-a-year school and all that fine Southern blood your mother gave you. How is school?"

"A's in World Literature, Beginning Algebra, Spanish, and Fizz Ed."

"And . . . ?"

"That's pretty good right there."

"What about History of the Confederacy?"

"C minus. I don't think I see it their way."

"Neither do I. What happened?"

"I said I thought Sherman was as good a general as Jeb Stuart."

"Anyplace else but here, that would be debatable. Don't they give any courses in tact?"

"I had a little trouble in Life Science, too. Not really trouble, but old Henlien caught me helping Courtney out with her frog. He told her to take the scalpel and separate out the tendons in the thigh, and she said she wasn't going to touch the nasty thing with a ten-foot slaughter pole. So he caught me cutting on her frog."

"Very chivalrous of you. Are you going to miss Point Clear?"

"I guess so. I'm used to it, even that lousy lunch they give you."

14

"You feel going to a public school is going to ruin your social standing?"

"I hope so."

"You'll make out. It's wartime. Everyone has to make sacrifices."

"Dad, I told you, I'm really looking forward to it. I like Sagrado, anyway, even if I haven't been there for a long time."

"We'll see if you like the winters, too. You've never seen any snow, have you?"

"No, but I hear it's cold and white."

"That about sums it up. You've been doing some research, I see."

I don't remember when we started this kind of conversation, but we've had a lot of them. The general theme is that I'm barely able to keep from drooling on my collar, and require full-time professional help so I won't injure myself through stupidity. Dad blames it all on his family, who he claims have set records for Scandinavian incompetence since the days of Leif Ericson. While Ericson was discovering Nova Scotia, he says, a dragon boat commanded by one of his own ancestors—they were named Arnulfssen in those days—got lost sailing across the Oresund Strait from Köbenhavin to Malmö, a fifteen-mile stretch of smooth water which could be navigated by a springer spaniel with a mallard in its mouth. He often spoke of Uncle Sven, who couldn't wave bye-bye until he was eighteen; of his great-grandfather, Gunnar, who was fired from his post of Village Idiot in Viborg because the quality of his work wasn't high enough; of Aunt Minna, who announced, at the age of twenty-five, that she was tired of speaking Danish because it was "too hard," and spent the rest of her life not talking at all, just pointing and gesturing and being misunderstood. It seemed to give Dad a kind of pleasure to downgrade the Arnolds. It was a relief, too, after a spell of listening to Mother or Jimbob drone on about their families.

We sat on the bed, and he told me what a dope I was, and how he wished he could find a kindly, understanding institution to put me in while he went off to the Navy.

15

"But no kidding," he said finally. "You be nice to your mother. You watch out for her. There aren't going to be any Southerners out in Sagrado to keep her feeling good, so go easy."

"Doesn't she like it out there?" I asked him. "She was out there with you almost every summer, before the war. I never heard any complaints."

He re-examined the end of his cigar. "I heard a few," he said. "It isn't that she doesn't like it there; it's just that . . . well, I suppose she gets jumpy when she's some place else. She said once that almost anywhere in the South—Natchez, Baton Rouge or Savannah, anywhere— she can always find a Devereaux or a Dabney headstone in the cemetery, and feels right at home."

I nodded, but I couldn't see getting comfort from dead relatives. "I'm a Southerner too, even if I do believe Farragut won the Battle of Mobile Bay, and not Buchanan."

"What you are," he said, "is more of a water rat. You're going with your mother because your brain needs drying out. In my opinion, there are barnacles inside your skull." Another reason for leaving, this one the feeblest yet.

He looked at his wrist watch, a heavy, complicated piece of equipment he'd bought when his commission came through. "It would give me considerable peace of mind if you got your ass in bed. We have a long drive ahead of us tomorrow." He opened the door to the hall. "You know, I'm still not sure about you. You're strong, but you read books. Are you going to be Art or Football?"

"I've been reading too many books," I said. "When I was kissing Corky tonight, all I could think about was Ernest Hemingway."

Dad shook his head. "Your great-great-grandfather Gunnar would have been proud of you. Good night."

"Good night, Commodore."

3

WHEN I WAS TWO I began to get things like Indian fire
and ringworm in the summer, on top of the prickly heat.
My father stood it for two years, and then said, "God
damn it, Ann, I'm taking Josh out of this swamp before
some hot-shot skin doctor puts him in the Carville Le-
prosarium. He's one big open sore."

He got a lot of advice from his friends, sent away for
bushels of Chamber of Commerce literature, read
weather charts, and finally decided it was a tossup between Tucson and Colorado Springs. The summer that I
was four, we drove west to look them over and decide.
Dad called Paolo Bertucci into his office and asked him
if he could handle the shipyard for a couple of months,
and Paolo said, "You want us to keep on building from
the keel up, or can I try out my idea about building from
the funnel down?" Then they fought out another episode
in their standing argument about whether Scandinavians
or Italians had a nobler maritime tradition, and whether
Ericson or Columbus discovered America. Paolo said the
squareheads sailed west looking for beer, and Dad said
the dagos sailed west looking for poontang. They decided
that Paolo could handle the shipyard for a couple of
months. As Dad was leaving, Paolo said, "There is one
thing, Frank. There's this one point I'd like you to clear
up. Does the deck go on top and the keel on the bottom,
or is it the other way around?" Dad stomped out, and

told my mother that afternoon that they'd probably be paupers when they got back from the trip west, and she'd better start learning how to use a sewing machine.

We drove around the Southwest all that summer. I don't remember the trip very well, but I recall that as soon as we got into West Texas the Indian fire and the prickly heat disappeared. Dad showed me the itinerary once: San Antonio, El Paso, Lordsburg, Tucson, Phoenix, Bountiful, Ely, Tuba City, Denver, Laramie, Butte, Ketchum, Cortez, Prescott, Albuquerque, Gallup, Taos. He scouted each recommended city thoroughly, entered a belittling comment on his list, and drove on.

It wasn't until late in August that he found the place he was seeking, and he'd never heard of it before.

We had spent two days in Albuquerque, the last major city on his list, and he was getting desperate. "Maybe they'll find something new to cure Josh's horrible diseases, something like cautery or arsenic pills. Maybe we can stay in Mobile during the summer."

"I wanted to stay there all along," my mother said. "I *like* Mobile. What's a little warm weather? And Indian fire is something all little boys and girls get. I had it. He'll grow out of it. Doctor DuBose says that tincture of iodine is still the best treatment." I began to howl along in there somewhere, remembering how the charred skin peeled off my knees after three months of iodine, so they let it drop.

My mother looked out the window of the old black Studebaker as we drove north through New Mexico. "I haven't seen one green thing all summer, Frank. Not one living green thing. Not since we crossed the Sabine River. Just dust." When we drove, she soaked small pieces of cotton in eau de Cologne and placed them on her wrists and her eyes. She hadn't seen much of anything.

"Sure, there's been some desert, but there's been some pretty country, too. Don't forget Estes Park. Don't forget the Grand Canyon. And anyway, look at Josh's knees." The state of my knees had brought about the whole trip. They'd looked at them every night, and by this time there wasn't anything to look for. They were just a pair of four-year-old knees, the knees that launched a thou-

18

sand ships. "What about it, Josh? Would you like to spend your summers out here somewhere?"

"I want to see the bears, Daddy." The only thing I really remembered about that 5,000-mile drive was a bear cub chained to a post behind a gas station, a "See the Ferocious Grizzly 25¢" bear. He was in the hot sun with nothing in his water dish and, when I filled it up for him, he went "whuffle."

"I'm sorry, Hoss," he said. He'd taken to calling me Hoss during the trip; something he picked up from a cowboy. "That bear's all the way back in Williams, Arizona."

"No, Frank. It was in Marfa, Texas," my mother said.

"That was the five-legged calf," he told her. We drove on, toward Colorado, through miles of tumbleweed. greasewood, yucca, horse skeletons, red dust and misleading signs reading "Last Chance for Water."

The ice in our water jug melted, the fine dust from the road rose from the wheels of cars ahead and settled on the windshield. Sometimes Dad would stop and slosh a little water on the windshield so he could see. When he saw the sign "Corazón Sagrado—58 Miles" pointing up a narrower road toward a distant line of blue mountains, he turned off.

"It isn't on our route," my mother said.

"The hell with it. If we keep going this way we'll dehydrate and start to crinkle like paper bags. It's probably cooler up there."

They drove that same 58-mile-long stretch of road every summer for nine years after that. The state paved it in 1940, but otherwise it didn't change. At first the road wandered through the same desert and horse skeletons, but at an arroyo, a waterless gully in which a white-faced steer was decomposing, it climbed to a plateau. No one had blasted a highway there; the road followed a natural path, doubling back on itself, skirting red pinnacles, twisting through narrow canyons as close together as the walls of a tunnel. At the top, a thousand feet or so higher, the hot, dry desert air vanished, to be replaced by air with a completely different set of qualities; mountain air, cool, fresh and joyous to breathe, as clean in its own way as a breeze from the Gulf.

Ahead of us, stretching to the foot of the mountain range, was a great pasture that sloped gently upward, a carpet for a million sheep whose clusters speckled the plain for—I measured it roughly, years later—a thousand square miles. As we topped the plateau, and my father stopped the car to let the engine cool from the climb, a boy with a herd of sheep took off his broad-brimmed hat and waved it at us. My father said, "My God!"

Across the pastureland, the road ran straight, to end in a vague patch of green at the flank of the mountain, twenty miles away. There was nothing else to indicate that there was a town there, no tall buildings, no buildings at all that we could see. The boy, dark-skinned, wearing what appeared to be his fat grandfather's clothes and a wide felt hat, stood in the center of an eddying flock of sheep a few yards from the road, and my father hailed him. "Is this the way to the town?"

The boy and a ragged-looking sheepdog walked over to the car. He smiled and the dog lay down to watch. *"Cómo?"* the boy asked.

After looking at the map again, my father pointed toward the mountain and said, "Corazón Sagrado?"

"Sí, claro," the boy said. "Vayn-tay my lace." He smiled again and whistled to his dog, who arose and went back to the sheep.

"Wonderful," Mother said. "Nobody speaks English."

"The map shows a circle with a dot in it," Dad said. "That's supposed to mean five to ten thousand population. I'll bet somebody there talks the language."

We parked beside a grassy square in the center of Corazón Sagrado that afternoon, and bought a roast chicken and some Coca-Cola. Dad spread a blanket under a tree for a picnic, and as we ate we watched a string of donkeys carrying wood. "Just like Mobile, in its way," he said. "More jackasses than people."

When we were halfway through the chicken, a big man wearing a badge walked up.

"Tourists?" he asked. "From out of estate?"

20

"Yes," Dad said.

"It's my juty to inform you that it's agains' the ragulations to sit or estand on the grass in the plaza."

"Sorry," Dad said, "we didn't know." He began to gather up the food.

"No, no," the man continued. "Jew don' have to move. Enjoy the lonch. It's only my juty to tell you. There ain' no panalty for it. Hell, Mayor Chavez, he eats his lonch here every day. That your little boy?"

"That's right. His name's Joshua."

"Oh, *Josué*," the man said, pronouncing it Ho-sway. "Me, I'm Procopio Trujillo. They call me Chamaco. I'm the shariff." He took off his hat, and we shook hands. "Jew from around sea level?"

"Mobile, Alabama."

"Jew better buy some big hats, and don' ron aroun' too much. A lot of people, they think it's nice and cool here, they go ronnin' aroun' and drop dead from the sun estroke. Estick aroun' for a while, we gonna have a fiesta after Labor Day. An' don' forgat about sitting on the grass. Jew been warned. I won' tell you more than three, four honnerd time, and then I'll clamp down. Hokay?"

Later that afternoon, after getting us a room at La Posta Hotel, Dad went to a real-estate agent and bought nine acres of land at the top of Camino Tuerto, which means One-Eyed Street. The agent said he was sorry the price was so high, but the property had a good view of the mountains. Dad said he didn't think four hundred fifty dollars was unreasonable, and could the man recommend a good building contractor?

"We don't have any real contractors here, Mr. Arnold. What we have is people who can build houses. I can recommend a man named Amadeo Montoya from up in Río Conejo, that's in the mountains. He'll build you any kind of house you want, as long as you want adobe. Adobe bricks are two for a penny. I'm sorry, the price went up last year."

I don't remember these conversations. My father told me about them later. He and mother argued for a week in the room at La Posta. Corazón Sagrado was too small, she said, too lonely and isolated. She didn't speak

21

Spanish. The town was full of Catholics. Why couldn't they spend their summers at Sea Island, like everyone else. She had to rub cold cream on her arms because the air was so dry. The streets were full of donkey manure. They'd never find anyone to play bridge with. Most of the population had dark skins. They *said* they were Spanish, but how could you be *sure?*

But he wore her down, finally, and until the war they drove in the early summer from Mobile to Corazón Sagrado when the first wet heat from the Gulf sloshed in. Dad would hand the shipyard over to Paolo, turn the car west on Highway 90 and race through the swelter until they topped the plateau and saw the sheep, the pasture land and the blue mountains. The same boy or another like him would be standing among his sheep as they drove over the top. Dad would point and ask, "Corazón Sagrado?" He knew it was the right road, but he would always ask. *"Sí, claro,"* the boy would say. "Vayn-tay my-lace." Twenty miles.

Amadeo Montoya, from Río Conejo, built three adobe rooms on our land that first year, and planted apple and peach trees. The next year he built three more rooms, planted poplars, and dug irrigation ditches. He and my father worked on it together in the summers, digging foundations, forming the big adobe bricks, plastering, setting pine beams in place, whitewashing, putting in Mexcian tile they brought up from Juarez. My mother, who had filled the house in Mobile with all the fragile and antique crap she could find, had exhausted her interest in decoration, so Dad furnished the house himself with sturdy, handmade tables and chairs, Navajo rugs, bright Southwestern paintings—many of them involving horses—and the delicate Pueblo Indian pottery from the area, that would hold anything but water. The thick-walled house seemed to grow naturally from the brown earth.

The two men worked well together, my father middle-sized and lithe, like a handball player; Amadeo like a round-headed bull. Dad could never get his Baltimore tongue around Spanish, but as the years passed he became roughly fluent in the Sagrado dialect, which was

22

full of English words. Once, before the house was finished, Dad was stirring some enamel and asked, *"Que pasó con el* paint?" Amadeo answered, *"Yo lo* diluted *con* turpentine."

My knees gradually lost their importance as an excuse for the summer house. Sagrado was my father's personal retreat, a refuge from the damp, noisy problems of a shipyard on Mobile Bay. He spoke of Sagrado as if it were the Lost City of the Incas, but it wasn't really that obscure. Tourists wandered in sometimes, usually lost; many of the residents had come to cure themselves of tuberculosis or asthma in the thin, clean air, and remained because life there was easy and undemanding.

I went there every summer until I was ten, the year I discovered the joys of catboating. After that my parents went without me, and I stayed behind with Lacey in the big house, sleeping and eating just enough to keep up my strength for sailing. There was nothing for me in Sagrado. It was two thousand miles from salt water, and the movies were always two years old.

4

I HAD BEEN AWAY from Sagrado for seven summers, but nothing had changed. Nobody had built a defense plant there, or an Army base. There was talk of something warlike going on at Los Alamos, up in the Jemez Mountains, where there had once been a rustic boys' school, but we assumed it was just another boondoggle. "They're manufacturing the front part of horses up there," Dad suggested, "and shipping them to Washington for final assembly."

The streets in Sagrado were a little pockier than I remembered, and the few cars were fewer. While Mobile was growing and spreading out, raw, new and ugly,

Sagrado protected itself, as it had for more than three hundred years, by being nonessential. That's the best way to get through a war: Don't be big and strong, be hard to find.

The Montoyas—Amadeo and his wife, Excilda—expected us. They had put fresh mud plaster on the house, swept the fine dust from inside, and put a polish on the welcoming job by thrusting sprigs of piñon through the door knocker and piecing out the message *"Bienvenidos a los Arnold"* with gravel on the doorstep.

They expected us, but they weren't there to greet us. Because they renegotiated their contract with Dad every summer that he came, it was their custom to wait a few days before the talks started. Mother had to cook during that period, and Dad had to irrigate and keep the place going. The work was tiring and the food was terrible. We were desperate for the Montoyas' help when they arrived.

Dad let me sit in on the negotiations this summer. He said I could learn some hard business sense from the bargaining, which began when he spread pink oilcloth on the big walnut outdoor table under the *portal*, set out ashtrays and Lucky Strikes, and pulled the cork on a gallon bottle of La Voragine Sweet Muscatel-Type Vino Fresno California A Family Tradition Of Gourmets Since 1934.

Amadeo and Excilda turned up in their truck on the afternoon of the third day. There were enormous greetings all around. I had grown *"casi una yarda,"* my mother was *"mas bella que antes,"* and my father was *"mas gordito y rico que nunca,"* a cunning opening shot which described him as richer than ever, and even rich enough to put on waistline.

Excilda went into the house with my mother, to tell her about the new *primos, nipotes* and *nietos*. Ordinarily, my mother loved talk of family; she came from a large and undistinguished family herself, notable for poltroonery and the seduction of minors, as it later turned out when her great-grandmother's diaries were published by the University of Alabama Press. But she always thought of them as being rich in Southern tradition. However,

24

Excilda's family chatter annoyed her; there were never any grandchildren or cousins named Ashley or Lucinda; just Osmundos and Guadalupes, Alfonsos and Violas, all suffering from infant diarrhea.

My father and Amadeo Montoya and I sat around the walnut table, and the two men cracked the jug.

"How have you been, Amadeo?" It was plainly the wrong question.

"Well, Mr. Arnold, you remember that cold spell we had back around Old Christmas. It got fourteen, fifteen below for almost a week. The Indians couldn't even open up the ditches 'cause the sluice gates were froze."

"It was nice and warm down in Mobile in January. Maybe you should have written me a letter about it. We don't get the Sagrado weather report down there."

"Well, this cold didn't hurt your house any, except for some windows cracked on the east side from some water got under the putty and froze, but up in. . . ."

"How many window panes?"

"Five or six, I forget. I got a receipt for glass from Roybal. It's somewhere in the *troca;* I can go get it in a minute."

"We'll come to that later."

"Up in Río Conejo there was this *chingao* wind that came straight out of Texas, killed two calves. They were gonna be fine calves."

"Where was that Archuleta boy that takes care of your stock in the winter? He's supposed to get your animals in the barn."

"You're right, Mr. Arnold. You're right about that, but that *cabrón* didn't show up. I think he got married."

"Married! He's only ten years old!"

"You're thinking about Epifanio. Epifanio went to live with his uncle in Arroyo Coronado. This was his brother Wilfredo, he's about seventeen. He didn't show up. He went to work for the Park Service over by Ute Mesa and had this girl with him. If it wasn't for that *chingadero* I wouldn't of lost two calves."

"You're not trying to blame me for those calves, are you? I told you to get winter help on the place in Conejo, and said I'd pay half your help's salary, didn't I?"

"Sure you did, Mr. Arnold. I didn't say it was your fault. How could you help what happens up there in Río Conejo when you're down there in Alabama on the beach watching those sailboats in the warm. . . ."

"Amadeo, wouldn't you like another glass of vino? I'm going to have one."

"*Un traguito, no más.*"

Amadeo and my father drank off a glass of wine, commenting on its smoothness and power, and silently prepared for the next round of negotiation.

"You have a real nice garden here, Mr. Arnold."

"Thank you, Amadeo. I owe much of it to you."

"Aw, well, I'm no gardener. My brother Esteban is the man who can make things grow. Me, I just slap a lot of manure on the plants and pray for a little rain in April. You know."

"A little rain in April is always a good thing, Amadeo."

"A gift from God. A true gift, because it doesn't rain much in April."

"How were the April rains this year, Amadeo?"

"There wasn't one. Not a drop. Dust blowing all the time. If you could have seen that *chingao* dust you'd have thought you were in Texas. I can still taste the dust."

"The rose trees look very good, in spite of all the dust. They should bud out very well in July. Did you water them?"

"Oh, sure. Your ditch was running sometimes. They got enough water. But it was the manure."

"The manure . . .?"

"Sure. I put a lot of manure on the roses. You know Excilda's brother-in-law, Cruz Gutierrez, got all those horses?"

"How much manure?"

"Four truckloads?"

"Are you asking me? I was down there on the beach in Alabama watching the sailboats go by."

"Make it two truckloads. Prime horse manure. Fresh. I had to wear a bandana over my face."

"Amadeo, we haven't even started on this wine. It's going to turn sour if we just sit here and look at it."

"*Una copita, nada más. Gracias.*"

"*Salud.*"

"*Salud, patrón.*"

"Now don't start calling me *patrón.* I'm not your *patrón.* Those days are gone forever, thank God."

"You said it." They drank another glass of muscatel, and noted that several minutes in the sun had baked some of the impurities from it.

"I hear Excilda telling my wife all about the new grandchildren in Conejo. How many?"

"Four this winter. Three living. Margarita's little girl died. Named Consuelo."

"Oh, I'm sorry, Amadeo. I'm very sorry. How old was she?"

"Two and a half months. Pretty little girl, *rubia,* looked almost like a *gringa.* She died in April."

"What was the matter?"

"She had the shits. Goddamn, Margarita told all the kids to boil water before they gave it to the baby, but somebody forgot. Probably Francisco, that stupid *pendejo,* but he says it wasn't him."

"You had a doctor for her?"

"Sure. Old Anchondo. He couldn't do nothing for her, but he sure sent his bill to us."

"I think your glass is empty, Amadeo. There's plenty of wine left, and if you'd just pass your glass. . . ."

"I don't think I want any more just this minute, Mr. Arnold, thank you."

The preliminary negotiations were over.

"Would you and Excilda like to work here again this summer, Amadeo?"

Amadeo thought this over very carefully, and seemed doubtful. "Gee, I don't know about that, Mr. Arnold. Roybal offered me a job for the whole year, full time, driving his *troca.* No paperwork or anything. I just drive his machine."

"Roybal doesn't pay very well; he never has."

"No, well, but he offered me thirty-five to start, five

days, half a Saturday, drive the *troca* home at night, he pays gas."

"Thirty-five! You know Roybal's never paid anybody thirty-five dollars a week in his life. Not even that dumb cousin of his that can't tell piñon from mahogany."

"He pays old Bernabe forty now. They're paying sixty up at Molybdenum, bucket man."

"Amadeo, that mine must be more than a hundred miles from Conejo. You want to drive a hundred miles twice a day?"

"No, Mr. Arnold. I don't want to, but man, sixty dollars, that's a lot of money."

"What about thirty for you, twelve for Excilda, I pay gas from here to Conejo, no Sundays? I'll let you use my gas coupons."

"I don't know. Excilda says she has to do a lot fancier cooking around here than up at home. She says it takes a lot out of her."

"Thirty-five for you, fifteen for Excilda, but by God we get *cabrito en sangre* at least once a month, from one of your own kids, and that goat better not be more than two months old."

"Thirty-five and fifteen. That only makes fifty a week, Mr. Arnold. Up at Molybdenum. . . ."

"Thirty-five and fifteen is all I can pay this year. I can always go talk to the Maldonados."

"Mr. Arnold," said Amadeo after reflection, "you think maybe your wife and my wife would like some of this good wine before it all turns to vinegar? Man, I sure hate to see this good wine go to waste."

That night, my father asked me if I'd learned any hard business sense, and I said I thought I had, but I wasn't sure.

But it was a good summer, the best summer ever, from June to August, 1944. My mother found lots of people to play bridge with at La Posta Hotel and almost forgot that she was living in a mountain town full of Catholics and dangerous people who felt, however vaguely, that Lincoln Was Right. Dad would have to report to the Navy in late August, and he said he took his commission seriously. "I'm out of shape," he said, short-

28

ly after we arrived. "They're going to run my fanny off with a bunch of callow college boys when I show up. I'd better take off some flab." We rode almost every day, or hiked—we didn't swim; there were no swimming pools in Sagrado; water was too precious—and once we made a two-week camp in the Cola de Vaca Peaks in the Cordillera, carrying all the gear on our backs.

For an old man (he was forty-one) he did pretty well. I still didn't understand why he'd insisted on joining the Navy at his age. Mother didn't understand, and neither did Paolo Bertucci. The War Production Board didn't think it was a good idea; they had told him his patriotic duty was to stay in Mobile to build landing craft and small, fast tankers with shallow drafts; but he had scurried around and snapped at people, threatened bureaucrats and finally called the Secretary of the Navy in Washington—a man named Knox—and got his commission at the same time as the Normandy invasion, an operation which employed more than a hundred of his landing craft. "You see," he told Paolo one evening in Mobile, when he'd dropped by to argue, "they're fighting the rest of the war on land. They won't be needing Arnold-made craft any more. The yard can go back to making shrimp trawlers and garbage scows. You can handle that sort of thing yourself."

"I think you're just like a little boy playing sailor," Paolo told him.

"You're right," Dad said. "I am. And don't try to stop me, or I'll put a six-pounder into your poop deck. You swab."

In August, after running me around the mountains until my nose bled every afternoon, he declared he was fit to wear the uniform. On his last day with us, my mother forewent her bridge game at La Posta and stayed home. Excilda roasted a kid, we each had a glass of Harvey's Bristol Cream before dinner, and Dad cracked a bottle of Chambertin 1934, which had probably never been drunk with goat meat before. We toasted the President, John Paul Jones and Lord Nelson. My mother refused to toast David Farragut, but I went along with it. After dinner, he telephoned Paolo Bertucci in Mobile.

"Papa's off to the seven seas," he said. "Everything going all right down there, you loathsome wop?"

"I think so," Paolo said. "We're squirting boats like a machine gun. I'd say as many as twenty-five per cent of them stay afloat when they hit the water, although they don't all float right side up."

"That's a pretty good average for a Genoese landlubber."

"I do have one question, though," Paolo said. "Some of the men asked me, and I thought I ought to check with you. When you're standing at the back part of the boat, facing toward the front of the boat, what do you call the right-hand side? Is it starboard or larboard?"

"The right-hand side is called the mizzenmast," Dad said. "You call the left-hand side the fo'c'sle. I knew we'd have a language problem if we let a dago run the yard. Maybe I ought to resign my commission and get back there."

"We'll make do without you, Frank," Paolo said. "Hell, all you ever did was get in the way. I'm already saving twenty thousand a month by using oakum instead of rivets."

"The paper said some landing craft sank halfway across the Channel on D-Day. Any idea who made them?"

"Couldn't have been us," Paolo said. "Ours don't sink; they capsize. Well, keep your powder dry, Olaf. My respects to your family. Tell Josh we always have a job for him as ship's cat."

"I wish you wouldn't let him talk to you that way, Frank," my mother said, when he reported the conversation. "It wasn't too many years ago that he was a carpenter or something."

"I'll work on the dignity angle when I get back," he said. "Right now Paolo's building boats and keeping five hundred men occupied. If I want deferential language I'll hire a butler to run the yard."

He left the next morning, wearing his new suntans. "Practice your Spanish, you ape, and be nice to people," he said. "Make new friends. Get a haircut once in a while. Don't suck your thumb. And don't get cute with your mother. A little flippancy goes a long way with her." He set his suitcase down on the gravel driveway and gazed around him, sighing. "God, I'm going to miss this country."

"I'll try not to set fire to it," I said.

"Good-by, Hoss."

"Good-by."

He got into the car with Amadeo for the long drive to the train. I went into the kitchen, where Excilda was preparing lunch.

"Can I have a *burrito?*"

"Say it in Spanish."

"Puedo yo have un burrito?"

"That's the way they teach it in school down there in Mobile, huh? Your father ought to get his money back."

"Dame un burrito, pues."

¿*"Por favor?"*

"Por favor."

Excilda gave me a *burrito.* You have to work for everything.

5

THE NIGHT BEFORE school started I did ten push-ups in my bedroom, and had to quit. With all the sky in Sagrado there simply isn't any air in it.

Next morning, when the home-room teacher called the roll, I listened for familiar names, but the only one that rang a bell was Stenopolous. There was a Doctor Stenopolous I kept reading about in *The Conquistador,* the Sagrado newspaper, who seemed to be the only obstetrician in the area and was constantly on the jump. When local news was slow, and it generally was slow, the paper would run a baby story. "Woman Gives Birth in Mayor's Office," a headline would run, or "Baby Delivered in Wagon on Load of Melons."

At the recess break I introduced myself to William Stenopolous, Jr., a chunky, brown-haired boy who looked as Greek as Eric the Red. "Call me Steenie," he said. I asked him about athletics, and he said that Helen De Crispin High School had a track team, despite the lack of breatheable air.

"We're conditioned to it," he said. "Now, you take Swenson . . ." He pointed across the schoolyard to a tall, bulgy-looking brute surrounded by girls. "Swenson's a borderline moron and a prime horse's ass, but he has a forty-seven-inch chest. He's all lung, like those Peruvian Indians that carry grand pianos up and down the Andes."

"He seems to be in good shape," I said.

"Oh, he's got a good musculature on him," Steenie went on, "and some primitive bones to hang it on. Like all Scandinavians, he tends to run to calcium. I tried to get the calipers on him once, for some skull measurements, but he threatened to pound me. My guess is, his head's solid bone down to the center of it, where there's a cavity just big enough for his pituitary gland."

"I don't want to start off on the wrong foot," I said, "but my father's a Scandinavian clear back to Sven Fork-Beard. We're not *all* idiots."

"Don't take anything I say personally," Steenie said. "I have Sagrado-itis of the mouth." Sagrado-itis is the local name for violent diarrhea. "And there are exceptions about Scandinavians. I even heard once that Ibsen was a Norwegian. I doubt it, but that's the story." He backed away and looked at me searchingly. "You from the South?"

"Mobile, Alabama."

"There's a Negro in school here, in the tenth grade. Are you going to lynch him?"

"Not unless he tries to marry my sister," I told him. "As long as he stays in his place."

"And calls you 'Boss'?"

"Well, sure."

"All right, then. We don't want racial trouble out here. And don't call him a Negro. He thinks he's an Anglo. We only recognize three kinds of people in Sagrado: Anglos,

Indians and Natives. You keep your categories straight and you'll make out all right. Do you have anything against your sister marrying an Anglo?"

"To tell you the truth, I don't even have a sister."

"Now, you see that girl over there by the cottonwood tree? The one with the knockers?" I saw her. She would have stood out in any crowd. "What would you say she was?"

"She looks like a Creole," I said.

"Arnold, you have a lot of work ahead of you. She's a Native. Her name's Viola Lopez. She speaks Spanish and English, and she's a Catholic. Don't ever make the mistake of calling her a Mexican. Her brother will kill you. Of course, if you call her a Creole she'll get confused as hell and think you mean she's part Negro—that is, part dark-skinned Anglo—and her brother will kill you again. So think of her as a Native, unless you're comparing her with an Indian. Then she's 'white.' Got it?"

"I think so," I said. "But what about the Negro?"

"I already explained that to you. He's an Anglo. That is, he's an Anglo unless you're differentiating between him and an Indian. Then *he's* 'white.' I admit he's awfully dark to be white, but that's the way it goes around here. You have to learn our little customs and folkways, or it's your ass. And if you've got any Texas blood in you, you'd better take 'spik' and 'greaser' out of your vocabulary. If there's a minority group at all around here, it's the Anglos. By the way, do you know any judo? I taught judo to a Commando class this summer."

"Aren't you a little young for that? You don't look any older than I do."

"Uncle Sam takes his talent where he finds it. There's a war on. Now, you be the Kraut and come at me with a knife." Steenie showed me some judo holds that I'd read about in *Life* magazine a year or so earlier.

"You'll learn," he said, afterward. "If the war turns against us, and we get invaded, this knowledge will come in very handy. My plan is to head up into the mountains and hold out, like Mikhailovich, harassing the enemy. I wish there was a railroad around here. I know how to blow up a railroad. You know anything about boats?"

33

"That's about all I do know anything about," I said.

"Do you know how to sink one?"

"Anybody can sink one. It's learning how to keep one afloat that's hard. My father told me once I'd foundered more catboats than anybody my age and weight. He said I hold the Southern Conference record in poor seamanship."

"Well," Steenie went on, "bad seamanship or not, it won't do you any good out here. That's the trouble. All this military talent going to waste. Sagrado is the worst place to fight a war I ever saw. You know, they've got people up there in La Cima"—he pointed to the mountains—"that don't even know there *is* a war. The last one they heard about was when the Spanish Armada got sunk. Second Punic, I think it was, or Jenkins's Ear."

"I think it was the War of the Roses," I said, "but I'm a little rusty on it myself."

"What does your old man do for a living?" he asked suddenly. "Mine runs a chain of whorehouses in Juarez. I helped him pick the girls for it this summer. Exhausting work, let me tell you."

"I thought you said you were teaching judo to the Commandos."

"That was the early part of the summer. No, really, what does he do?"

"He's a Navy officer right now," I said. "Before that he ran a shipyard. He built the *Serapis,* the *Bon Homme Richard* and *The Golden Hind."*

Steenie thought that over. "I think you're crapping me," he said finally. "It's just what I deserve."

I had lunch that first day with Parker Holmes, leaning against a mud wall behind the school and eating from our lunch boxes. Excilda had packed mine, but Mother had supervised it: sliced ham between two slices of soggy bread, no mustard. A gangly boy with ears that reached out sideways for the most subtle sounds, Parker was munching something he claimed was elkburger, "cut off from around the brisket." His father was a game warden, and brought home lots of confiscated, illegally shot meat.

"This country," Parker said, grinding his sandwich, "abounds in game. Abounds. Elk, like this here, Rocky

34

Mountain Mule Deer, bear, antelope, rabbit—both jack-
ass and bunny—grouse, bandtail pigeon, snipe, rail, gal-
linule, *gallopavo merriami* and pea fowl. We also got the
inedible, like feral dogs and pussycats, *zopilote,* fish-
eating beaver and two-stripe skunk." He waved his arms
to indicate vast populations of fauna. "A game biologist
can go ape in this country. Ape."

In the afternoon, after a clumsy speech of welcome by
the school principal, a small, pop-eyed man named
Alexander who got tangled in the microphone cord and
fell heavily, I found Steenie in the baked-mud schoolyard talking to a girl, medium-sized, slim with black hair
and fair skin. Steenie appeared to be examining her face
closely as I approached them.

"Not a blemish," she was saying. "You see? It
worked."

"I still insist," Steenie said to her, "that acne is caused
by psychiatric imbalance and not by chocolate malts.
You could have drunk six a day and still not had a
pimple. You deprived yourself for no reason."

"Well, how about this?" she said. She turned her back
to him and pulled her skirt tight against her behind. "I
didn't put an ounce of lard on it this summer. It's hard as
a rock. No, don't touch it. Take my word for it." She saw
me and smiled. "What do you think? Isn't that a pretty
behind?"

"Turn around, Marcia, and I'll introduce the front part
first," Steenie said. "Marcia Davidson, Jericho Arnold.
Marcia's old man is rector of St. Thomas's Episcopal,
but don't bother watching your language."

"It's Joshua," I said. "Jericho's where I fit the battle."

"That's a cute little scar you have," she said. "Are you
sensitive about it?"

I noticed that she had dark circles under her eyes, like
mice. "Did you get those shiners from asking rude questions?"

"No," she said. "They're functional. I've been getting
them every month since I was twelve. Steenie's been
giving me some exercises to help the cramps."

"How are they working, by the way?" he asked her.

"The cramps are better, but I still get that gicky feeling."

I knew I was beginning to turn red, and I started to get that gicky feeling myself.

"Couldn't we just talk about something else?"

"All right," Marcia said. "If it upsets you. But Steenie's my medical advisor." She said she was pleased to meet me, and walked away after shaking hands again. Her hand was cool and dry, and not gicky at all.

"Nice kid," Steenie said. "My only patient. She draws the line at examinations, of course. . . . Now, turn your back to me and bend your right arm as if you were carrying a rifle at shoulder arms. Ordinarily, I'd use a three-foot length of piano wire for this maneuver, if you were a real Kraut, but I'll let you off easy."

I turned my back and bent my arm, and he whipped his rolled handkerchief around my neck and assured me I was a dead Kraut.

When the bell rang for the last class of the first day, Steenie and I joined the herd and began to push through the double doors. There was the usual amount of shoving and bad manners and goosing and giggling; Point Clear behavior wasn't any more courtly. But in the middle of all this happy horseplay, somebody jammed an elbow into my ribs, a deliberate and painful jab.

I scanned the unfamiliar faces, most of them dusty from an hour spent on the grassless playing ground; Point Clear was lush and its grounds were closely covered in fine golf-course lawn. I saw a few faces that I recognized: Steenie, Parker, the white-haired look-alike Cloyd girls, and Viola Lopez, whom Steenie had pointed out to me because of her enormous, precocious bosom. None of these people had jabbed me in the side.

To my left, burning out of the sea of pink and tan faces, was the meanest-looking human pan I'd ever seen, a brown, flat face with hot black eyes, a mouth so thin and lipless and straight that it seemed like the slot in a piggy bank. The face was framed by rich, thick, black, shiny hair, long and carefully combed; it swept around the top half of the ears on its way to the duck's ass arrangement in back, and the sideburns reached nearly to the bend of the jawbone.

By the time I saw this last face we'd all broken through the jam-up at the door and were pouring untidily down a corridor. Hate-Face fell into step beside me, shoving gently and insistently with his shoulder.

"Jew are a fahkeen queer," he said pleasantly. "I am goeen to bahss your ass."

I brought a right up from around my ankles, forgetting what science I knew, and landed it on his cheekbone.

His head rocked back perhaps half an inch, and a small spot of red appeared on the dark tan skin. He turned the lips upward, showing handsome teeth, and said softly, through the smile, "Jew heet like a fahkeen gorl. Now I am goeen to cot you estones off." He presented an upraised middle finger to me, said *"Toma, pendejo,"* and walked away toward music class, his long arms brushing against his thighs.

My legs were quivering, and I was having some trouble getting my breath as I followed him to class, wondering whether estones meant what I thought it did. Steenie was waiting near the door.

"I don't want you to think me crude," he said, "but may I perform the autopsy? I've never had a real cadaver to cut on, and what I really want to see is whether your brain is as small as I suspect."

"I guess I started school on the wrong foot," I said.

"Let's say you've just committed suicide," he said. "Why did you pick Chango? You got something against living?"

"Chango?"

"Maximiliano Lopez. Chango is his nickname, but don't use it to his face. No, in your case it's perfectly safe to call him Chango. You're going to die anyway. It means monkey; did you notice his arms?"

"Yes," I said, "they're long."

"That's only part of it. They're strong, too. I estimate he spends three hours out of every twenty-four hanging by his hands from a branch. Sometimes, the story goes, he hangs by only one hand, while he feeds himself bananas with the other." Steenie patted me tenderly on the shoulder, and sighed. "I don't think you've learned enough Commando to protect yourself."

"Why did he jab me? He damn near broke a rib for me when we were coming in."

"Did you by any chance stare at his sister's tits today? It's a natural thing to do, of course. I did it myself, once, and got off with a chipped incisor and some minor gum damage."

A small, blonde woman with pale skin and thick glasses came out of the music room and faced us, her hands on her hips. "Are you coming in this minute, or do I tell Mr. Alexander? It's your choice."

A large clot of native boys, led by Chango Lopez, provided a chorus of loud, boisterous monotones during the singing. The woman who'd accosted us in the corridor played a chipped and out-of-tune baby grand piano in accompaniment. She never paused during the singing to correct even the most flagrant examples of poor musicianship. Chango's crew sang loudly, on only one note, and made up their own words as they went along. As they sang they passed among themselves a small book of obscene cartoons. One of Chango's friends, a bow-legged, squinty boy with boils on his neck, crept on his hands and knees to a vantage point under the piano where he could see between the pianist's legs. No one in the music room took any notice of him. The woman, Miss Rudd, gave him about a minute of uninterrupted viewing, and then removed her right foot from the hold pedal and kicked him neatly on the chin, causing him to bump his head sharply on the underside of the piano. He wobbled out from underneath, his eyes faintly crossed, and made his way back to his seat, while Chango's bunch laughed coarsely. No one paid any attention to this tableau, and I took it for daily ritual.

At the end of the singing, which had become increasingly painful, Miss Rudd said, "Fight Song, everyone. Lots of spirit!" We all rose and sang "I'm a Crispin Boy."

It wasn't easy for me to follow the words, for I was sitting near Chango and his cronies, whose version of the

38

song was *"Chinga chinga, oh, chinga chinga, chingadero chingadero. . . ."*

As we left the room Chango kneed me in the tailbone so hard my legs almost buckled. "Jew gone look fahnny weeth your *chorizo* cot off," he whispered.

Steenie walked part of the way home with me, up the long fragrant hill to Camino Tuerto. "I think you'd better get a pistol," he said. "It won't kill Chango, of course; nothing can kill him but a wooden stake through the heart. But it might make some holes in some of his honchos."

"You must be exaggerating," I said.

"Can you get hold of some war-surplus hand grenades?"

I asked him about Marcia Davidson. "I know her father. St. Thomas's is the church we go to here, when we go. How come I never saw her around?"

"Church camp," he explained. "She spends every summer at a church camp in Colorado. She comes back with a tan and the scroungiest jokes I ever heard. This year she brought back a song called 'Ring Dang Do' that would make your hair turn white."

My mother was drinking sherry and listening to the radio when I got home. She'd become pale and slightly shaky in the few days since Dad had left.

"Did you have a nice time at school today?"

"Same old stuff," I said.

6

Dear Josh:

I haven't got a letter from your mother yet, but I assume you're behaving like a brave little lad and not blubbering and wetting your bed. I am in no danger as yet, other than the ever-present fear I may laugh so hard during indoctrination classes that I fall off my chair and injure myself.

The Navy, after having generously given me the rank of Lieutenant Commander, assumes that I am a stranger to salt water, and is re-teaching me all the fundamentals. (I was happy to learn this afternoon that the rear, or back, part of the boat, or ship, is known as the "stern," and that objects in that section are said to be "aft" or "abaft.") The officer who told us this, a young JayGee named Garrison, with a slight facial tic and a large behind, seemed very proud of his knowledge, and is eager for tomorrow's class to begin so that he can tell us the Navy names for right and left. I read the next chapter in the book, and have discovered they're called "starboard" and "port" but I'll pretend it's all a surprise when he breaks the news to us.

I believe I'm to be executive officer on a DE (destroyer escort), but I'll never make it at this rate. The Japanese and Germans will rule the seven seas by the time I've been taught the difference between a reef and a bowline, and President Roosevelt will be in a concentration camp with Eisenhower and Halsey and those other Jews.

Have you been getting long, intense love letters from little Corky, or has she fallen under the spell of Bubba Gagnier's heavy-handed charm? I don't want to sound patronizing, but I don't think 17 is the proper age for maintaining a love affair at a distance of 2,000 miles. Maybe you'll find some pretty little native girl—to your mother's horror—and begin taking instructions as a Catholic. Amadeo and Excilda have a daughter about your age, pretty as I recall. Still, don't let me push you into anything.

You're an adolescent, I realize, and not a very bright one, but you must keep an eye on your mother. She's away from her friends, and I don't think she's terribly fond of Sagrado, or the Southwest. She can, thank God, play pretty fair bridge, and that should keep her occupied, and she's out of the reach of some of her strange Mobile friends, who will remain nameless. I honestly couldn't think of a safer place for you and her than our house in Sagrado. There is still a possibility of bombing and shelling on the mainland, and Mobile's a fat sitting duck.

Please write me an occasional letter; use the FPO after December, and the Cambridge address until then. I will appreciate it if you don't use the rank "Admiral of the Ocean Sea" on the envelope. The Navy is deficient in humor.

Since there's no sailing in Sagrado, you might do some riding and hiking. Hiking is an old form of locomotion in which the leg muscles are employed. You may learn to enjoy it.

Back to the books. This weekend Garrison is going to take us to Boston harbor to show us what a sea looks like, and next week we'll learn all about buoys.

Keep up the calisthenics,
Dad

7

LAS FIESTAS del Corazón Sagrado is an annual event, celebrating the town's escape from the famous smallpox epidemic of 1705 which scourged the countryside and reduced the Indian population to a manageable size. It comes in mid-September, a cool and beautiful time of year in the mountains, when the scent of burning piñon is in the air and the first snow lies on the peaks. I'd always had to return to Mobile before Fiesta.

Steenie and Marcia and I met on the Plaza, the main square of Sagrado, surrounded by the town's historical buildings—J. C. Penney's, the Sagrado State Bank, Romero's Pool Room, Wormser's Dry Goods and the New Shanghai Chinese-American Eats.

During the night a dozen or so painted stalls had sprung up in the Plaza, and the proprietors were selling native food. Excilda knows how to cook this sort of thing, which is fiery but good. The chefs on the Plaza fried it all in last year's grease, producing a nauseating smell.

"Let's get some *tacos*," Marcia suggested. "With green chile and a Dr. Pepper."

"You'll get diarrhea," Steenie said. "As your medical advisor I strongly recommend the *burritos*. The worst they can do is constipate you."

"I'll get both," she said sunnily. "That way I'll come out even."

"Can't you two talk about something else?" I said. "I'm embarrassed all the time."

41

"Don't be ashamed of your body," Marcia said. "It's God's temple. Oh, look! Now that's what I call a real Fiesta costume!"

A conspicuously drunk native came toward us, almost unconscious, weaving along the flagstone path in a perfect zigzag, like a sloop tacking on a measured course. He wore no shirt, and someone had drawn concentric circles, like bulls-eyes, around his nipples in lipstick. He wore a policeman's cap and his fly was gaping open, revealing the head and front paws of what appeared to be a spaniel puppy, hanging out of the opening like a baby kangaroo. He halted in front of us and, dimly seeing Marcia, he removed the policeman's cap and bowed deeply. *"¿Cómo está, señorita?"* he said with dignity. "Don' tahtch the dog. He's a mean sonoma-beech."

Marcia made a grab for the puppy, who had long and silky ears aching to be scratched, but Steenie and I stopped her. The man with the ornament wobbled past us, having himself a hell of an old Fiesta.

"Couple of prudes," Marcia said.

We bought the *burritos,* having decided to come out even, and leaned against an ancient cottonwood near the center of the Plaza to watch the uneven procession of revelers. I don't know what went on in the thirties, but the war hadn't made much of an imprint, except for the tourists. Steenie, a veteran of many Fiestas, said they were missing.

Marcia said there wasn't enough hot sauce on her *burrito,* so I made a very sharp business proposition at one of the stalls for a nickel's worth of hot sauce. The *burrito*s themselves were just flour tortillas wrapped around beans. In Mobile we caulk catboats with paste like that.

"Burritos ordinarily give me gas," Marcia said, "if you know what I mean."

"I know what you mean," I said. "Be quiet about it."

"Bicarb," Steenie said. "Exercise."

"Clean thoughts," I said.

"I might as well be out with a pair of nuns," Marcia said, licking the hot sauce from her fingers. "Mmm, that's good! Burns going in and burns worse coming out."

"This is just like having a date with a Marine," I told Steenie, "but a Marine would watch his language."

"Talking isn't doing," Marcia said. "I'm still virgo intacta. Right, Doctor?"

"So you say," Steenie said. "I could be more certain after a fast pelvic, of course."

"Well, *I* couldn't be *more* certain," she said. "What do you think, Josh? Are the Cloyds virgo intacta?"

"What's it mean?" I whispered to Steenie.

"Cherry," he said, more loudly than necessary.

I started to turn red again, and then got hold of myself. "They don't talk as if they were. Not that you do."

"Definitely not," she said. The Cloyds were sisters, Velva Mae and Venery Ann, girls with pale dirty hair and four identical sharp breasts that they might have loaned to each other, like hats, while one pair was out being blocked. "I think Bucky Swenson's planking both of them."

We walked a few times around the Plaza, going generally against the crowd, and stopped once more to eat chicken *tacos* that had been boiled in what seemed to be sewage. I wanted to take them home and let Excilda cook native food for them the right way, but they enjoyed it.

They led the way north, across the Plaza and down Fillmore Avenue toward the edge of town. As we passed a convent, they proudly pointed out the cornerstone. Chiseled into granite were the words:

The Sisters of Our Lady of Succour
Laid April 14, 1873
By
The Most Reverend Francis X. Brady
Bishop of Corazón Sagrado

"Reading that always cheers me up for some reason," Marcia said.

On its north side, Sagrado ended suddenly at the base of some small brown hills. The dry earth was pocked with little holes where prairie dogs made their homes, and as we began to climb they poked their heads out and barked at us with a sound like "churp." The hills were steeper than they seemed. I started puffing from the altitude, and every ten steps or so I had to grab for the branch of a piñon tree and hold on. Steenie and Marcia didn't appear to mind the climb; they dodged and pranced on the incline, tossing pebbles at each other. Sometimes they stopped and waited for me when I fell down or halted to gasp, and said uncomplimentary things such as "Eeho-lay, *que* bum!"

We topped one rise and started down the other side. The town disappeared, and we seemed to be out in the country with no hint that there were any people for miles. *"Vamos al* dump," Steenie said. *"Al* dump," Marcia echoed.

We walked along a dried stream bed with high walls, and I lost my sense of direction immediately. The packed sand was easy to walk on and, with the climb ended for the time being, and the cool breeze blowing, it was pleasant. The stream bed turned, and as we turned with it a horrible choking odor surrounded us.

"Dead cow?" Steenie said.

Marcia stopped and sniffed the wind like a bird dog. *"Caballo,"* she said with finality. "Let's have a look."

I followed them around some more bends, and we emerged at the city dump, five acres or so of tin cans and bottles and old sofas with the stuffing coming out of them. Near the center of the refuse was a dead horse, surrounded by clouds of flies, giving off a visible green mist. I took my handkerchief out of my back pocket and tied it around my face.

"Would you say that horse is really dead," Marcia asked Steenie, "or it it playing possum?"

"Good question," Steenie said. "Shows an alert mind, a mind that doesn't accept the obvious. Josh boy, throw a rock at it and see if it wakes up."

"If I move one inch I'll get sick," I said. "Let's get out of here."

"First," said Steenie, "we have a little game. It's a little game we call *gallina*."

"It means 'chicken,' " Marcia said.

44

"The object of the game is to walk, or run, to the horse, touch it with your hand, and walk, or run, back to the starting point, which is here."

"Can you hold your breath?"

"You *have* to hold your breath. Otherwise it's *mucho vomito.*"

"Mucho puko," said Marcia, with relish.

"Now, if you walk to and from the horse, it takes longer, naturally, and you have to hold your breath longer. If you run, you get out of breath faster. Either way it's rough. We've played the game since we were six or seven."

"Why do you play it at all?"

"A feeling of accomplishment," said Marcia. "I'll go first."

She stood still and took several deep, noisy breaths, exhaled about halfway and, crossing the fingers on both hands, began a slow and deliberate walk toward the horse. As she entered the blue-green cloud that hovered around the corpse she hesitated briefly, then plunged forward to her knees, put the palm of her hand on the horse's flank, stood up and whirled around. Her eyes were closed.

"No running," Steenie yelled. "You have to walk back." Marcia nodded her head and, with her eyes still closed, walked back, her face red from stored-up carbon dioxide.

"Good girl," Steenie said when she returned and let her breath whoosh out. "A true champion."

"He's a good one," Marcia said. "He's falling apart and there's maggots."

"Do you want to go next?" Steenie asked me.

"I'm not sure I want to go at all."

"If you don't go, you're *gallina.* If you get a reputation as *gallina* around here you might as well go back to Alabama."

"Nobody likes a *gallina,*" Marcia warned. "Girls won't neck with a *gallina.*"

"Dogs bark at *gallinas,*" Steenie continued. *"Gallinas* are a hissing and a byword."

45

"It goes into your file. You never live it down. You lose your voting rights."

"I'll go if you go," I told Steenie.

Steenie was a runner, not a walker. After the usual deep breaths he took off at a sprint, knelt at the horse and slapped him with both hands. He ran back even faster, and collapsed at our feet, taking huge staggering breaths.

"He's really a beauty. A textbook study in decomposition. It's days like this that really make the game worthwhile."

"Your turn, Josh," Marcia said. "You'd do better if you ran."

If I hadn't tripped just as I got to the horse, I believe I could have made it. It's hard to hold your breath for a long time when the air's thin, and I wasn't used to the altitude yet. I honestly think I could have carried it off if my foot hadn't slipped on a beer bottle. When my chest hit the horse about midships it made a noise like an orange being squeezed, and the horse's ribs began a slow caving-in movement. I pushed myself away and my hand went through his skin, surprising me so I took a deep breath without meaning to.

Later, still pale and weak-kneed, I told Marcia and Steenie that they didn't need to help me walk and they let go of my arms and stood back.

"A real sport," Steenie said. "Just threw himself on that horse and hugged him like a brother."

"I didn't realize until now that we've been playing the game wrong all this time," Marcia said. "It doesn't mean a thing until you crawl right *into* the horse."

"I'd throw up some more if I had anything left to throw," I said.

"*Mucho puko,* guy."

"Maybe it was something you ate," Steenie said.

We climbed some more hills and came back into sight of Sagrado, now perhaps a mile away, peaceful-looking. We admired the view; even old-time residents of Sagrado liked to spend part of each day looking at the landscape. Soon the wind blew away the lingering scent of deceased horse. Clouds began to build and the air became chilly, so we tramped back to the Plaza.

Near a cotton candy booth we saw Chango Lopez, holding his beautiful sister's hand. Viola's face was calm and happy, like a saint's. Chango was trying to look mean, but her presence seemed to embarrass him.

"Hello, Viola," Marcia said. "Happy Fiesta."

"I think I have a vocation," Viola said. "I'm going to be a nun."

"That's wonderful," Marcia said. "You must be very happy."

"Jew are a *pendejo* bahstair," Chango said softly to me. "Eeef I deen have my seester weeth me, I bahss your ass."

"And a happy Fiesta to you, Maximiliano," Steenie said heartily. "Are you going to follow your sister into God's service?"

"Estoff eet op your *culo*," Chango said. "I gat you too."

"Reverend Mother's been telling me all about it," Viola continued. "You can't talk to anyone for a whole year, and they cut off all your hair."

"It sounds very . . . exciting," Marcia said.

"I'm going poot on my boots and estomp the cheat out of you, *jodido*. Jew batter keep your eyes open."

"Chango," Marcia said. "You give me a pain in the behind."

Chango fell back alarmed. "Don' talk dorty," he said in anguish. "Not een front of my seester."

"No seas tonto, hombre," Viola told him. *"Tú lo hablas así tú mismo.* You talk the same way all the time."

"Ees deeferent. I got a reputation."

"I tried to get him to talk to Father McIlhenny about the language, and he said something dirty about the Church."

"Come on," Chango said. "Less geet outa here. I don' wan talk to bonch of Anglos."

Viola took her brother's hand and led him away, like a nanny and a little boy. He turned around and gave me

47

the finger. *"Toma, pendejo,"* he yelled. Viola jerked his arm and he nearly stumbled.

"Viola's a nice girl," Marcia said, "but she has endocrine trouble. She began getting breasts when she was nine."

"And they're still growing," Steenie pointed out.

"Don't talk dorty," Marcia said, imitating Chango. "Not een front of my honcho."

With the cooling air the crowd in the Plaza began to thin out. Only a straggly group of tourists remained to buy the *burritos* and the *tacos* and the Indian pottery. A wind was coming from Bernal Peak, scattering paper cups and wooden spoons in the street. On the bandstand, Chamaco Trujillo, who combined the job of sheriff with that of uncrowned King of Fiesta, was exhorting the people vainly through a public-address system. "We going to have folk dancing in jost a few minutes, folks. Estick around and have a good time. We got the Mariachi Bustamente up from Mexico gone play your old time favorites. Whatsa matter? You escared of a little wind?"

"Hey, Chamaco," Marcia called to him. "You better get home before you catch pneumonia."

Steenie joined the chorus. "I saw the bass player from the Mariachis piled up drunk behind the Elks Club. He had puke all over his costume."

"Why don' you kids try to have a good time and estop *chingando* with the Fiesta?"

"Why don't you get your *taco* salesmen to put some fresh grease in their griddles?" Marcia asked him. "They're giving the trots to all the tourists."

"It's snowing," Steenie told him.

"It never snows in September," Chamaco yelled back through the p.a. system.

"Suit yourself," Steenie said.

It was snowing, heavy wet flakes that stuck to people's hats and fringed the *taco* stands with white awnings. I had never seen snow before, except in photographs. We walked through the deepening slush to the hotel and stood under the arcade, watching the snow drive the tourists off the streets. We could see Chamaco dimly through the snowflakes on the bandstand, still trying to get the crowd in. As we watched, the folk dancers came into the Plaza in a bus. They were dressed in the national costume of Lithuania, or Liechtenstein. Chamaco hollered once more into his microphone before the snow shorted it out. "Look, everybody, here's the dancers." The male dancers were wearing short leather pants and their knees were turning blue. The women had their overcoats on, and wouldn't take them off. There wasn't anyone around to watch the dancing, anyway.

"Poor old Chamaco," Marcia said. "He tries so hard."

"Is it always like this?" I asked her.

"It doesn't always snow," she said, "but something always happens. One year his bandstand collapsed and the dancers got all cut up. One year everybody in the band got thrown in jail for illegal entry. One year we had a rabies epidemic and the tourists went to Colorado instead."

"Last year was the best," Steenie said. "Chamaco arranged with the Elks Club for a fireworks demonstration out by the ball park. Some Elk got drunk and fell into the fireworks with a lighted cigar. They all went up at once, like dynamite. Half of the Elks got their hair burned off."

The snow had become so heavy that we couldn't see the bandstand, but we could hear Chamaco screaming, even with his p.a. system shorted out. "Dance! Dance! I paid you to dance, and you're gonna dance!"

We decided to go home before the snow got too deep. Camino Tuerto is half a mile from the Plaza, uphill, and I was almost frozen before I arrived. By that time I knew all I needed to know about snow. Excilda met me at the door, looking like the Madonna of the Chile Peppers. "We got company," she told me. "Three weeks Mr. Arnold's been gone, and we got company already."

"What kind of company?"

"I don't know. He looks like some kind of *maricón* to me."

My mother came to the door, with a glass of sherry. "Joshua," she said, "I have a wonderful surprise for you."

"Is the war over?"

"Better than that." She took my hand and led me, still dripping melted snow, into the living room. A piñon fire was blazing in the corner fireplace, the curtains were open to let in the cold, snowy light. The Navajo rugs were bright and cheerful, and the sherry bottle sat nearly empty on a copper tray.

"Well, now. How's our little cowboy doing?" Jimbob Buel said from my father's leather armchair. "I'm sorry I can't offer you a glass of sherry, but it just isn't good for growing boys. Excilda! Bring this growing boy a glass of milk."

8

THE WONDERFUL SURPRISE turned out to be permanent, and Jimbob stayed on, giving orders to Excilda and Amadeo, helping Mother get rid of all that sherry cluttering up the cellar, taking over the spare bedroom and complaining about the cold weather. Mother was drawing five hundred dollars a month, which should have been plenty, but it didn't seem to cover Jimbob's expenses. He didn't like the way Excilda ironed his shirts and had the laundry do them. There were never quite enough eggs in the morning, even though he contributed his ration cards, a point Mother liked to bring up. He had a big collection of ascot cravats, and wore a different one every day, with the same tweed coat. He didn't like Excilda's cooking, and made some nasty scenes about it, but even he couldn't change that, and the food was still good. Mother and Jimbob played bridge almost every day with her summer friends, and he seldom left the house. He brought news from Mobile.

"That delicious little Courtney Conway was just sailing her pretty head off the last time I saw her," he told me.

"She was always with Earl and Mary Gagnier's boy. Aren't you sorry you let that slip through your fingers?"

"Not very."

"What are you doing for companionship here in the desert? Have you got some little squaw girl on the string?"

"I got a whole tribe of them. They fight among themselves all the time to see who gets to sew moccasins for me."

"That's very nice to hear. I thought you'd go native as soon as you left civilization."

"Mr. Buel, how come *you* left civilization? Isn't life around here a little too crude for you?"

"I thought it would be beneficial if I brought a little breath of culture here. There apparently isn't a decent bridge player or a drinkable bottle of bourbon in the area."

Excilda grumbled to me about him, but she liked her job and she liked me. When Jimbob got too arrogant, and started shouting orders, she pretended she couldn't understand English. Amadeo spoke to him only in Spanish, and as I got more familiar with the language from the chatter at school I enjoyed the conversations.

"Amadeo," Jimbob would say, "now that the last snow has melted, don't you think it would be a good idea to mound some humus around those rose trees?"

Amadeo would touch the bill of his hat. "I think you have a face like a peccary and smell like a Taos whore."

"I thought you'd see it my way. We don't want Mr Arnold's roses to die, do we?"

"You can make a rose tree die just by walking past it, with all that whore's perfume you wear. Why don't you come out to my place and make love to one of my goats? It might be a change from all those sheep you're so famous with."

The Conquistador carried a story in the society column about James Robert Buel, scion of a distinguished Virginia family, who was a house guest of Mrs. Francis Arnold and her son Joshua. (Mr. Arnold, a well-known summer visitor, is serving in the U. S. Navy.) I cut it out and mailed it to Dad, just the clipping. The boys overseas like to get news from home.

"Who's that guy staying at your house?" Marcia asked me one day. "An uncle or something?"

"Not a relative," I said. "Just a friend."

"Your mother just doesn't look like the type," she said.

"If you want to stay honchos with me, you'd better lay off," I said.

"Don't be so sensitive. War is hell."

"Maybe you'd better go study up in your venereal disease book," I suggested. "You know the name for everything, but that's all you know."

"Maybe I'll go out to the football field and watch Bucky flex his muscles. He's got the best-looking greater trochanter in town." She looked at me sharply, and pointed to my scar. "That's cute," she said, "but it isn't as cute as Bucky's greater trochanter."

Marcia walked away, and I picked up some rocks from the De Crispin playground and threw them at the big cottonwood tree where we parked our bicycles, missing the tree and breaking someone's taillight. The sound of breaking glass attracted one of the Cloyd girls, and she jounced over.

"You busted the livin' crap outa somebody's taillight, boy," she said, licking her lips. "You must be pretty mean."

I threw another rock, which hit the tree without causing breakage. "I'm feeling mean," I told her, pushing my jaw out. There was something about those girls that made you want to strut. "Which one are you?"

"I'm Velva Mae," she said, swinging the lower part of her body so that her skirt swished against her legs. "Venery Ann's yonder by the drinkin' fountain wavin' her butt around."

"How do people tell you two apart," I asked her. They did look alike, both growing out of their clothes at about the same rate, both with dirty knees.

"I'm the friendly one," she said. "You got a car?"

"Bicycle," I said. "A Schwinn."

"Not even a motorcycle?" She looked very disappointed.

"Can't you be friendly on a bicycle?"

"You kin stick your little old bicycle," she said prettily. "I'm too old to go muffin' around on bicycles."

I felt low and sad about having only a bicycle to muff around on with Velva Mae, but I didn't know what to say to her. She stood there, swishing her skirt, and looking up sideways at me, as if anything went as long as I came up with a 1940 La Salle. Her knees were really dirty, with old mud ground into the wrinkles and a gray blotch down her calves, but her dress was clean and her short socks were shiny white. Her mother probably had a washing machine but no bathtub. "Maybe I can get hold of a car," I said. "Maybe you and I could double date with old Parker or somebody." If she had just stopped swishing her skirt I might have stopped all this silly talk, but she went on swishing away.

"That's a deal, Arnold," Velva Mae said. "Me and Venery Ann and you and Parker can drive out somewhere and watch the moon come up. You just get the car." She paused and looked down, and took her dress hem in both hands to spread it out. "We'll wash up," she said. "Just stay away from Davidson in the meantime."

I saw Parker later that day; he'd shared his roast javelina sandwich with me at lunch, and said I was the first guy he'd ever seen that didn't gag on it the first time. I asked him if he could get his father's car for a date with the Cloyd girls.

"Which one you got, Velva or Venery?" he asked.

"It's Velva, I think."

"It's one and the same," he said. "They're just like a couple of she otters anyhow. Maybe Daddy'll loan me his car, if he doesn't have to drive out to Seven Springs and plant trout. He don't mind. He's real keen on nature study, and damn if the Cloyds ain't nature study. Venery like to bite my mouth off one time. Hey, who's that guy staying up at your place I heard about?"

"Now don't you start on it," I told him.

"Just bein' friendly," he said. "Forget it." The bell rang in the playground just then. "Let's go on in and sing that cute little song about the caterpillar," Parker said. "Somebody told me Miss Rudd's got on red lace pants today, and I love music just as well as the next man."

I tried to catch Marcia's eye during the singing, but she was too busy staring at Bucky. After the last class I saw her walking with him. I would have thrown a rock at him, but I might have hit Marcia.

There was no one around for me to walk with. Steenie said he was going to his father's office to pick up some more books on childbirth or venereal disease. Parker had a special package to get at the post office, something he said he'd ordered all the way from Tennessee. The Cloyd girls had probably found a couple of guys with motorcycles. I started home alone.

Camino Tuerto crosses an *acequia,* an irrigation canal, at the bottom of the hill, and Chango Lopez was sitting on the stone bridge railing, waiting for me. He'd been giving me nothing but lip for more than a week, and wasn't making me as nervous as before. I was beginning to believe he was all talk. "Hallo, you sissy queer *pendejo* bahstair."

I stopped near him. "Chango, why don't you go get a haircut. You're getting grease all over your collar." It wasn't very sharp, but it was the only thing that came to me.

Chango whistled through his teeth, and another boy crawled out from under the bridge—the *acequia* was empty at the time—and began to climb the bank. He was a stranger, but mean-looking, with pocks on his face and half a right ear. There wasn't any point, that I could see, in staying around for a discussion. I pushed Chango in the chest, and he fell backwards into the *acequia* as I started running.

Home was uphill, a bad slope to run, so I turned left along Camino Chiquito, which paralleled the canal, and ground down the dusty road between high adobe walls. Driveways cut the walls on both sides, and as I ran, hearing Chango yelling "Hey, Tarzan! Gat the son of a beech!" I looked down each one for a place to hide. Chango's friend was behind me when I turned my head to look. Chango himself wasn't running very fast, and was limping. He'd apparently sprained his ankle when I pushed him off the bridge. The one with the ear was in the lead, running very fast and lightly, like a gazelle. As usual, the altitude was beginning to get me; it was hard to breathe and my chest hurt.

On my right I saw a break in the wall, and a compound behind it, with a turning circle and some small houses grouped around it. I skidded into it, ran behind a house and through a patio gate, and dived behind a pile of neatly stacked piñon wood. I could hear Chango and then the other one, crunching on the gravel in the drive, and then leaving and walking back out to Camino Chiquito. The patio I was in was full of boulders, pushed against the wall and scattered around on the flagstones.

Each of the boulders was about a hundred-pounder, white or tan, and some of them were carved into heads and faces. But they weren't marble or tombstone granite. They were just big rocks, the sort that lie all over the hillsides around Sagrado. I went over to one of them; it was carved like an Indian's head, with the hair cut in bangs and a cloth band tied around it. I don't know much about art, and I don't think that's what it was, but it was a professional job of carving.

The patio gate was still open where I'd busted through it. It was just good luck that Chango and his honcho hadn't noticed it, and come in to drag me from behind the woodpile. Or maybe they did their stomping only on public streets, and had a rule about not invading private property. I walked over, still panting, to the patio gate, but before I reached it I glanced into a window of the house to see if anyone had seen me. I believe that technically I was trespassing.

Inside was a naked woman, standing on a table. Her feet were slightly apart and her head was held back, her long brown hair reaching almost to her waist. She didn't seem to be doing anything, just standing there and looking at the ceiling. I turned my head and felt my face turning red, then looked back at her. She didn't appear to see me. She was pale and well-built, and it was an interesting view. I'd never seen a woman completely undressed before; it was fancier than a statue. She was

55

talking to herself, or to someone I couldn't see. Her lips were moving, but I couldn't hear what she said. I stood in the shadow of the wall and just watched. My breathing was more regular now, and the spots before my eyes were clearing. I always got them when I ran too hard or too far without warming up, even in Mobile.

The woman relaxed and stepped off the table onto a chair, and then onto the floor. She still didn't look at me, but reached for a bathrobe hanging on the chair and put it on. Then someone came into the patio through the open gate.

"Are you a lover of art, or are you just a dirty little boy?"

A large bald man with a black mustache stood at the gate with his hands on his hips, smiling at me. His forearms, sticking out of a stained khaki shirt, were as large around as my head. There was nowhere to run to, and if he caught me I knew he could pluck me like a rose. I just stood there and tried to look like an art lover.

"She's beautiful, isn't she?" he said. He had a rich accent which sounded European, not the harsh mushy Sagrado-Spanish accent. "She can hold any pose I give her for fifty minutes and her muscles never start quivering. She doesn't mind being looked at, but she doesn't like to be leered at. Were you leering at her?"

"No sir," I managed to say. "I didn't even know she was there until. . . ."

"Until you saw her. That sounds reasonable. Would you like to come in? I think you're still frightened."

"I'm not frightened."

"You're not? If Tarzan Velarde were after me, I'd be frightened. Well, maybe I wouldn't, but most people would. You really shouldn't make enemies of the Spanish boys. They can be very cruel. Come in. Come in."

I followed him into the house, through the patio door near the woodpile. He went to the woman, who was sitting next to the table and smoking a cigarette, and said, "It's all right, Anna. He's an art lover after all. This is Anna. Anna, this is. . . ."

"Joshua M. Arnold," I said. "How do you do. I didn't mean to peek. It just took me by surprise." She blew

56

smoke slowly at me, and didn't change her expression, which was neutral and bored. "We're going to have some coffee now, Mr. Arnold," he said. "Would you like a cup?"

"Sure. Thank you." He went over to a hot plate on a counter that ran along one side of the studio, and poured coffee from a pot into three heavy china mugs.

"I want some sugar this time, Romeo," the woman said. "I don't like it black."

"Sugar will only make you fat, Anna," he said gently. She lapsed back into neutral silence and puffed on her cigarette. I thought she was pretty, even without any lipstick on, but she looked . . . not stupid exactly, but as if she never thought about anything.

The sculptor sat with us at the table and we drank black coffee, which tasted faintly of clay. He had clay on his hands and wrists, and on his shirt and the fly on his trousers and in his ears. The statue he was sculpting was on a small pedestal and it seemed to be nearly finished. He'd caught the pose pretty well, but it still wasn't art. He saw me looking at it.

"I know," he said happily. "It isn't going to threaten the reputation of Praxiteles. When it's finished it will look like Anna, and I will sell it for a hundred dollars, maybe a hundred and fifty, and it will decorate a concrete fountain in Grosse Point, Michigan, or Bend, Oregon. I'm not a very good sculptor, but I like to do it better than carpentry. I'm a very good cabinet maker, and people tell me I could make much more money that way, but I am very bored with chairs and breakfronts and credenzas and bookshelves."

"I think it's very good," I lied. "It looks just like her."

"You can do a better likeness of her with a box camera," he said.

"I don't like it," the woman said flatly. "It doesn't have enough plastic integrity."

"Anna," he said. "Don't use words you don't understand. You're too beautiful to use words like that, and they'll give you lines on your face." He pulled back her long hair and kissed her behind the ear, and she said, "Hmmmmmm."

We finished our coffee, and Anna went into another room to put her clothes on.

"Aren't you Ann and Frank Arnold's boy?" he asked me, and I told him I was. "Sure," he said. "I haven't seen you since you were eight or nine. Frank's an old friend of mine. Tell your mother Romeo Bonino says hello."

I promised I would. I didn't remember him, and I couldn't picture him at our house playing bridge or listening to my mother talk about her kinfolk in Atlanta and Louisville and Charleston.

"Where is Frank, by the way? I haven't seen him this year."

"He's in the Navy," I said. "He's in Massachusetts right now for training, and then he'll go overseas somewhere."

"Are you as tough as old Frank?"

"I can outrun him," I said. "I don't think I can outwrestle him yet."

The woman, Anna, came back into the studio and without saying anything began to rattle pots and pans in the cooking corner of the room, and to slice some salami. I stood up and thanked Mr. Bonimo for his coffee and for letting me hide in his patio. "Tell Mrs. Bonino I'm sorry about staring at her." The woman said "Hah!" and kept slicing salami.

"Sure, sure," he said. "Listen, when do you have to get home? Does your mother worry about you?"

"No. She doesn't worry about me. I can get home any time. If those guys don't jump me again."

"I want to take some rocks back to the mountain before dinner. It won't take long. Why don't you come with me?"

"Some what?"

"Come along. I'll show you."

We left Anna with the salami and went out to his garage. He backed an old truck to the patio gate. "We'll just take the ones with faces on them," he said.

He and I rolled and carried the boulders to the truck and hoisted them into the bed, where he'd laid some army blankets. There were seven of them, and they were heavy.

I climbed in, and he drove out between the compound walls and northeast toward Teta Peak, so called because it was shaped like a breast, with a big pink rock nipple on top of it.

"Anna isn't exactly Mrs. Bonino," he said after a few minutes. "She's more of a friend, and she models for me."

"Oh, that's okay," I said, not knowing what else I should say. "She looks very nice."

"She isn't," he said. "She's a rotten model and a bad cook, and she doesn't shave under her arms often enough and she's stupid."

"I'm sorry," I said.

"Don't be. We get along very well, and when she gets tired of me, or when I get tired of her, she'll go live with someone else. I'm about number fifteen for her. She's about number twenty for me."

"Oh."

We turned off the road and onto a rutted track that led to the foot of the hill, and stopped. "Here we are," Romeo said. "Time to sweat."

We unloaded the carved boulders, and he chose the heaviest one to start with. "These came from up there," he said, pointing to a small clearing far above us. We got behind a boulder and began to roll it slowly uphill. When we came to a nearly level place we'd carry it together, but mostly we had to roll it. It was hard, sweaty work, and we were gasping when we reached the clearing. Romeo found a stick and scratched a shallow depression in the earth, and we rolled the carved rock into it so that it sat on what would have been a neck if he'd carved a neck. "Much better," he said, and we started down for another boulder.

"Frank and I used to do this, sometimes," he said. "He was one of the few people who didn't think I was crazy, and he said he liked the exercise. Do you think I'm crazy?"

"I guess not. Who are you doing this for? I mean, who owns the hill?"

"Owns the hill? Nobody owns the hill. It belongs to the state, or the Federal government, or something. It's a public hill. I'm simply improving the land."

We rolled rocks up the hill until the sun went down and it was too dark to see where we were going. Once, halfway up, with a boulder carved like a Negro's head, our hands slipped and it rolled downhill away from us, knocking over small trees. We scrambled after it, with Romeo screaming "Come back, come back, you son of a bitch!" He tripped and banged his knee on a root, and I tripped over him, and for a few seconds we lay there, laughing, and listening to the carved head crashing and bouncing down the slope. We found it ten minutes later, after a lot of thrashing around, and put our backs in it, and got it to its original spot.

"Maybe my father didn't think you were crazy," I said, as we went down for another one, "but I'm not so sure."

"As I said, I'm improving the land. I'm improving on Nature, and I don't believe I'm arrogant to say that Nature can be improved. Now a tree: As Mr. Kilmer said in his awful poem, only God can make one, and I know of few ways to improve upon trees. Cutting them down to make paper for income-tax forms, or carving them into chairs, is not really an improvement. But these boulders are an ugly shape when I find them, and Nature isn't going to make them more beautiful. All that will happen to them is that the rain and the wind will erode them, make them smaller and smaller, until they're turned into dust, which will be washed down this hill into the Rito Sagrado, and then into the Río Grande, and from there into the Gulf of Mexico. Do you see what I mean?"

"I think so."

"Good. So I beautify them myself. I take them from the mountain, temporarily, and I carve good strong faces in them, and I put them back. All of my friends and most of my relatives are on this little mountain. I'm careful to carve only admirable people."

We were exhausted when we'd rolled the last of the heads up Teta Peak, and it was dark. He drove me home, told me to be careful of Tarzan, and said to come over any time and learn to sculpt. "Any idiot can do it," he said.

Jimbob and my mother were having a little snort when I came in, a peaceful and homey scene. "Where have you been?" Mother asked, looking a little cross-eyed.

"Your mother's been terribly worried about you," Jimbob said. "She's been just frantic." She looked stoned to me, and not frantic at all.

"Who was that driving you home?" she asked. "It looked like someone in a truck."

"A friend of yours," I said. "A man named Romeo Bonino. He says he knows you."

"He's a friend of your father's," she said. "He's a dirty, filthy man. He's an Italian."

"He's bearing up all right under the disgrace," I said.

"Don't you dare be sharp with your mother," Jimbob said, rising to his feet unsteadily and trying to put a fierce look on his face, which was getting red and puffy. "She's been frantic about your safety."

"Frantic," she echoed, having herself another little old *traguito*.

"You're too old to thrash," Jimbob said, "but you deserve a thrashing." It was such an old-fashioned word that I began to laugh, and his face got redder and fatter.

"Thrashing," my mother said. "Frantic, frantic thrashing."

"*Mierda de toro*," I said. I'd been improving my Spanish here and there.

Jimbob thought that one over. "I'm sure that's something vulgar, but I'm proud to say that English is my language."

I said "excuse me" and went into the kitchen. Excilda and I had a bowl of *posole* together, a kind of hominy cooked with hunks of pork and beef and boiled in red chile. She spoke to me in very slow, simple Spanish, so I could get it.

"I know Amadeo and I made a contract with your father," she said, "but there wasn't anything in it about him." She indicated Jimbob with her chin, which is what

61

the people in Sagrado do instead of pointing, which is considered impolite. "He called Amadeo a nigger the other day; Amadeo almost hit him with a shovel. He's giving all the orders around here, and most of the time he doesn't know what he's talking about. I sure wish Mr. Arnold were back."

"I wish I knew what was the matter with my mother," I said. "She's not acting right."

"I know what's the matter with her," Excilda said. "She doesn't like it here and she's drinking all that wine so she can forget she's in Sagrado instead of back in Alabama. She doesn't like this dry air, and she's not going to like the snow when it gets heavy. She's not used to being without her husband. She doesn't like the food I cook, even though everybody says I'm one of the best cooks in the county. She doesn't even like this," she said, indicating the *posole*, which was great.

"And," she continued, "I don't think she likes Catholics."

"Now I don't know about *that*," I said. "The woman who worked for us in Mobile was a Catholic."

"Then maybe she doesn't like me because I'm Spanish. Her and her family. Jesus, man, my family's been around here for three hundred and fifty years."

"Her family was just a lot of horse thieves, anyway," I said. "She talks about them a lot, but she doesn't let you meet any of them. I think most of them make whiskey and run barefoot."

"Well, if she doesn't like Spanish people she sure came to the wrong part of the country. You're learning Spanish pretty good. Do you like Spanish people?"

"Some of them. There's a couple of guys I don't like any too well. I think one of them wants to kill me. Maybe both of them do. Do you know a guy named Chango Lopez?"

"Is that Maximiliano?"

"That's the one," I said.

"I know his mother and father. He was a wood carver from around Ojo Amargo. A *santero,* you know, he carved little saints out of wood. He works in town now. What's Maximiliano got against you?"

"I don't know. Something about his sister, as I understand it."

Excilda cupped her hands in front of her chest. "The one with these?"

"More like this," I said, cupping my hands and holding them farther out.

"You been playing around with her? If you have, you asked for trouble. Those Lopez people are real backcountry, and they get proud sometimes."

"No," I said. "I've never touched her. Chango's just imagining things."

"You have a girl?"

"I thought I did, but now I don't know. She's sore at me about something."

My mother came into the kitchen, weaving slightly. "Thick as thieves," she said. "You two are just thick as thieves. What are you talking about in here?"

"Joshua's just practicing his Spanish on me, Mrs. Arnold," Excilda said. "He speaks it very well for an Anglo, when you consider he hasn't been here very long."

"I wish you wouldn't call my son an Anglo, Excilda. It just doesn't sound very nice."

"Well, whatever he is, he's learning Spanish pretty good. Do you want some dinner? I've got *posole*."

"I recommend it," I said. "It'll tear the top of your head off."

"Can't you make anything without chile in it?" my mother said. "Mr. Buel has a delicate stomach."

"I suppose I can cook some hamburgers," Excilda said, sighing.

"You just do that little thing," my mother said.

So Excilda did that little thing, and my mother and Jimbob ate hamburgers which they were probably too loaded to taste, and exclaimed over good, wholesome American cooking which was so simple that even a Mexican could manage it.

9

PARKER GOT HIS father's car the next evening, which was Friday, and we made dates with the Cloyd girls. After I asked Velva Mae if she'd like to see a movie, and then assured her that the automobile was ours for the night, she made me describe it carefully. It was a dark blue 1939 Plymouth sedan with fuzzy gray upholstery and a six-cylinder engine. Parker told me that Venery Ann was just as inquisitive. The girls were really making a date with the car, and letting us go along like a pair of little brothers. Never, not before or since, have I known girls who were so carried away by the internal-combustion engine.

My mother hadn't been showing much interest in what I did or where I went recently, but when she saw me putting on a tie she got curious.

"A tie!" she said. "I'm so happy you're beginning to care about how you look again. You've been going everywhere in blue jeans for so long I suspected you'd forgotten how to dress."

"Your mother's quite right," Jimbob put in. "You've been looking terribly tatty recently. Practically sharecropperish."

"I know," I said humbly. "I've been letting myself go. But this girl is different. This just isn't the sort of girl you can wear blue jeans with."

"Of good family?" my mother asked.

"Well, I don't know about that. Rich, though."

"Old money?" said Jimbob, "or new money?"

"Banking," I said, making it up as I went along. "The oldest bank in West Texas. Rancher's National of Amarillo."

"Oh, yes," Jimbob said.

"Also insurance. You know; Panhandle Life Assurance. A billion something in policies."

"A fine old firm," he said, looking only a little puzzled.

"And ranching, of course. That's where it all came from. The Circle Bar Four. The longhorn and Guernsey cross-breed. I forget what they call it, but the steers are resistant to heat and mosquitoes and give nothing but T-bones. I think they had a big contract with the Confederacy. Jefferson Davis was a great fancier of Mr. Cloyd's beef."

"Of course," Jimbob said. "Cloyd. That's old. . . ."

"Chester Cloyd," I said. "He started the ranch. His grandson Felix runs the business now. I mean, the empire."

"You mean you're going out with Felix Cloyd's daughter? Well, I must say I'm truly impressed. It's certainly a fine old family. I believe my father used to do business with them."

"What's this young lady's first name?" my mother asked me, brightening up.

"Amanda Sue," I said. "I call her Susie."

"Imagine that!"

Parker's car came into the driveway, and I said goodnight and went out through the kitchen. Excilda was mashing red chiles through a sieve, and peering through the window, trying to identify the car. "Who are you going with tonight?" she asked.

"A girl named Cloyd," I told her. "You know her family too?"

"I know everybody's family around here. That one's about the worst there is."

"You'd better not tell anybody."

"You'd better not come back here with the crabs," she said.

Parker had his hair slicked with water, and had made a little wave in the front of it. He'd also had a haircut, and his ears stuck out. The car smelled like fish.

"Daddy went and used his own car this morning," he said. "The Game Department has this truck, but Daddy likes his own car. He carried four thousand rainbow fry up to the Pecos, and then hit a rock by Cañón Seco. The goddamn fish sloshed all over the back seat, and he had to spend an hour picking them up by hand."

"It smells pretty strong," I said. "Will the girls mind?"

"Shoot, they'll ride on top of sacks of wet horseshit if they can do it in a car. Hey, you got boots on?"

"No, why? Are we going hiking?"

"You better go back in the house and get a pair of boots or galoshes or something, if you don't want to ruin your shoes. Just get 'em. You'll see why."

I went back inside and got my knee-high rubber fishing boots, and came back to the car. "Just sling 'em in back," Parker said. "You'll need 'em."

We drove west through town, past the Plaza and out across some arroyos to where the street lights stopped and the houses leaned sideways, or had the melted look that adobe gets even in a dry country, when every little rain washes part of the walls away. None of the streets were paved; nobody in this part of town paid any taxes, so they didn't get any paving. In the part of town I lived in, everybody paid taxes, high ones, but the streets weren't paved there because the residents thought asphalt would destroy the charm. They were right; it would. It would destroy the dust, too.

"What does Mr. Cloyd do?" I asked Parker, who wasn't talking much because he had to drive his father's car very carefully around chug holes and sleeping dogs.

"Do? Shoot, old Black John don't do anything," Parker said. "He's a sewer."

"What do you mean, a sewer?"

"I mean that's all he does. He sues people."

"Oh."

"He's got something wrong with his spine, and he can make his backbone pop out of place whenever he wants, like it was doublejointed. It makes a hell of a big lump, like a baseball. When he's getting short of money, and that's most of the time, because he don't do regular work, he bumps up against some moving vehicle and then falls down and lies there moanin' and raising seventeen kinds of hell. He generally picks on cars or trucks that have some kind of company sticker on the side, because he figures they got more insurance than just people."

"Isn't that called fraud? Don't they ever catch up with him?"

"Well, yes, I suppose they do. He moves around the country a lot, Velva Mae told me, and he's pulled it three times already here in Sagrado. He got five thousand from Wormser's Dry Goods when he let their panel truck bump him, and about the same amount from the State Corporation Commission. He's in the middle of a deal with Big Pepe's Lumber Company right now."

"That sounds like a pretty good way to make a living, if you have the backbone for it," I said. "I'm looking forward to meeting him."

"He's in kind of a bad frame of mind right now, from this last thing with Big Pepe," Parker said. "The thing was, he got himself in position for the lumber truck to sideswipe him down at the corner of Wilson and San Policarpio, but the driver made too sharp a turn. Old Cloyd threw his back out all right—he does it by turning his shoulders one way and his hips another—but as he was goin' down a piece of Ponderosa pine two-by-four slid off the truck bed and caught him right in the thigh. Busted his leg all to hell, and now he's really hurtin'. He's workin' a suit for ten thousand now, but the pain in his leg's so bad he can't get any fun out of it."

Parker pulled the car off the road, onto a dark shoulder that seemed to be mud and sand, mixed, and turned off the engine. "Get your boots on," he advised me. "We're gonna have to slog for a while."

Between us and the light from the Cloyds' house was a hundred yards of what looked like Alabama swamp. The ground was mushy and covered with water and high grass and weeds, and I could see the dark shapes of cottonwoods and poplars. Parker led the way with a flashlight, and I sloshed after him.

"I didn't know there was this much water around Sagrado," I said. "The Sagrado River's been dry since I got here."

"This is a *cienega*," Parker said. "It's some kind of underground spring, but it's not good for anything but making the ground wet. Costs a fortune to drain it or pump it off, and Cloyd isn't about to spend money for things like that."

"Does the whole family have to walk through this stuff to get to their house? You'd think they'd build a duckwalk or something." Parker said Cloyd would rather swim than build something useful.

A door opened in the house ahead of us, and I could see someone standing in the yellow rectangle of light. "It's Parker!" Parker yelled quickly. "Don't go shootin'!"

"Get offa my proppitty, you goddamn weasel!" Mr. Cloyd yelled back, in a voice like a trawler scraping a dock.

"There goes the evening," I said, and turned around to head back to the car.

"Don't pay any attention to him," Parker whispered. "He always says something like that. It's his way of welcoming people."

"You dirty little polecat son of a bitch," Cloyd hollered. "You take one more step and I'll blow a big hole right through you. Who's that you got with you? I'll blow a big hole right through him, too."

"It's just me and a friend, Mr. Cloyd. We came to pick up the girls and go to a show."

"You try to put one finger on my girls and I'll pour kerosene down your britches and light the match myself. Is that boy a Mexican?"

"No, sir, Mr. Cloyd. He's not a Mexican."

"I don't want no Mexicans playing around with my girls. This is a proud family."

The house was on land slightly higher and dryer than the *cienega*, and as we walked up to the front steps I could see that Cloyd wore a beard, a big crushed black hat and a dirty union suit, and carried a heavy 12-gauge

68

double. The right leg of his long johns was split to make room for the cast, which stretched from his waist to his foot. Velva Mae and Venery Ann were standing behind him, almost hidden by his bulk, peeking at us.

"Hey, Parker," Venery Ann said. "Did you bring your car?"

"You shut your whorin' mouth," Cloyd said, "or I'll lay a gunstock across your butt. You boys, you just stand right there while I lock these two strumpets up in the storeroom."

"You got enough gas for a good long drive?" Velva Mae asked. "Me and Venery want to ride that big wheel."

"I got half a tank," Parker said. "Mr. Cloyd, the movie starts in about thirty minutes, and we better start now, if it's okay with you. How's your leg?"

"You never mind my leg, you little stinkpot, or I'll throw you and that jellybean friend of yours in the cesspool."

The girls squeezed between their father and the door frame and joined us, wearing cotton print dresses and knee-high wading boots, and carrying their city shoes in their hands. "We'll be home around twelve or one, Papa," Venery Ann said.

"And you better come back in the state of purity you left in, you little chippy, or I'll sell you to an Ay-rab whoremaster."

We waded back to the car while Cloyd yelled curses at us. Velva Mae held my hand and told me she'd ridden in a Lincoln once in Las Cruces, and still got the shivers from it, it was that dreamy. She said she'd swallow her pride for tonight for a ride in Parker's Plymouth, because it was wartime. We put our boots in the trunk, changed to more civilized footwear, and started back to Sagrado.

"The whole car smells like fish," Venery Ann complained.

"We can always walk," Parker told her.

"I don't mind a little old fish smell," she said.

We saw a movie about Sergeant York. Velva Mae said she couldn't understand how a big hero like Gary Cooper would come back and marry a little flat-chested thing like Joan Leslie when he had all those bazoomy French girls to choose from. Parker and Venery Ann spent most of the movie kissing each other and going out to the lobby for Black Crows and popcorn. When we'd seen the cartoon twice, we walked across the street to Rumpp's Pharmacy and choked down some mooncakes and strawberry malts. It was nearly ten when we returned to the Plymouth.

"We got two, three hours yet," Velva Mae said. "Let's go up to North Hill and watch the moon come up."

"It looks like snow," Parker said. "Can't see the moon tonight."

"I can always go right back in the movie and find somebody else to give me a ride," she said. "We gonna drive or not?"

We drove slowly to the top of North Hill, the site of a fort the Americans built when they first took Sagrado away from the Mexicans a hundred years before. If there had ever been a fort there, it had since disappeared completely. There wasn't even an outline; just a wide flat space on a hill that looked south over the town, with piñon and juniper trees scattered around. At night, there were cars or pickup trucks parked behind most of the trees. Steenie and I had walked up there one night, and whenever we kicked a stone or brushed against a tree branch, startled faces popped up from back seats to identify the disturbance. "If the entire nation operated on the North Hill plan," Steenie had said, "we'd have a larger population than China in twenty-five years."

Parker pulled his Plymouth behind a broad juniper, and opened a window to air out some of the fish odor. The sky was covered with low, thick clouds, and neither moon nor stars were visible. The lights of Sagrado were only a sprinkle; we didn't have to dim out that far inland, but there was no night life in the town and people tended to go to bed early. I put my arm around Velva Mae, whose sharp little teeth were chattering.

"It's pretty up here, isn't it?" I said, making some of the brilliant drawing-room repartee for which I was famous on three continents.

70

"If you're gonna try to make out, you better not talk," she said. "I don't like a lot of conversation."

Parker put his elbow on the back of the front seat and turned to face us. "My package came in from Tennessee," he said. "Cost me three-fifty plus postage, but it sure is worth it."

"That's great," I said. "Why don't you tell Venery Ann about it?"

"Shoot, she's not interested, are you, Venery?"

"Uh uh," she agreed.

"I'm not interested neither," Velva Mae told him, "so why don't you just turn around and get to doin' whatever you got in mind?"

"It's not something that would interest a girl," Parker continued, "but old Josh is interested."

I took my arm from around Velva Mae's neck. "Okay," I said to Parker, "I'm all ears. What did you get from Tennessee that cost three-fifty plus postage? I haven't eaten a thing for three days just worrying about it."

"I got a half-pint of fox urine," he said triumphantly. "I figure it to last me the whole winter."

"If you drink it real slowly," I said, "it might last you *two* winters."

Velva Mae had started slightly beside me, and was looking at Parker as if he'd just sprouted snapdragons from his ears. "You got a half a pint of what?"

"Fox urine," he said. "Vixen urine from Tennessee foxes."

"You mean . . . pee?"

Parker looked injured. "In game conservation work, we call it urine. We use a lot of biological terms like that."

"I think it's cheap of you to hog it all to yourself, Park," I said. "Shouldn't you share the good stuff with your friends? I'll pay my half."

"What in the world would you do with that?" Venery Ann asked from the gloom of the front seat.

"Bait fox traps with it," Park said. "What else would I do with it?"

"Are you tryin' to make fun of us?" Velva Mae said.

71

"We may be country, but we don't have to stand for nasty talk."

"You see what happens when you try to have a little intelligent conversation," Park said to me. "The girls get all foolish and start dancing around calling names."

"You can drive us home right now, Parker Holmes," Velva Mae said.

I grabbed at her and tried to get back in our former position, with my arm around her. "You don't want to go now," I said. "We just got here. The moon hasn't even started to rise yet."

"Well. . . ." I could tell that Velva Mae didn't really want to go home. I kissed her and she bit me lightly on the lower lip, not too painfully. Parker wasn't concentrating on Venery Ann. He was still half turned in his seat, with an arm hooked over the back, looking at us.

"At three-fifty for a half a pint, I make it fourteen dollars a quart. That's a lot more expensive than whiskey."

"Don't pay any mind to him," Velva Mae whispered into my ear, and then nipped me on the ear lobe and ran her fingers around the scar on my temple. "How'd you get that little scar?"

"A doctor took out a piece of skull to look inside. Said he'd never seen anything like it in thirty years of medical practice. Say, why don't you bite the other ear for a while? I think this one's starting to bleed."

"I dearly love to chew on boys," Velva Mae said. "Here, you stay where you're at, and I'll scrunch over." She heaved herself up and sat on my lap, and slid off slowly to the other side. "That was fun," she said. "Let's have a bite off that other ear."

"Don't you go marking him up," Venery Ann said from the front seat, where she was fiddling with the dials on the dashboard. "Hey, Parker. Where's the headlights?"

"It's that little knob right there," he told her. "Don't go turning it on. You'll run down the battery."

"I'll just give it a little flip," she said. "I want to see who all's in that car up ahead." She turned the lights on briefly, and illuminated a 1934 La Salle with a broken rear window. "I bet they're cold in there with their clothes off and all that air comin' in."

"That's Chango in that car, isn't it?" Parker said. "He must be following you around."

"Let's get out of here, Park," I said. "I don't want to get blood all over your car."

"You're not afraid of Chango Lopez, are you?" Velva Mae said. "I thought you were a man."

"One of the things that doctor saw when he looked inside my head was that I was a *gallina*. Come on, Park, let's go."

Parker turned on the motor and the girls began to whine. "There isn't no place else to park," Velva Mae said. "There's policemen all over with flashlights, lookin' in at you."

"If we don't leave right now," I said, "I'm taking off on foot down the hill. The last time I saw Chango he and a friend of his were waving knives around."

Parker backed around through a clump of juniper and started down the hill. Velva Mae pushed me away and sat close against the back door with her arms folded, pouting. I took out my handkerchief and wiped off my ears, which were sore and wet. "I'm sorry, Velva Mae," I said. "You don't want me to get killed, do you? What's the fun of that? You'd be a witness, and have to answer questions in court. Some smart lawyer would say 'Miss Cloyd, the body of the deceased showed forty-three stab wounds in the chest and abdomen and a chewed condition of both ear lobes. Would you tell the court, please, whether. . . .' "

"You just run on, Arnold, and my daddy'll jump up and down on you when we get back to the house, if I tell him to. I'm not ever goin' out with you again."

We made the long trip back to the Cloyds' *cienega* in silence, and it began to snow before we got there. "This is going to be the first big one," Parker said. "That one back at Fiesta time was just a starter. Be eight, ten inches on the ground by tomorrow morning."

"It sure gets cold in that old swamp in winter," Venery Ann said. "I wish Daddy'd move into the city, but he likes it out there. He says he can always hear people coming through the water, and no one can sneak up on him and steal his pigs."

We all put on our boots for the long hike through the *cienega*, and went single file. I tripped once and fell on my knees and hands, and Velva Mae giggled. I was freezing and wet when we got to the darkened Cloyd house, and said good night to the girls. Venery Ann and Parker kissed each other.

"I'm not gonna kiss you," Velva Mae said. "You're all wet."

The front door snapped open and Mr. Cloyd put his head out. "You're goddamn rootin' tootin' you ain't gonna kiss him good night, you little two-bit tart. You get your little tail inside right now or I'll put a boot up it."

"That's Daddy," she told me, as though the fact weren't already clear. "I think I better go in. Come on, Venery."

"Good night," I said.

"Good night."

"See you at school."

"You two little whorehoppers better move out smart or I'll start kickin' asses," Mr. Cloyd bellowed. When Parker and I were halfway back to the car, we could still hear him yelling at us through the night: "Them two girls better be pure!"

10

A LETTER CAME from Dad:

Dear Josh,

Well, I was a little afraid of that, but Jimbob's harmless, at best, and at worst he's irritating. You probably don't know this, but he hasn't got a nickel of his own; his family was a power before Reconstruction, but the Buels sold their land in

74

the 1880s at something like two dollars an acre. Jimbob's four years at the University of Virginia took care of the last of it, and he's been a semi-professional house guest ever since. He has many talents and no skills, and the sort of short-lasting charm which comes from having learned good manners as an exercise. He's a useless man, intelligent enough to know it and decent enough to hate himself for it. It's difficult to say what your role should be in this. Just be yourself, and I hope I'm not unleashing a monster by saying that.

You may use the FPO address from now on. I'm executive officer on a DE (that's a destroyer escort, as if you didn't know) and never mind where. I'm also the ship's censor, and read everyone's mail. I'll be happy to tell you about some of the hair-raising things sailors write to their wives and girlfriends when you're old enough, say in about forty years.

If you haven't already met him, look up an old friend of mine named Romeo Bonino. He's a sculptor and lives, or used to live, on Camino Chiquito with a girl named Georgine. It was Georgine two years ago, at any rate. The civil arrangement is always rather loose-jointed at his place, if you know what I mean. Your mother can't stand him, for various reasons. You'll like him, I think. In a strange way, he may be a good influence on you.

The Armed Forces Radio Service says there was a big storm over the Rockies a few days ago. How do you like snow, you swamp rat?

Enclosed check is for Amadeo. Don't make deals with him; just give it to him.

Love,
Captain Bligh

And a letter from Courtney Ann Conway:

Dear Josh,

How are you? I am fine. I've been sailing a lot because it's still warm, and Bubba says to tell you hello. School is as much fun as always (ha ha, joke). The paper said there was a German submarine in the bay the same day we were out in the sloop but it didn't sink us. All the niggers are working at the plants and making just scads of money and Daddy says it's going to ruin the economy.

Bye now.

Lotsalove,
Corky

And a letter from Lacey:

Dear Little Boss,

Paul and I are both working full-time and over-time at the boat plant, sometimes 60 hrs. a week making as much as $110 each and saving up to buy a house in Rosewood for after the War. Your Daddy said he'd carry our paper when he got back but at the rate we're going he might not have to. We get letters right along from your Daddy and a check sometimes also. Looks like you forgotten how to write. It's been some hot here all along right through the middle of October and isn't rained hardly any so the crawfish holes has dried up and they're bringing 49¢ a pound, hows the crawfishing out where you are? Paul says are you getting into that wine like before.

Love and kisses to your Mother,
Lacey Robinson XXXXXXXX

This is Paul writing now. Lacey is still snapping mackerel and she's going to be the biggest thing in the Church maybe Pope. Like in the song, I'm a Methodist till I die, but come Friday Lacey still cooks up Pompano and man, who can call that fasting? Lacey says if I go Catholic I get a spot in heaven and I sure hope it's cooler than what it is here in Mobile.

Your friend,
Paul

And, finally, a note on light blue paper from Marcia:

Dear Josh:

I'm sorry I've been acting like such a nut. Will you forgive me? The biggest muscle Bucky has is the one between his ears, and I feel as if I've been talking to a loaf of bread for two weeks. Will you talk to me at school tomorrow or will I have to become a Lesbian, which I just found out about and they're fascinating.

Your honcho,
Marcia

11

WE WERE IN ENGLISH class one morning, making faces at the Lucy poems, when Chamaco Trujillo came in with Ratoncito, the principal, and began to whisper something in Miss Jefferson's ear. Steenie stood up and announced, dramatically, that he was the guilty party and to please take him away so he wouldn't do it again. He was giving an involved, psychological explanation for his crimes, whatever they were, when Miss Jefferson said, "Steenie, be quiet. Joshua Arnold, will you come here, please?"

Chamaco, acting in his capacity as sheriff and not as Fiesta impresario, was in full dress, Southwestern version of cop. He was wearing mostly khaki uniform with a neat black tie, but he set it off with high-heeled boots, a big Stetson and a service revolver hung low with the holster thong tied around his thigh. He was about forty pounds overweight, and a lot of him was hanging over his belt, but he looked serious.

As I walked between the desks toward the front of the room, Steenie muttered, "Breakout tonight in Wing D, pass it on," but Chamaco and Miss Jefferson and Ratoncito were all looking at me, and it wasn't time to laugh. I caught Marcia's eye on the way; she looked interested and alert, but not particularly sorry to see me taken away by the police. I believe she was figuring out a way to meet this new challenge; I pictured her, briefly, standing at her kitchen counter with an open cookbook before her and a messy array of cake-baking materials cluttering up the work space: flour, eggs, sugar, baking powder and a Nicholson file, recommended for sawing through three-quarter-inch chilled steel bars.

Ratoncito, Chamaco and I walked single file to a small room near the principal's office, and Ratoncito left us there. Chamaco told me to sit down, and sat across from me.

"Mr. Trujillo," I opened, "I'm really sorry about yelling at you in the Plaza. I mean, I know you were doing your best with those people, and of course it wasn't your fault it started to snow. They say it never snows here in September, and that was just a freak storm, but I really know how hard you were working and it wasn't nice to try to kid you about it, and I'm very sorry."

Chamaco stared at me during my little speech and kept on staring after I finished, as if he were afraid I might vanish in a puff of green vapor. He eventually reached into his breast pocket and withdrew a cigarette, which he lit. He blew smoke slowly and thoughtfully.

"What the faulk are you talking about?" he asked.

"Fiesta," I said. "You remember, this Fiesta when it started to snow and some friends of mine and I. . . ."

"Arnole, I been having a bunch of esmart-ass kids yelling at me since before you was born."

"You have?"

"Jess. That ain' what I come about." He blew some more smoke and stared at me again. "You know a boy name Tarzan? Tarzan Velarde?"

"Yes, I've met him."

"When's the last time that you seen him?"

"A couple of weeks ago, on Camino Chiquito."

"What did you talk about?"

"We didn't really talk about anything. He was chasing me, and I was running. He had a knife. I think it was a knife, anyway."

"Jess, it was a knife. He likes to go aroun' esticking it in people's tires. Lahs' night he estock it in a fren' of his. You prob'ly know him too. Maximiliano Lopez, goes to school here."

"You mean somebody stuck Chango Lopez with a knife?"

"Thahs right. Through the gots and part of the liver."

"Kill him?"

"No, didn't kill him. He's in the hospital, be there for a couple of weeks."

"Well, Sheriff, how come you're asking me about it? I hardly know Tarzan, just that time on Camino Chiquito. He's not what you'd call a good friend of mine."

"The reason I asked you is 'cause Chango tole me in the hospital, 'Ask Chosh Arnole.' Maybe he think there's something about it you know."

"I'm sorry, Sheriff, I don't know anything about it. I don't even know where Tarzan lives."

"Oh, we been to his house. He's not there, and his father tole us to go take a ronning faulk. So we think he's hide out somewhere, maybe in the hills north of town, maybe he hitch a ride somewhere."

"Mr. Trujillo, I swear I don't know anything about Tarzan Velarde, but if I see him I'll come tell you, and not stand there and argue with him."

Chamaco extinguished his cigarette and lit another one. "That's a good idea. His mother tole me she thinks he's crazy and ought to be lock up somewhere. Me, I jos' hope I don' have to shoot him." He blew some more smoke, and sought Tarzan in the swirling pattern. "You a good friend of the Lopez boy, huh?"

"No, sir, I don't think you'd say Chango and I are exactly friends, either. As a matter of fact, he doesn't like me very much. Of course, I'm sorry he got knifed in the liver."

"I known Lopez since he was confirmed. He's toff, an' he's mean-talking, bot he ain' as moch trouble as a lotta boys. He wouldn't tell me how come Tarzan estock him. He says he's gone get Tarzan himself, which I don't think is ver' likely in his condition right now. Are you sure you're not a good fren' of Lopez's? He sure was talking there in the hospital like you was."

"If he thinks we're friends he's got a funny way of showing it. He keeps accusing me of messing around with his sister."

79

"Oh, jess. His sister. That's Viola." Chamaco made the cupped hand gesture in front of his shirt.

"That's the one," I said.

"Hokay, why don't you get back to the classroom. I'll tell Mr. Alexander to spread the word about keeping a lookout for Tarzan." He heaved himself out of his chair, and paused. "Nex' year, if I see you yellin at me by the bandstand, I'm coming offa there and kick the cheat out of you. Hokay?"

"Okay, Sheriff."

After classes that morning, Marcia and Steenie and I walked over to Rumpp's Pharmacy for one of their double-thin chocolate malts. The snow was beginning to melt, and was piling up gray and sad against the hedges. The gutters were full of brown water and in spite of the blue sky it was a depressing day, cold and slushy. I wanted some fresh snow to fall and cover up the ugly places.

Steenie felt it, too. "One more good snow," he said, "and we can go sledding down Otero Hill. You like to sled, Josh?"

"We didn't do too much of it back in Alabama," I said, "there not being any hills or any snow."

"We have a little game we play on the sled," Marcia said, "that we call *gallina.*"

"You mean you go sledding on a dead horse?"

"No, this is another kind of *gallina.* We'll show you when the time comes."

We sat in a booth, and Marcia tried to pump me about my date with Parker and the Cloyd girls.

"I assume you comported yourself like a man," she said. "I mean, after all, it's a simple biological urge, like eating and self-preservation. It's nothing to be ashamed of."

"Everybody else has made it with the Cloyds," Steenie said. "Well, almost everybody. I personally keep myself pure for my work, like a monk."

"As a matter of fact," I said, "we spent the whole evening talking about the price of fox urine. According to our computation, it comes to $14 a quart."

Marcia ignored me. "Was it a beautiful and tender

80

experience," she asked, "or was it mechanical and sordid? I understand it can go either way."

"It can be frightening and repulsive, too," Steenie added. "Or mystical and religious. There aren't any hard-and-fast rules."

"I'm sorry," I said. "I don't want to talk about it. If you talk about something too much it sort of takes the bloom off. Just let me say it was a night I'll always treasure."

"You're a liar," Marcia said. "You didn't touch either one of them. You're a show-off."

Steenie patted her hand. "Don't try to take the lad's memories away from him," he told her. "Don't try to embarrass him. It's a decisive emotional experience for a boy, just as it is for a girl."

"Right," I said.

"Nuts," Marcia said. "I want another lousy malt, and if I get one my lousy face will break out and I'll put another lousy inch on my lousy hips, and I'll look even more like Sophie Tucker than I do now."

"That's ridiculous," Steenie said. "You're the most beautiful girl west of the Allegheny River. Josh and I are both blinded by your beauty. It's like going out and having a malt with Notre Dame Cathedral."

"You make Betty Grable look like a sack of oyster shells."

"You have hair like the mane on a clean lion, not that I ever saw a clean lion."

"You could drive whole regiments mad with your looks. Picasso is dying to paint you, with two noses and seven eyes."

"Natalie Kalmus wants to do you in Technicolor."

"José Iturbi wants to play the Minute Waltz in fifty-seven seconds, just for you."

"If your ankles weren't just a little thick, Gary Cooper would. . . ."

"What's that about my ankles?"

"Well," Steenie said, "they're not what you'd call gross, but maybe a half-inch less wouldn't hurt."

"Marcia," I said, "believe me. I think your ankles are fine. You're perfection just the way you are, and maybe a couple of inches more up on top there would do the trick."

"What's the matter with up on top here?"

"Matter? Nothing's the matter. It's delightful, what there is of it, and I guess it's enough."

"Technically speaking," said Steenie. "Medically speaking."

"I don't know why I let myself be seen with you two *pendejos*," she said. "Bucky Swenson said only nice things about me."

"Like what?"

"He said I was cute."

"That's my Bucky," Steenie said. "A master of sweet talk. He purrs those golden words in your ear. . . ."

"Those honeyed words. . . ."

". . . those honeyed words in your ear, and you swoon. You turn over the keys to your jewel box to him. You let him drive your Rolls-Royce."

"I wish I could talk like Bucky Swenson," I said. "I get all tongue-tied around girls."

"Me too," Steenie said.

"Why don't you and Josh go fly a lake?" Marcia suggested.

"How about if we go jump in a kite?" Steenie asked her reasonably.

"You know what I mean."

I took her hand and looked earnestly and, I think, soulfully, into her eyes. "Marcia, we love you. We really do. We think you're the swellest girl on the block." Steenie took her other hand. "Nobody can play marbles or get scabs on her knees as well as you," he said.

"You're just like one of the fellows. Nobody would ever know you were a girl."

"Now, stop it!" she said briskly, her eyes beginning to get red. "I told you I was sorry about going around with Bucky. I crawled on my hands and knees to you. I humiliated myself."

I kissed her on the cheek. Steenie kissed her on the other cheek.

"You're both a couple of never minds," she said.

"A couple of whats?" Steenie asked her.

"My father doesn't want me to use the word. He says it's a sign of a weak vocabulary. But you are. Both of you."

"Are what?" I asked.

"Bastards."

Steenie dropped his spoon and looked at her aghast. "Marcia! A word like that coming from your sweet lips! I'm disgusted."

"I'm going to throw up my malt, right here on the table," I said. "Language like that makes my stomach turn over. Argghhh! I'll never be the same again; I've been in contact with true filth."

Marcia looked solemnly at Steenie and then at me. "Oh, shit," she said evenly.

"That's my girl," Steenie said.

"Now you're talking," I said. "That's my good old Marcia."

We each had another watery chocolate malt, a genuine wartime confection, and wondered where all the chocolate, and malt, and ice cream went in wartime. Steenie felt that it was converted into explosives at a secret arsenal near Bunkie, Louisiana. Marcia claimed it was dropped on Tokyo, so that the Japanese would eat it and break out in acne, thus bringing a swift conclusion to the Pacific war.

As we walked back to school, Marcia suggested that we visit Chango in the hospital. "Poor guy," she said, "lying there with plasma dripping into his veins, and nobody to stomp on. Too sick to protect Viola from a fate worse than death. Why is it called that, by the way?"

"Don't ask me," Steenie said. "I don't call it that."

"Well, I'm perfectly willing to visit Chango," I said, "if you can promise the strain of entertaining visitors will kill him. Maybe we can all sit on his bed and bounce up and down."

"That's a horrible and nasty thing to say," Marcia said, "and I know you don't mean a word of it."

"I can always pick a bouquet of chamiso for him. If he sneezes enough it might break open his stitches."

"There's something about injecting an air bubble into the vein," Steenie suggested. "A painful death, and no trace. I can probably sneak a syringe out of my dad's bag."

"You guys are just ghoulish," Marcia said. "There's nothing wrong with Chango that a little love and tenderness won't cure."

"Love and tenderness and a new liver," Steenie said.

The afternoon went slowly, and the classes buzzed with talk about Tarzan and Chango, neither of whom was in the running for Best Personality to begin with. The boys all swore they were going to carry side arms until Tarzan was captured and brought to justice, but the only one who owned a side arm was Parker, and he wasn't going to wear his. "A gun is a tool of game management," he announced, "and not a weapon. We use them for killing predators."

"I can't think of a better word for Tarzan Velarde," I told him.

"Don't try to mix me up," he said.

The nurses on duty pointed out Chango's ward to us that afternoon. Apparently we weren't going to get him alone. There were four beds in his room, two of them empty. An old man lay in one of them, his face turned toward the wall. A group of what could only have been relatives sat on chairs in a semicircle around his bed. Chango was lying next to the other wall, looking pale and small under the white sheet. Someone, probably a doctor with a strong sense of hygiene, had washed his hair. He lay with both arms above the sheet, and raised one weakly. "Hi," he said. "It's nice of you to come." He'd lost his *pachuco* accent, too.

Over at the other bed, the relatives were alternately grieving—a little too soon, I felt; the patient wasn't dead—and discussing the division of the property. One of them, a strongly built young man who should have been out earning a living by himself, was saying: "Papacito, you know I should get all the land east of the big cottonwood, because it was me told you to plant alfalfa there in the first place. I mean, Jesus, Papacito, what the hell can Ramon do with six acres, anyway?"

Marcia picked up one of Chango's tough brown hands and patted it, something she'd never have done if he'd

84

been on his feet. "You look terrible, Maximiliano," she said solicitously. "What does it feel like to get stabbed all the way into your liver?"

"It hurts," he answered. "It feels like I'm on fire in there."

Over at the other bed, where the agony was taking place, one of the women said, "The big room has eighteen *vigas* across the ceiling, and if you're going to divide it equally, Carmen and Consuelo and I should get six each, and since I'm the oldest I ought to get the six in the middle, with the fireplace."

Steenie stuck his fingers out straight and flat, and pointed them down, over Chango's stomach. "I'm going to probe a little, Chango. Scream out if I hit a tender spot."

Chango turned even paler, and sweat broke out on his upper lip. "Jesus, please for God's sake don't poke me down there. Christ almighty, *te ruego, hombre.* I'm not kidding, man."

"If you touch him, William Stenopolous, I'll never speak to you again," Marcia said.

Steenie emitted a professional-sounding hum, and let his fingers relax. "Perhaps actual palpation won't be necessary," he continued. "You notice what happened with the mere threat. He said 'please.' This may be a medical miracle, like sulfa or anesthesia."

"Please, please, please, man," Chango said.

"By God," Steenie said. "A complete change of personality. I wonder if *The Lancet* would accept an article from a seventeen-year-old American amateur. It would be a nice thing to show the faculty when I enter medical school."

At the other bed, one of the sons or nephews was saying, "Well, hell, old man, if you won't say where you got the silver plates hidden at least tell me where to get the keys to the pickup."

"How you doing, Chango?" I said. "Aren't you going to call me any names?"

"Man," Chango said, "I'm real sorry about that. Real sorry. You never did anything to me, and I want to get that off my conscience."

"Chango, how come you're talking so fancy? What happened to that greaseball accent?"

"I just talked like that 'cause I thought it was tough. I was, you know, *muy macho*."

"You don't look so *macho* now, guy," Marcia told him. "You look like you just had twins."

The tender scene at the other bed was getting noisier. The sick man had turned around to face his family, and was giving them all the finger. "I told you I already had confession and the last rites and all that, so my soul's clean and I'm not going to talk about business. The lawyer's got the will, and after I'm gone you can all have a look at it. If you don't like what you find, you can fly up to heaven and kiss my ass."

Chango gestured at the bereaved family. "They been going on like that all day. That's a tough old man over there, but they'll kill him sooner or later."

"And you, you *perezozo pendejo*," the old man was saying to the largest and huskiest of the men, "if I leave you any property you'll have to get off the welfare and either work the land or find a job. Do you think at forty years old you'd be willing to make such a big change in your life? Hah? Get out of here, all of you, before I blaspheme and have to do the whole extreme unction all over again."

The oldest woman of the family said. "Let's all pray for the soul of your father," and the children obediently arranged themselves in pious attitudes and began keening in Latin.

"The Good Lord won't listen to a word you say," the old man told them. "He doesn't hear it when a weasel prays to Him to let him get into the hen house." He flipped around and faced the wall again.

Marcia was looking at Chango as if he were a wrapped Christmas present. "Can I pull down the sheet and see where the knife went in?" she asked him. "I've never seen a real stab wound."

"It's all covered over with bandages," Chango said. "They got a rubber tube stuck in there, and they feed me through the . . . they don't let me eat the usual way."

"I know a joke about that," Steenie said. "This guy was being fed rectally, and he asked the doctor. . . ."

"I know it too, man. Don't tell it in front of the girl," Chango pleaded.

"I swear," Steenie said, "if I'd known a knife could do this I'd have used one on you years ago. You going to take holy orders as soon as you get out of high school?"

"Chango," I said, "what was all that crap you told Chamaco? You know I don't know anything about Tarzan, except that he scared the hell out of me that day by the *acequia.*"

"Man, I thought Tarzan would come to see you after he stuck me. He's crazy. He wants to stick a knife in everybody. That day on Camino Chiquito I didn't even know he *had* a knife. I just asked him to help me some. We were gonna knock you around and kick you a little bit so you wouldn't wise off. Man, I really didn't know. And then you took off like a coyote and ran into that guy's patio. Hell, I knew where you were. I could see your shadow there by the woodpile, but I was afraid if I told Tarzan he'd go in there and cut you. And then last night I saw him down by the river, and he'd been thinking about it all that time and he was in a real bad mood. He said I was chicken. He said I practiced running fast so I could catch rabbits and make *pinche* with them. So then I told him to go to hell and he said, '*Tómalo, cabrón,*' and stuck me with his *hojita,* and man, I went down. Then while I'm lying there he bends over and says, 'I'm gonna finish the job on *Josué*' and then he kicked me in the . . . and then he kicked me and took off. So, man, I thought if he hadn't got you already you might at least know where he is, so I told Chamaco. Does Chamaco know where he is?"

"Chamaco told me he could be hiding out north of town, or he might have hitchhiked somewhere."

"No, he isn't gonna leave town unless the cops really get after him."

"Well, who's this *Josué* he's after? Me?"

"That's you, man. I mean, he knows where you live and which way you walk to school. You better look out.

87

He's not young like us. He's twenty years old. He spent three years in the sixth grade."

A nurse came in briskly and said, "Here's your dinner, young man. Your visitors will have to leave." An orderly was wheeling in a stainless steel hatrack with some bottles and tubes hanging on it.

"Mmm," Steenie said. "Looks delicious."

"Don't kid around about that, man," Chango said. "It ain't funny."

The family at the other bed finished their prayers and put their beads away. The old man was still facing the wall.

12

IT SNOWED FOR THREE DAYS in early November, and the people of Sagrado put their cars in garages and walked everywhere. Amadeo, who came in from Río Conejo every morning in the pickup, put snow chains on the rear tires and loaded the truck bed with three hundred pounds of concrete blocks to get traction. An entire family of Navajo Indians froze to death in a drafty hogan near Beclabito, when the temperature went to 46 below one night. Forest Rangers on snowshoes hiked up to Bernal Peak and announced that the 117 inches of snowpack promised a good spring runoff. *The Conquistador* ran a picture page called "Winter Wonderland," which showed primarily that one of their photographers didn't know how to compensate for the glare on snow and had overexposed a lot of film. Amadeo and I stacked three cords of foot-and-a-half split piñon for the fireplaces, and the whole town smelled like a campfire. Parker gave me a venison hindquarter and my mother told me to take the filthy thing out of the house, so I gave it to Excilda. She and Amadeo and I stuffed ourselves on venison chile for a week, and then she made *sopa de albondigas* with what was left. I went sledding with Marcia and Steenie, on Otero Hill, the three of us piled up sandwich fashion on one sled, Marcia on top. We just missed getting creamed by the Blue Goose Laundry truck. Nobody knew what had happened to Tarzan Velarde; we all hoped that he was now lying, stiff as a plank, under a juniper tree in a nameless arroyo. Bucky Swenson set a new conference record for rebound baskets and gave a modest interview to *The Conquistador's* sports editor, in which he said that regular church attendance played an important part in his training. The highways were closed for almost a week. When a Highway Department employee named Orlando Lucero drove the first snowplow into town, opening the roads again, the mayor declared it Orlando Lucero Day, and the Chamber of Commerce gave a dinner for him. Lucero got drunk at the dinner and smashed the window of Wormser's Dry Goods while driving his snowplow recklessly around the Plaza. The snow drove a herd of elk into town. One of the bulls wandered into the Sagrado State Bank and got an antler caught in a teller's window. They called Chamaco, after the Game Department tried ineffectively to lure the elk outside with a bale of alfalfa. Chamaco shot it with his service revolver. The animal weighed 900 pounds and the depositors had to stand on top of it that morning to get their banking done, because it was too heavy to drag out. After Orlando Lucero got out of jail, where he served three days for drunkenness after the incident with Wormser's Dry Goods, he went back to his job with the Highway Department and ruptured the town's main gas line with his backhoe the same afternoon. The mayor and the City Council met and, for the first time in three hundred and fifty years, withdrew a proclamation—the one establishing Orlando Lucero Day—and issued another one banishing Lucero from "the hospitality and usufruct of La Villa Real del Corazón Sagrado." Jimbob Buel went outside in his slippers to berate Amadeo, who was shoveling snow, noisily, beneath Jimbob's window one morning, and caught a head cold, which turned into a chest cold, and then into lobar pneumonia. He went into the hospital the same day that Chango was released.

I'd been visiting Chango fairly regularly after school, and sometimes I walked there with his sister Viola. She was moody and withdrawn, a little too wrapped up in Holy Mother Church for my taste. Out of respect for her beliefs, and equal respect for Chango's former bad humor, I tried to keep my eyes off the front of her blouse. When she took the veil, the ecclesiastical tailors were going to have trouble fitting her into a habit. Viola and I were on hand, along with Steenie and Marcia and Chango's parents, the day he got out.

He was still slightly pallid, and his Levis hung loosely around his hips, but he looked ready to go. The knife had truly frightened him, he said, and knowing what it felt like to be on the receiving end he claimed he was through with being a professional *macho,* unless someone really insulted him. He still had the arms and shoulders of a medium-sized gorilla, and I didn't think it likely that anyone smaller than Primo Carnera would think of trifling with him. He chivalrously took off his shirt to let Marcia see the scar, which she'd begged him to do every time she came to see him. Viola turned her head delicately while this coarse disrobing took place. Chango's scar ran from his navel to the right side of his ribcage; the first inch was thick and crooked, where Tarzan's knife had penetrated. The rest of it was thin and surgical. The surgeon had opened him up like a gored bullfighter to clean the wound.

"Eeho-lay," Marcia said. "That's a beauty!"

"You feeling all right?" Chango's mother asked him in Spanish. "You feeling pretty strong?"

"Sure, Mama," Chango said.

She cracked him a stiff one on the cheek with her open hand. "Maybe now you'll stay away from *pachucos* like Tarzan Velarde, may the root of his tree be torn out and burned on the Fourth of July."

"Aw, Mama," Chango said, rubbing his cheek.

"It's cold as ice cream outside," Mrs. Lopez said. "I brought you a sweater, *carito mio,* you with your big ideas."

"They didn't find Tarzan yet, did they?" Chango asked.

"No," Steenie answered. "They'll dig him out next spring sometime, if the coyotes don't get to him first."

"Ojalá que tengas razón," Mrs. Lopez said. "I hope you're right."

Mr. Lopez had brought his pickup—you just weren't anybody around Sagrado unless you owned a pickup—and we drove slowly, with lots of skids, to Chango's house. I'd never been there before; I'd always assumed he lived in a cage. It was an old adobe on the west side of town, with an acre of kitchen garden, now snow-covered. I don't know how Mr. Lopez made the worthless soil in Sagrado produce, but he said he got three grades of chile, cucumbers, squash, tomatoes, corn, *frijoles* and asparagus out of it. Mrs. Lopez gave us coffee and we sat around and kidded Chango about what a brave little trouper he was. Mrs. Lopez slapped him again, and then gave him a big hug. Pale as he was, we could see the blushes clearly. Marcia insisted on seeing his bedroom. He showed us a bare, monastic cell with an old photograph of Vincent "Mad Dog" Coll on the wall.

Mr. Lopez offered to drive us home, but we declined. It was a fine, cold evening, and we felt like walking. Marcia said on our way home that she'd always known Chango couldn't be as bad as everyone thought he was. Steenie said the conversion was less medical than he'd first suspected, and more mystical. "That dirty bandit has had a first-class religious experience," he announced, "and it was Tarzan's knife that did it to him. I'm going to write directly to the Pope and suggest that he equip all of his missionaries with six-inch shivs. 'Do you believe in Holy Mother Church, infidel? No? Then, *tómalo!*'" Steenie stabbed an imaginary unbeliever in the navel with an imaginary knife, and converted an imaginary heathen. "I may go into church work," he said. "Convert 'em first, and sew 'em up afterwards. I'll be a medical missionary with a built-in practice."

"Steenie," Marcia said, "you lie better and more often than anybody I know. I don't think you'll ever make it to medical school. You're going to be a career grocery-bagger at Safeway, and get a testimonial dinner after forty years of putting the lettuce and the eggs at the bottom of the sack, with the cans on top."

We walked Marcia home, and then I walked Steenie home. His father was asleep, fully dressed, on the living room couch. Mrs. Stenopolous shushed us and we tiptoed into the kitchen. "Your father's been delivering babies since six this morning," she told Steenie. "Why do these women always wait until the snow's three feet deep before they have labor pains? He delivered four at the hospital, two at home and one in the drunk tank at the Police Station. Then an hour ago a police car radioed in to headquarters and they telephoned him to hustle out to the Texcoco Road and deliver twins in the back of a pickup."

"It sounds like a very exciting life, Mrs. Stenopolous," I said.

"Oh, God!"

"Can Josh and I go into Dad's study?" Steenie asked.

"Sure," she said. "Go look at the gruesome pictures. Go look at photographs of breech deliveries. Why can't you get your sex education in the gutter like the other boys?"

The *Handbook on Obstetrics* was a revelation, and I learned a number of new and useful words, but I didn't see how Dr. Stenopolous could look at that sort of thing all day and remain interested in Mrs. Stenopolous at night.

It was good, later, to get back to a house without Jimbob Buel in it. Mother was on the telephone, talking to someone at the hospital, and saying, "You mustn't forget that Mr. Buel has asthma, too, and finds breathing difficult under any circumstances."

"And don't forget to send the bills to you," I said.

"Oh, yes," she went on, "and send all the bills to me, Mrs. Francis Arnold, Seven-Nineteen Camino Tuerto."

After she hung up, she turned to me and said, "You think this is all very funny, don't you? Of course, you've been blessed with good health. You don't know what it's like to have pneumonia."

"I'm from the South myself," I said, "but I know

better than to go stomping around in the snow with bedroom slippers on. I'm surprised Amadeo didn't bean him with the snow shovel."

"Amadeo," she said, "seems to be forgetting that he's a servant and not a member of the family. Your father's always been too lenient with both of them. He seems to lose all perspective whenever he comes to Sagrado, and forgets his class distinctions. Class distinctions are extremely important, because without them nobody knows where his place in life is. A stable society is a society in which everyone knows his situation."

"And anything else is Red Communism, right?"

"Don't you dare be sarcastic with me. Don't you dare be snotty. You're already picking up a lot of filthy manners from those tacky trash you go to school with, that Greek boy and that Davidson girl. Do you know that she's Jewish?"

"I thought her father was the Episcopal minister," I said.

"He is," she said. "That's just the point. That's the first thing they do, become Episcopals."

"Well, if they're Episcopals, how can they be Jewish? I mean, if you switch from being a Baptist to being a Methodist, you're not a Baptist any more."

"I don't care how Episcopalian they pretend to be. I don't care if one of them becomes the Archbishop of Canterbury."

"Okay," I said. "First thing tomorrow I'll go out and paint a swastika on St. Thomas's."

"You just shut your mouth, Joshua M. Arnold, or I'll come over there and slap it shut for you. I'm going to write your father about your behavior."

"You might mention in the same letter that Jimbob's got pneumonia. Dad might need some cheering up."

She got up from her chair and walked three or four steps and slapped me on the cheek with her right hand. I didn't even have time to flinch; she'd never slapped me before. It didn't really hurt, but it stung, and it made me sick to my stomach. I felt as though I'd been hit by a crazy stranger. I wanted to hit her back, to slug her a good one, so I locked my hands behind my back to be sure

I wouldn't. She cracked me another one, backhand, on the nose, and it made tears come to my eyes. I could feel my nose starting to bleed. There wasn't anything I could do. I just stood there with my hands behind me, wondering what was happening, and what was going to happen. I was much bigger than she was, and heavier and stronger. I'd never noticed before what a little woman my mother was. I looked at her face closely while she was hitting me, and it was a stranger's face. Her cheeks were fuller than they'd ever been, and her skin was gray. There were tiny grape-colored lines in her cheeks near her nose, and the whites of her eyes were pink, as if she'd been swimming in a chlorinated pool. Each time she slapped me I caught a whiff of sherry.

She said, "Apologize! Apologize! Apologize!" and each time she said it she slapped me. But when I opened my mouth she hit me in it. I don't know how many times she slapped me. My face was getting numb, and the slaps sent little dark red drops of blood from my nose flying around the room. After five or six blows, I realized, in a detached and clear-headed way, that I wasn't angry any more, just bored. So I finally brought my hands around in front of me and grabbed her wrists and held them. They were thin and without strength. I said, as slowly and clearly as I could, "I'm sorry Mother," and dropped her wrists and walked into my bedroom. It was only after I'd sat down on the side of the bed that my legs began to tremble.

I sat in the dark for several minutes, waiting for her to come in and start again, but she didn't. I turned on the light and went into the bathroom and wiped the blood off my face with a wet washcloth, and then I threw up the coffee that Chango's parents had served me.

When I was in bed, Excilda came in with a grilled cheese and chile sandwich and made me eat it. I finished it quickly and she said, "Me and Amadeo just got fired. She just came into the kitchen while I was doing the dishes and Amadeo was having a cup of coffee and said 'You're fired. Both of you. Get out of my house.' What's the matter with her? Is she crazy?"

"I don't know what the matter with her is, Excilda. I don't even think she can fire you. I don't think anybody but my father can fire you, since he hired you, and he's not about to do that."

"So what do you think we ought to do? Write him a letter? He's out there floating on the ocean shooting Germans. There's nothing he can do in Sagrado until he comes back, and he's not coming back for a long time. You can't be a *patrón* when you're some place else."

"Maybe I can talk to her," I suggested. "Maybe she'll be in a different mood tomorrow."

"Me and Amadeo don't want you mixed up in it," she said. "You're just a boy, and we don't need help from any boys." She paused and looked down at her hands. "You know, we worked for your father for thirteen years, since you were a little baby. We talked it over every summer with your father, and every summer him and Amadeo had the same argument, and we always got a raise. And you know, he made me have my babies in the hospital and he paid the doctor for it every time? You know when Osmundo was born with the funny-looking mouth he paid for the dentist and the braces? You know he sent us money in the winter sometimes, and once he even bought us a new cow when the old one died? You know my eight-year-old boy is named Francisco after your father, and he came to the church up in Río Conejo to be godfather to him? How can your mother just tell us we're fired after all that?"

"That's what I mean," I said. "She can't fire you. She doesn't have the authority."

"You want to be the one to tell her that? I don't and Amadeo don't. She says we're fired, and we sure feel fired, so I guess we're fired. Maybe when the war's over and your father can come here and give us the job again, but I don't know if we want to work here any more. There's no pride in working for somebody who doesn't like you."

Amadeo came to the bedroom door, and said, "Come on, Excilda. Let's go." He kept his head down and wouldn't look at me. Excilda took the sandwich plate and said, "Let me wash this up, and I'll come. You come up to Conejo and visit us when you can. I'll teach you how to milk a nanny goat."

I heard Amadeo start his old pickup, and heard the wheels with the tire chains spin in the snow, and then it went off down Camino Tuerto, sounding very loud without its muffler. Amedeo had been planning to get a new muffler with his next pay check.

It was impossible to sleep because I couldn't stop crying. I got up and put on a bathrobe and knocked on my mother's bedroom door. She didn't answer, and by listening closely I could hear her snoring. I'd never heard her do that before, and wondered if sherry did it. Back in my own room, I got one of the Max Shulman books and one of the H. Allen Smith books from the shelf and tried to cheer myself up. The story about the biggest goddamn hippopotamus in the world that sank to the bottom of the lake and never came up almost did the trick, but I couldn't concentrate very hard, and I got sleepy about three in the morning. It was difficult to get up at seven-thirty for school, and when I tried to make my own breakfast the eggs stuck to the pan because I forgot to put the margarine in first. I left the dishes for my mother. When she woke up she'd need the exercise.

Lack of sleep made me dopey and depressed all day. Looking at Marcia or the Cloyds, or any of the girls, all I could think about were the photographs in the *Handbook on Obstetrics,* all the blood and pain and stretching. Chango was in class, and being very good. He carried himself gently, and said "Yes, ma'am" and "No, ma'am" as if he'd been a model student all his life. I think that at first Miss Jefferson thought he was being sarcastic. He read aloud "My heart leaps up when I behold" without any accent, and a good deal of feeling. Some of his Native buddies laughed when he sang out "Or let me die!" with a lot of fervor. He gave them an approximation of the old mean look, but it faded into a self-conscious blush. It was a notable change and Miss Jefferson remarked on it. The last time Chango had recited, before the trouble with Tarzan, he'd read in his thickest *pachuco,* in a perfect monotone:

Meeltone! Dow shoos be leeving at dees hour;
Englan'hat needs of dee; shee ees a fan
Of estagnant gwatters.

I had had the feeling then that the door of the classroom was going to fly open and William Wordsworth would come bulling in, yelling, "Stop it!" This time, Miss Jefferson said, "That's quite an improvement, Maximiliano. Will you turn to page three-eighty and read 'Lines, Composed a Few Miles Above Tintern Abbey?' " And Chango read the whole bloody business, as if he both liked and understood it, which I sure as hell didn't.

Because of his still fresh scar, he was excused from basketball practice that afternoon, so I couldn't tell if he had completely reversed his character or not. He generally had a way of dribbling that involved leading with his thumb. If you tried to move in on him the thumb got in your eye. Since he wasn't practicing with us, he sat it out on the bench and applauded the bad plays along with the good ones, yelling things like "Nice try!" when someone missed the rim by seven feet.

I thought I saw a trace of the old Chango when Bucky Swenson came up to the line for two free throws. Just when he got set for the toss, Chango yelled, "You can do it, Bucky," and Swenson flinched and missed. On the second shot, Chango just *looked* as if he were going to yell something, but didn't, and Bucky's eye was off because he kept expecting something, and he missed that one, too. Then Chango said, "Nice try, Bucky!" and you could almost hear the flames crackle inside Swenson's head.

I walked home alone, and saw that the frying pan from breakfast was still in the sink where I'd left it. My mother was still in her room; I could hear her humming tunelessly to herself. I washed the frying pan and put it away, and then went down the hill, turning left on Camino Chiquito to go to Romeo's studio.

He had a dirty white bandage wrapped around his head, and a purple bruise extending down his jaw. He pointed to it. "Anna moved out, and left me with this. She hit me with an iron saucepan during a perfectly civil discussion about art, and when I woke up she was gone, along with eighteen dollars and several cans of Vienna sausage, which I'd been saving for when I was really broke. Come in. I want you to meet Shirley."

Shirley was sitting at the table, smoking a cigarette,

and wearing the same dirty bathrobe that Anna had worn. She was very large and sleepy-looking, and acknowledged my presence by slowly nodding her head. Her bathrobe was untied, and she was naked underneath it. She arranged it around her very deliberately, without changing her expression. "Romeo," she said, yawning, "I'm tired. Can I rest now?"

"Shirley, dear, you've been resting for half an hour. Don't you remember? Look at all the cigarette butts in the ashtray."

"Oh," she said, "half an hour. I'm so-o-o tired." She cradled her head on her arms and conked off.

Romeo took the burning cigarette from between her fingers and put it out. "You want some coffee?"

I nodded, and we walked over to the kitchen area. "Have you been giving her sleeping pills?" I asked him.

"No, it's her thyroid. When she first came three days ago I took her down to my doctor, and he gave her a basal metabolism test. He told me that clinically she's been dead for some time. Has no thyroid gland at all. He wrote a prescription for thyroid stimulants, but I like her this way. If I gave her the pills she might get jumpy and start throwing things, like Anna. This way she's easy to handle."

"Can she model?"

"She's a terrific model. She's like a catatonic. I can arrange her in any position, standing, sitting, kneeling, leaning over, balanced on one toe, and she falls asleep and never moves. Of course, she's not any good as a housekeeper, but she eats very little. It doesn't take much fuel to keep an engine that sluggish moving. All in all, I'd say she was about perfect. She may even be intelligent, but she can't stay alert long enough to let me know."

"I know a girl who'd be a good model," I said. "She has a good figure, anyway."

"Good figures have nothing to do with it. Or very little. A model has to have some imagination and lots of muscular control, and she has to know how to take orders. If she looks like Miss America she'll probably be a lousy model. Girls like that are always preening themselves and showing you their profiles and wondering if they have a pimple on their behinds. How old is this friend of yours that has the figure?"

"My age. Seventeen."

"My God, are you insane? I already have a civic reputation as a lewd old man."

"This is really a nice girl. Her father's a minister."

"Worse and worse. I can see that you have no appreciation for the niceties. Here, drink your coffee. It may help to clear your mind."

We leaned against his little waist-high refrigerator and drank coffee and watched Shirley sleep. She was a big-boned woman, long in the legs and small-waisted, with a rosy skin. Somewhere, at some time, she must take exercise, I thought, because you can't get a figure like that by sleeping. "She's from San Francisco," Romeo said. "She said she got tired of looking at the ocean and took her money—she didn't have much—and bought a bus ticket and three pounds of Monterey Jack cheese. The bus ticket ran out in Sagrado, but the Monterey Jack ran out in Elko, Nevada. When the bus driver made her get off in Sagrado she began walking, but said she kept falling asleep. The last place she fell asleep was against my gate. I opened it three days ago to put the trash out and she fell backwards into my arms. Didn't even wake up. It's just my dago luck; whenever I need a model, God sends me something."

"I think you ought to give her the pills," I said. "She's missing all the fun of life this way."

"That's a very considerate thought," Romeo said. "When I get starved for conversation or love I'll give her five or six grains and see what happens. She'll probably turn into a harpie, though, and begin to whine and move things around the studio and want me to buy clothes and cosmetics, and tell me to shave my mustache and vote Republican. You remember Anna? The one who gave me this?" He pointed to his bandage. "When she wasn't talking to me about plastic values and economy of line and masses and thrusts, she was telling me that I was a political juvenile and should join the Communist Party and man the barricades. Now I ask you, where the hell should we put up a barricade in Sagrado? Where's a

Winter Palace for us to storm? Can't you see me charging into the city council meeting some Wednesday night and telling Mayor Chavez that I represent the revolution of the proletariat?"

Shirley began to stir, and her bathrobe fell open again. Romeo walked over and put his hand on her shoulder. "Cover up, dear one," he said. "You're exposing the Piazza di Spagna."

She yawned. "Can I have a sandwich? Anything but Monterey Jack."

"All right," Romeo said. "We'll have dinner. Do you want something to eat, Josh?"

I thought about the dinner Excilda would have ready, and then remembered with a sharp pang that Excilda wasn't going to be cooking at home any more.

"I ought to be going home for dinner," I said.

"Nonsense. The Montoyas left yesterday, and I know from agonizing personal experience that your mother is a vile cook."

"How did you. . . ."

"Amadeo came in this morning and asked for work. Believe me, if I had any money to spare at all I'd have been delighted to hire him, but I'm as poor as he is. Now, please stay to dinner. Will sardine and onion on rye bread be satisfactory?"

"Sure," I said.

"It had better be. It's all we've got."

Shirley dragged herself off the chair and tied her bathrobe. "I want to wash up before dinner, Romeo," she said, in a dazed way. She walked dreamily across the studio and opened the door to the patio, went outside, and closed it. Romeo and I watched the door for half a minute, and then heard the sleepy knock. He opened the door, and Shirley stood there in the snow, barefoot, looking puzzled. "This is outside," she said.

"That's right, *bellissima,* you did it again."

"But I wanted the bathroom."

"Right over there," Romeo told her gently, pointing toward another door. "If you wish, I'll paint 'Ladies' on it. Nothing's too much trouble for my Shirlina *bella.*"

Shirley smiled vaguely. "You're nice," she said, and

walked across the studio to the bathroom, tracking snow on the floor.

"I have to watch her," Romeo said. "Sometimes she goes to sleep in the bathtub, and sometimes she dozes off when she's on the toilet."

"She's really beautiful," I said.

"Yes, she is. Beautiful and ornate and serene, like an artichoke. I'm thinking of doing a massive work of Shirley, in marble, called 'The Vegetable.' "

"You really ought to give her those pills, you know," I said. "She might drown in the bathtub sometime."

"All right," he said. "I will. You've convinced me. But I won't like her that way."

Shirley made it out of the bathroom all right this time, and the three of us sat around the scarred round table and ate onion and sardine sandwiches. Romeo let me have a small glass of the red wine he served from a gallon jug. It tasted a little like paint.

"Have they found that Velarde boy yet?" he asked me when we'd finished. "The one with the knife?"

"No, we think he's dead from the cold. The sheriff said he was either hiding out somewhere in town or he's run away south to Mexico, where carrying a knife doesn't make you stand out in a crowd. Where did you get this stuff?" I asked him, referring to the wine.

"It's local," he said. "There's a man named Northrup in the valley out east of here who has a little vineyard and makes his own red. He did a lot of research on the soil and the climate and decided that Sagrado wasn't too high to be good wine country. What do you think of it?"

"It's awful."

"You're right," he said. "It is awful. Northrup was wrong, but he won't give up. However, it costs only sixty-eight cents a gallon, and it does have an alcoholic content."

"Would you like something a little better? Dad has a little cellar at our house, and nobody's drinking it right now, except Mother, and she's sticking to the sherry. I think I could arrange for a few bottles."

"That's stealing, Josh, I won't hear of it."

"There's some Châteauneuf-du-Pape, some Nuits-

101

Saint-Georges and some Clos de Vougeot," I said. "I don't think I should take any of the clarets. Dad counted them pretty carefully before he left. He said he'd see that swift justice came to anyone who touched his case of Château Margaux 1929."

"Your offer is falling on deaf ears, Josh. I am a man of stern principles when it comes to other people's property. Although it isn't very good, I am perfectly happy with my gallon of Flor de Yunque. Shirley likes it too, don't you dear?"

"Mmmm?" Shirley said.

"Romeo, this wine is all from the thirties, and it won't last forever. If someone doesn't drink it now it'll lose its power and go downhill. The Clos Vougeot should be at its peak right now. Another few months and it will start tasting like a raspberry phosphate."

"For a minor you seem very knowing about wines."

"I belonged to a little wine-tasting society in Mobile. The president of it was Paul Robinson, the noted Southern connoisseur and gourmet. He always said a robust Rhône or Burgundy was the best thing to accompany onion and sardine sandwiches."

Romeo poured another glass of Flor de Yunque, and when he drank it off it made his mouth pucker, as though he'd bit into a lemon. "I'm weakening," he said. "This stuff really isn't fit for human consumption. Do you honestly have Châteauneuf-du-Pape?"

"About a case and a half, all lying there getting corked."

"If you get caught at it I'll deny everything. I'll throw you to the wolves."

"Can I lie down for a spell?" Shirley asked.

I left soon after Shirley hit the sack, and walked home. Nothing had changed in the kitchen, and I knocked on my mother's door and went in. She was lying on the bed, dressed as she had been the night before, with two empty bottles of Pedro Domecq on her night table.

"Mother, do you want something to eat?"

"No, thank you."

"I can fix you some eggs or something."

"No, thank you."

"How's Jimbob? Did you talk to the hospital?"

"I don't know. Why didn't Excilda come in today? I couldn't reach her anywhere."

"I thought you fired her last night. That's what she told me, anyway."

"Don't be ridiculous. She's been with us for years. It isn't like her not to come like this."

"Mother, you fired her. Her and Amadeo. Don't you remember?"

"You were very cruel last night. I'm not hungry now, thank you."

"Would you like some more sherry?"

"Maybe Excilda will be in tomorrow. It isn't like her to stay away from work without calling."

"I'll see if I can find her."

"Thank you for cooking such a nice dinner, Josh. It was delicious."

"You're welcome. Good night."

"Come again."

I closed her door and called Steenie's house. His mother answered the phone.

"Mrs. Stenopolous, this is Josh Arnold. I think my mother needs a doctor, and I don't. . . ."

"Is *your* mother going to have a baby?"

"No, she doesn't need that kind of doctor. I think she needs a psychiatrist. She's acting funny. Are there any good doctors like that in Sagrado?"

"There's one. Dr. Arthur Temple." She gave me his home phone number. "He's the only psychiatrist in town."

I thanked her, hung up and called Dr. Temple's number. A child's voice answered. "This is Tsigmoont. I can answer the telephone."

"Tsigmoont, can I speak to your daddy, please?"

"This is Tsigmoont. I can answer the telephone. Do you want to hear my song? *'Frère Jacques, Frère Jacques, dormez-vous?'* It's in French. I can sing in a whole lot of different languages. *'Muss ich denn, muss ich denn. . . .'*"

"I'll call back in a few minutes, Tsigmoont."

I waited ten minutes and called the number again, but the line was busy. Tsigmoont had probably left the telephone off the hook. I soft-boiled some eggs, made toast and a pot of tea, and brought a tray into my mother's room. She sat up and turned the lights on. "Isn't this nice," she said. "Dinner in bed." I watched her eat, and took the tray away. I called Dr. Temple once more, but the line was still busy.

I set the alarm clock for seven, and made my mother's breakfast when I got up. She was in a nightgown and looked better. "I'll be at school all day," I told her. "Will you be okay?"

"Of course I'll be all right," she said. "What a question! Excilda won't be in today, will she?"

"No, Mother. You fired her."

"Well, she shouldn't have been so sassy. I'll do the cooking from now on, and we'll find someone to clean. Your father paid both of them far too much. It was spoiling them. You run along, now. I'll have a nice dinner ready for when you come home."

"Would you like me to call a doctor? You were pretty sick last night." She didn't answer.

I telephoned her twice from school that morning, to see if she was still up and around, and she sounded cheerful and amused by my concern. "I can't imagine why you keep calling me," she said. *"I'm* all right. *I* don't need a doctor. The only person who needs one is poor Jimbob, and he has one. I talked to his doctor just a few minutes ago. Jimbob's out of the oxygen tent, and eating like a horse."

During the lunch hour I called her again, but there wasn't any answer. I told Marcia what had happened and, as usual, she was fascinated by the idea that my mother might be mad. Anything colorful, out of the ordinary, gory or violent made Marcia's eyes light up. "Is Dr. Temple going to see her?" she asked.

"I called him, but I couldn't get him."

"He's a weirdo," she said positively. "In one month last year three of his patients killed themselves."

"Thanks for telling me. I feel a lot better about it now."

"Well, *all* of his patients don't kill themselves. Some of them may even get well, for all I know. I've never heard of any that did, but I don't know who all his patients are. He and his wife live pretty high."

I hoped I wouldn't have to call Dr. Temple again professionally, I said, but Mother's behavior had been pretty strange last night. I told Marcia about all the sherry, and Marcia comforted me. "She was just stoned," she said. "Nobody acts right when they're really stoned."

"I know that," I said, "but this is the first time she's ever done this. She didn't drink back in Mobile. Not like that."

"She probably misses her husband," Marcia said. "You know."

After school I called home from the pharmacy, but there was still no answer, so I telephoned Dr. Temple at his office. I was afraid that Tsigmoont might be serving as his receptionist, too, but I reached him without any trouble.

"Did you call me last night?" Dr. Temple asked, after I told him who I was and about my mother.

"Yes, sir."

"Why did you hang up on Tsigmoont?"

"I'm sorry about that, Doctor, but he wouldn't let me talk to you, and he kept singing songs. I didn't want to talk to a little boy just then."

"Tsigmoont," he said crisply, "is a very *brilliant* little boy and a very *sensitive* little boy, and now he is a very deeply *wounded* little boy, thanks to you. You shouldn't be *brutal* to *children*. You should let them sing their little songs. The time of singing little songs is over too soon, too soon."

"I apologize," I said.

"Are you calling from your house?"

"No, sir. I'm downtown. It'll take me about twenty minutes to get home."

"What is the address? We'll meet you there in twenty minutes."

I told him the address, and started home, wondering who he meant by "we." Was he bringing the traditional

105

men in white coats with him? That seemed a bit prema-
ture; he hadn't even examined her yet.

He was on time. He and a woman were sitting in the
first Rolls-Royce I'd ever seen, a big catlike gray monster
that purred. The woman was driving, and Dr. Temple
was sitting next to her with an attaché case open on his
lap, making corrections on a thick manuscript. She
turned off the motor and they both emerged, looking
aggressive and competent.

"You are Arnold?" he asked me. "Of course you are.
My wife, Dorothy Temple." I shook hands with him, and
then with her. Her grip was far stronger. There was
something about her face, and the way her tweed skirt
hung around her rump, that reminded me of people who
owned Morgan horses and had tack rooms.

"Are you a doctor, too, Mrs. Temple?" I asked her.

Temple answered for her. "She is not a doctor, but she
accompanies me on many professional visits. You don't
mind." It was more a statement than a question.

"I'm glad you could come," I said. "It's lucky there's a
psychiatrist in town."

Mrs. Temple answered. "We came to New Mexico
because we thought Arthur had tuberculosis." She gave
him a look that could have withered a cactus. "It turned
out to be psychosomatic, all in the mind." Her husband
smiled wanly.

I unlocked the door, and immediately smelled something burning. I found the lights and ran into the kitchen.
The Temples followed me.

"In the oven," Mrs. Temple said. "There's something
burning in the oven."

"You can see why I ask her to accompany me on
professional visits," Dr. Temple said. "Her mind cuts to
the root of the problem at once."

I turned off the oven and opened the door. In a
casserole was what had been, once, a thick ham steak,
now crisp and feathery black. I recognized the odor of
carbonized Coca-Cola. "Mother's in there," I said, pointing to the bedroom door. "At least, I think she's in
there."

"We must go to her at once," Mrs. Temple said. Her

106

husband turned to me and gestured, as if to say, "You see? You see what brilliance she has?"

Mother was fully dressed, again, lying on top of the covers. There were two more Pedro Domecq empties on her table, and a half-empty bottle of Harvey's Amontillado. Dr. Temple went swiftly to her bed and picked up the bottle, opened it, and sniffed the contents. "I wonder where she got it," he said. "There hasn't been any in the liquor stores for months. Just that swill from California." Mrs. Temple touched him on the shoulder and pointed to Mother. "The patient."

"Ah. Your mother is drunk. She may or may not have a psychiatric problem, but at the present time she is drunk. Anyone who has recently consumed two and one-half fifths of sherry, even very good sherry such as this, will be drunk." He shook her gently by the arm. "Mrs. Arnold. Mrs. Arnold."

My mother opened one eye and said, "Who're you?"

"She is *very* drunk," he announced. Mrs. Temple whispered something in his ear. "Yes," he said. "Right. Being drunk, or rather drinking, is merely a symptom of a deeper, underlying problem, the nature of which must be brought to light by intensive probing. Profound analysis."

"I see," I said.

"Yes, but at the present time, as I pointed out, she is merely drunk. It is useless to discuss these matters with someone who is drunk. When she is no longer drunk, I will talk to her at my office. I suggest that you begin by making her sober."

"How?"

"How? How?" Mrs. Temple whispered in his ear again. "Coffee," he said. "Black, hot coffee. Make her drink black, hot coffee and then make her walk around."

"I don't think I can *make* her do anything, Doctor," I told him. "She's my mother."

"If you don't wish to cooperate with us, we'll never be able to help. Do you know where she hides her bottles?"

"She doesn't hide them," I said. "Why should she? This is her house. The liquor's all down in the cellar. All she has to do is go down there and open some."

"I've never heard anything so ridiculous in all my professional career," he said. "She *must* hide her bottles. It's all part of the clinical picture. These situations have a classic order about them, an order that must be preserved if therapy is to be effective."

"I'll look around the house and see if I can find some bottles stashed," I said.

"You will," he assured me. "Look in all the unlikely places, places where you are sure no one would ever hide a bottle. You will find them. These people are extremely clever and resourceful. There is no end to their ingenuity. Dorothy?"

"That's right, Arthur," she said.

"We are going now. Tomorrow, or whenever she becomes sober, call me either at my office or my home. If you call me at my home, Tsigmoont may answer. Please be courteous to him, and don't hang up on him in the middle of a song. That can be ruinous."

I went with the Temples to the front door and watched them climb into the Rolls-Royce. Dr. Temple reopened his attaché case, and immediately began to make corrections on his manuscript. Mrs. Temple drove. He obviously made the most of every minute.

It took nearly an hour to clean the burned food off the casserole. There was some canned tuna in the cupboard, and I made a sandwich for Mother, and fixed a pot of drip coffee. She ate the sandwich and drank the coffee without a word. She was getting very thin, I noticed, and her eyes were red. Her hands shook slightly as she held the sandwich.

"Mother," I said, "this is getting silly."

"I know."

"You're going to get sicker and sicker unless you start eating and stop all that sherry-drinking. I don't know how to run the house, and I don't know how to cook."

"I know. I know."

"We have to get Excilda and Amadeo back here. It's stupid to try to do everything without them."

"You're right," she said. She was crying.

"Maybe they haven't found another job yet. Maybe they'll come back if I ask them to."

"I'm so sorry," she said. "I don't know what came over me. Where's Jimbob?"

"He's still in the hospital," I said. "He caught pneumonia."

"Of course. I forgot for a minute."

"And that's something else," I said. "Maybe Jimbob ought to go back to Mobile. He isn't having a good time here."

"We can't ask him to leave when he's so sick," she said. "We couldn't ask anyone to do that."

"All right. When he's well we'll ask him to leave. If you don't want to, I will. He doesn't like me anyway, so I won't care if he gets sore. I don't think it looks right to have him living with us anyway. Not while Dad's away."

"That's a silly, provincial attitude. That's a very middle-class sort of thing to say. Jimbob is from the very best family. He's an ornament to any house, and a perfect gentleman of the old school."

"In my opinion," I said, "he's a lush and a bum and a sponge. And a snob. I didn't think gentlemen were supposed to be any of those things."

"We'll talk about it later. Who were those people in here? You shouldn't bring anyone into my bedroom without my permission."

"I thought you were sick, so I brought a doctor. The woman was his . . . nurse."

"Did he think I was sick?"

"He thought you were drunk. He said as much."

"Well, he was right. I was drunk. I still am, a little, even after all the coffee. I don't know any other way to get through these long, long days and nights. I don't know anyone at all here except some silly women who play bad bridge. I don't like this cold weather. I miss the sea. I miss the house in Mobile. I'm tired of living in this horrible mud house with tacky Indian rugs all over the floors and a garden you have to water all the time because it never rains. I'm sick of your father being away and having to make all of the decisions alone."

This last one didn't make much sense to me. The only decisions of any importance that she'd made since Dad left were to let Jimbob live with us and to fire the Montoyas. Both were rotten decisions, I felt.

"I'd be happy to help out with the decisions," I said. "Maybe the two of us together could make better ones."

"And I'm really sick of all the cute lip I've been getting from you. You haven't said a civil word to me or my guest for months. And I don't know who you're seeing. Can you imagine what it's like, sitting here alone at night and wondering what sort of sordid mess you're getting into with girls? You don't ever write to little Courtney any more. She's just pining away for you, and you don't even write her letters."

"I've made some new friends here," I said. "If I'm going to live here, I might as well make some friends. I'm two thousand miles from Mobile."

"Yes, friends, And what an assortment. There isn't one person, not one, who's had your advantages. Not one who's the sort of boy or girl you'd be proud to bring home and introduce to me. Just a bunch of tacky, dusty little Westerners who never go to the dentist."

"I don't know where you get your information," I said. "I think people like Marcia Davidson and Steenie Stenopolous go to the dentist as often as I do, and even if they didn't, I'm not sure I know what the connection is. Maybe you'd better get some sleep. Do you want me to call the doctor again tomorrow?"

"What sort of doctor is he?"

"He's a psychiatrist."

"You dreadful little snot. You've gone too far this time."

"Well," I said, getting up and taking the sandwich plate and the coffee cup, "I won't call him any more if you don't want me to. He seemed to think that your main problem was that you'd been drinking too much."

"That was perceptive of him. I wonder how big a bill he's going to send for that piece of diagnosis."

"Maybe we'd better talk this whole thing over some other time," I said. "Do you want me to try to find the Montoyas?"

"I can cook as well as I ever could," she said, "and

110

there isn't much outside work to do in the winter anyway. We can get along very nicely without them."

"Mother, I hate to tell you this, but you're a terrible cook. You're even worse than I am, and I'm not any cook at all. Let me at least get Excilda back here. What's going to happen when Jimbob gets out of the hospital? Are you going to cook for him, too? As I remember, he's a man that likes his meals on time, even if he complains about the way they taste."

"You can try to get her back if you want to. You can get every Mexican in Sagrado to stay here if you want to, and we can all sit around and eat tortillas and rattle Spanish at each other. Won't that be fun!"

"You won't mind if I write to Dad and tell him what's going on around here, will you? He still has some say about what happens."

"There is nothing, absolutely nothing, that happens here that needs to be told to your father. He went off to the Navy because he *wanted* to. He wasn't going to be drafted or called or anything, you know. He *wanted* to go. He *wanted* to leave us. He *wanted* to leave me with you on my hands *just* when you were starting to be difficult. He knows how much I hate it here. I've hated it every summer, and he knows it."

When her motor ran down finally she closed her eyes and turned her back to me, without saying anything. I turned out her bedside light and went to the kitchen to make a sandwich for myself.

13

A RATTLY BLUE BUS makes a daily circle of the little mountain towns in Cabezón County, from Sagrado to the valley at Yunque, and then up through the hills—San Esteban, Santa María, Villa Galicia, Ojo Amargo, Río Venado, Río Conejo, Amorcita and, at the end of the route, nearly 11,000 feet high, La Cima. No matter what the weather is like, the bus is always at full boil when it reaches the high point, and the driver has to give it an hour to cool off before he starts down again.

I skipped school the next morning and rode up to Río Conejo to find the Montoyas. Once before, when I was seven or eight, we had driven there for a Fourth of July dinner at their house, but I remembered nothing about the village except a tiny stream bordered by giant cottonwood trees, a little adobe church with a galvanized tin roof, and a baked-clay open space occupied by what seemed to be hundreds of sleeping dogs.

The bus stopped in front of Montoya's Genl. Mdse. U.S. Post Office Liquors Wines, a low, crumbled building that apparently served all the needs of Río Conejo. It was about eleven; the driver told me he'd be back through around three, and to be waiting at the same place if I wanted a ride. A young girl was behind the counter inside, and I asked her, pointing down the road, if the Montoyas lived that way. She said sure, and the other way too; everyone in Río Conejo was named either Montoya or Romero. She, herself, was a Romero. I asked specifically for Amadeo Montoya, the one with a wife named Excilda and twelve or thirteen children, and she gave me directions.

The road snaked between the hills, roughly parallel to the Río Conejo, lined with bare cottonwoods and poplars. The houses were scattered widely along the road, each with a rural mail box, each mail box painted with the name Romero or Montoya, distinguished only by first names or initials. Amadeo's was a mile uphill from the post office.

It was a fine house, solid, old and inviting. From the road it was difficult to tell how big it was. One story and pitch-roofed, it rambled and spread in several directions from the central room, which was log and mud, to the outlying bedrooms and storerooms of adobe brick, freshly mud-plastered in the fall. Several cords of wood were neatly stacked under the *portal* near the front door, and strings of dried red chile hung from the *vigas*. As I walked toward the house on a path shoveled from the snow, an immense dog, part shepherd and, to judge from his size, part horse, barked once and trotted to me for a scratch behind the ears, or a fight, whichever I wanted to offer him.

I was scratching him behind the ears when a small, round-headed boy opened the front door and looked at me gravely. I said hello, and he ducked back inside, to be followed by an older child, a girl. She disappeared, and other kids came to look at me, each one older than the last. A boy seventeen or eighteen finally asked me what I wanted. He was round-headed and heavy in the trunk, and looked like his father.

"I'd like to see Mr. or Mrs. Montoya," I said. "My name is Arnold, from Sagrado."

"Wait a minute," he said, and closed the door.

The dog and I walked back to the shelter of the *portal*, and I squatted on the flagstones and scratched him some more. He was in a thick winter coat, but glossy, as if he'd been brushed recently, and well-fed.

Excilda eventually came out onto the *portal* and asked me why the hell I didn't get inside before I froze to death, but not to let in that worthless brute of a chicken-stealing dog who, she was sure, was someday soon going to take her youngest child in its jaws and run away to a cave and eat him. I gave the dog a last scratch and he smiled and wagged his heavy tail. He didn't look like a dog that stole and ate children. He looked like a dog that might steal chocolate-covered Easter eggs.

The Montoyas' big farmhouse was bright and clean, with newly whitewashed walls and some good, simple homemade furniture. The Montoya family was well-known in the mountains for having always produced solid artisans in a number of fields, and while none of them ever became famous at any particular skill—saint-carving, for instance, or curative powers—the tribe could always offer a good carpenter and builder, with sidelines in veterinary medicine, midwifery, weaving, or just useful muscle. In recent years, various Montoyas had become famous as jackleg mechanics. They were never clerical or bookish, but they could all read.

I never got the count entirely straight, but there were

about a dozen people living in the house beside the Montoyas senior. Some were children, two were grandchildren, and one was a niece from an unfortunate branch of the family. There were some married sons and daughters living away from home; the oldest resident child was Tony, the seventeen-year-old boy, who was shorter than I, but as strong-looking as Chango.

Excilda asked me if I remembered Vicky, and I didn't. "Don't you remember that Fourth of July, ten years ago?" she asked. "I remember coming here for dinner, but that's all," I said.

"You followed Vicky around like a sheepdog all afternoon," she told me. "You held her hand and kissed her and told me and Amadeo you were going to marry her as soon as you could scrape up the money to buy a house and a diamond ring."

"I remember," Vicky said.

There is a Mexican movie star named Maria Felix with a symmetrical oval face that seems to be cast in porcelain and never ages. The Montoyas' daughter Victoria looked like her, but with skin softer than porcelain. Big eyes, Indian cheekbones and a pointed chin, a slim body that made her appear taller than she was, coarse black hair gathered by a clip in back and cascading down her back, a quiet, low voice with a faint Spanish rhythm to the words.

"If you're trying to embarrass me," I said, "you're doing a good job."

"You promised you'd become a Catholic and learn to speak Spanish if Vicky would marry you. I don't think your mother liked to hear that kind of talk, but your father thought it was real funny."

Excilda had an eight-burner black stove in her kitchen, and the whitewashed *vigas* were hung with herbs that she'd grown or picked herself. She named some of them for me, and when she got to Yerba de Lobo I asked her what wolf grass tasted good on. She laughed and said it didn't taste good on anything; you made tea with it and it kept you running to the toilet for two days. It was good for people who had ringworm, boils and bleeding gums. It was also good, she said, for kids who got out of line.

Instead of beating them, you make them drink a cup of Yerba de Lobo tea and it keeps them out of mischief for forty-eight hours.

Sitting at the kitchen table was a small Spanish woman smoking a cigarette and looking disturbed. She was Mrs. Saiz, Excilda told me, and was one of Vicky's teachers in Yunque. I could tell that she and the Montoyas had been involved in some sort of argument, because she kept saying, "*¡Jamás! ¡Jamás! ¡Es una tontería tremenda!*" which means, roughly, "Never! It would be real dumb!" That isn't a literary translation, but it gives the sense. Mrs. Saiz left when I came in, and when she passed Vicky she thumped her lightly on the forehead with the heel of her hand and said, "*¡Cretina!*" Vicky didn't look like a cretin. She was only sixteen, and already a senior.

I sat with Excilda, Tony and Vicky in the kitchen and drank coffee out of a bowl. Excilda hadn't asked me what I was doing in Río Conejo on a school day, and I knew it wasn't polite in the hills to come right to the point. When the Montoyas were in Sagrado they acted like town people, but at home they stuck fast to country customs.

Tony had said very little since I arrived, but now he asked his mother for lunch, because he had to go back. "Tony's helping a man rebuild his house. You know, Procopio Romero's house burned down last week? Was there a story about it in *The Conquistador?* No? Well, it was a big fire for Conejo, and he lost everything except a few crocks of cider and his family. Everybody's helping out."

From the oven she took a dish of *carnitas de puerco* which, after stuffed pompano, is my favorite food in the world, and gave some to Tony along with a few tortillas made of blue corn meal. He wolfed it down and had another cup of coffee, and then left, saying he'd be back for dinner.

"You hungry?" she asked me.

"No," I said, "I had a big breakfast and ate a sandwich on the bus." It was a lie. I was starving.

"Well, have some *carnitas* anyway."

"I couldn't. Absolutely. I'd bust."

"Vicky, give your *novio* here some *carnitas* before I get mad and push him out in the snow." While Vicky was dishing up the meat, she went on. "Look, *niñito,* we still have lots of pigs. We can last all winter on no money at all if we have to, and that's more than you can do. Eat your *carnitas* or I'll get insulted."

The little cubes of pork had been baking all morning, and each time I bit into one my eyelids got heavy, as though someone were rubbing warm butter on them. It should be against the law to do anything to a pig but chop him up into cubes for *carnitas*. No ham, no spareribs, no pork chops, no bacon.

"Amadeo should be back pretty soon," Excilda said. "He went up to Molydenum to see about a job in the mine there."

"That's what I came up here about," I said. "Can't you come back to work for us in Sagrado? We could really use some help."

"You better talk to Amadeo when he gets back. He's the one decides things like that. He was pretty mad when we left the other day. I've never seen him so mad."

"All right, I'll talk to him too. But I sure wish you'd come back."

"We didn't leave; we got kicked out. Oh, I don't want to talk about it now. Amadeo should be back pretty soon. Vicky, take your *esposado* back in the big room and send the kids in here for some lunch."

Victoria and I sat on a lumpy couch in the front room while the children ate. She was nearly my age and beautiful; I didn't know that girls sixteen could be really beautiful. I was nervous and couldn't think of anything to say, and she seemed very calm and serene.

"What's your dog's name?" I finally asked her, to break up the silence.

"Don Carlos," she answered.

"He's a nice dog."

"He's okay."

"What kind of dog is he?"

"I don't know. Different kinds."

The dog talk obviously wasn't going to get me anywhere with Maria Felix, Junior, so I tried Memory Lane.

"Do you remember that stuff your mother was talking about? Me chasing you all around?"

"I guess so."

"Well, I don't remember it at all."

Victoria didn't answer, and the conversation, never very lively, died again. The only things left to discuss were movies and school.

"Have you seen any good movies recently?"

She thought about that for a while, then said, "Abbott and Costello."

I was on sure ground. "Abbott and Costello in what?"

"In the Army, something."

"Sure, that's 'Buck Privates.' I saw it in Mobile. Did you like it?"

"I guess so." Her eyes wandered to a window and stayed there. I wondered whether I'd committed some serious breach of manners, or smelled bad. It came to me suddenly that it was a weekday, and she wasn't in school.

"Have you been sick?" I asked her.

"Sick? No."

"I was just wondering why you weren't in school today. Where do you go, here in Conejo?"

Some animation came into her face for the first time, and she focused on me. "No, in the valley, in Yunque. I used to go. I quit school when they—" she pointed to the kitchen with her chin—"lost their work. I have to go to work, now, and make some money." Her eyes began to sparkle, and she turned on the old sofa to face me directly. "I was doing real good in all my subjects at Yunque. I was getting A's in everything. Mrs. Saiz said she thought after I graduated I could get a scholarship to any school in the state. When I told her I'd have to quit school she told me I was crazy, even when I explained why." Her voice had become sharp and piercing, and she was spitting the words at me. Now she really looked like Maria Felix, when she told the bandit to go ahead and rape her, because no matter what he did to her body he couldn't touch her spirit. I forget the name of the picture, but it was full of corn like that, which I suppose they call *"maiz"* in Mexico.

117

Excilda heard Victoria's voice, and came out from her kitchen, holding one of the toddlers under one arm. "Mrs. Saiz was right," she said. "You are crazy. You should finish your high school, anyway. You don't have to work."

"I'm sixteen," Victoria said. "I can do what I want."

"Que no seas cabezuda," Excilda said, "don't be stubborn." But she said it in a way that showed they'd been all over the ground before, and that Excilda hadn't got anywhere. "This girl's just like a mule," she said to me. "Makes up her mind and that's it. Like a rock."

Don Carlos began to bark outside on the *portal,* and I heard a truck coming. "That's your father," Excilda said. "You better not give him any back talk."

We could hear Amadeo talking to Don Carlos, calling him affectionate names in Spanish: "Three times miscarried son of a sheep-stealing coyote," for example and "courageous fighter of blind kittens." Then he came in and took off his hat and fur-lined jacket.

"Hello, Josh," he said. "How you doing? You come up to see Vicky? That's a long way to ride just to see a stupid girl."

I stood up. "No," I said, "I came up to see if you and Excilda would consider. . . ."

"Never mind about that," he interrupted. "We got fired fair and square, and you didn't have nothing to do with it." He turned to his wife and said, *"El capataz me dijo que hubiera trabajo en dos, tres semanas."*

"Amadeo," I said, "you don't have to wait three weeks to get work. Really. And I remember you and Dad talking about that job. He said it was a hundred miles away."

"It's good money. Don't worry about it. I been a bucket man before."

"I'm sure it's all right with my mother," I pleaded. "She's so mixed up she doesn't even know why you're gone. She's been sick. We really need some help down there."

"Your mother," Amadeo said, "doesn't have anything to do with it. If she hadn't fired us we'd have quit anyway. There's no man around there to give the orders.

118

Your papa is out there in the Navy somewhere, and that *maricón* in the red bathrobe don't know what the hell he's talking about, and he's lucky I didn't kill him, some of the things he said to me."

"Well, *I* don't know how to be anybody's boss. And besides, you know more about what you do than I ever could. I'm only seventeen."

"When my grandfather was sixteen he had a wife and a baby and was farming four hectares right here in Conejo, with two Indians from San Ysidro helping him in the fall. I mean, goddamn, boy, are you gonna be Papacito for a while or you gonna let that . . . woman do the job?"

"Amadeo, I don't *know* anything about what you do."

"Damn, boy, that don't matter. You got what down there, eight, nine acres? You got forty apple trees, four of 'em dying, you got an *acequia menor* and ten ditches to work, you got some lawns and some roses and some flags and some Japanese plum and six lindens and a patch of tulips. About two times a year you got some carpentry to do, and some replastering. There isn't nothing you can tell me about how to take care of a place like that. All I need is some *gallo* in charge to let me do it, and maybe once in a while some business about money comes up to tell me '*Sí, lo podemos hacer*' or '*No, no lo podemos hacer*.'"

"That's all we want," Excilda put in.

"*Cállate,*" Amadeo told her, without even looking at her. "But she's right. Don't forget, that's not my land down there. That's your papa's land, and I just work on it. Up here, this is my land and I work it the way I want to. If I make a mistake, it's my own mistake, and I don't make many mistakes on my land. But down there in Sagrado, I'm not my own boss. Now, is there gonna be somebody around there to be boss, or am I gonna be a bucket man for sixty a week at Molybdenum?"

The whole business was getting over my head, and I sat down on the couch next to Victoria and pretended to be thinking. Victoria was no help; she simply sat there looking from me to her father as if she were enchanted by all the adult discussion.

119

"Amadeo," I began, "I don't know. . . ."

"No, that's right. You don't know. So I wrote a letter to your father last night to that crazy address that pretends he's in New York when he's really around Old Spain some place. Victoria, bring me that letter." Victoria got up quickly and went into another room.

"Excilda and Victoria and I stayed up until nearly eleven last night writing this letter," he went on. "Victoria spells the words better, and she wrote it down in pencil first and then Excilda wrote it again with ink. Excilda's got a good hand."

Victoria came back with two pages torn from a ruled notebook, and handed them to Amadeo, who reached into his breast pocket and drew forth a pair of spectacles I'd never seen before. *"Yo me vuelvo ciego por cierto,"* he said, referring to a mild nearsightedness. "I'm going blind for sure."

" 'Dear Mr. Arnold,' " he read, " 'Everything is going fine here except that we got fired by Mrs. Arnold. We don't know how come, because we were just doing our work like always.' "

"I told him that should be 'as always,' " Victoria said.

"You can say what you want to in your own letters," Amadeo told her. "This is my letter. 'We don't know anything about being a doctor but both of us think that Mrs. Arnold is sick and your son Joshua M. Arnold should give the orders if you can't be there to give the orders. If you will send me a letter saying this we will go back to work at your place. Meantime I am looking for another job.

" 'We hope you are feeling okay. Respectfully, Amadeo Lorenzo Montoya R.' "

"What do you think?" he asked.

"I suppose it can't do any harm," I said. "What does the 'R.' stand for?"

"For my mother's name: Romero."

"Well, there's one thing I'm sure of. All the money's in the bank, either here or in Mobile, and I can't write any checks. So I can't pay any bills or salaries. If my mother doesn't want the money to be paid out for something, there's nothing I can do about it."

"I'm sure your father will think of something to fix that," Amadeo said. "And we can work for a while without getting paid. All you have to do is tell your mother she can't fire us unless Mr. Arnold says she can."

"Oh, boy. She'll love that."

"I sent the letter air mail. I'll wait until your father gets it and sends me an answer before we go back."

Excilda said, "It'll do your mother good to eat her own cooking for a while."

"It won't do *me* much good," I said.

"If she has to do something, like cook, maybe she'll stop drinking all that wine," Excilda said. "When's Mr. Buel coming back from the hospital?"

"I don't know exactly," I said. "Pretty soon. Too soon. I thought this was going to kill him for sure."

"There's nothing the matter with him," Amadeo said. "He's healthy. He ought to be in the Army. He's younger than your father."

"He's a bum," I said. "All he does is visit people and hang around. I thought we were far enough away out here, but he'll go around the world for a free meal."

"Well," Amadeo said, "you'll be okay for a while down there by yourself. I got a few things I need to do around here anyway. I got to hunt some."

"Hunting season's pretty much over, isn't it?"

"When you got all these kids to feed, hunting season's never over. I know it's against the law, but letting kids go hungry is against the law too. If you keep your mouth shut, I'll let you go elk hunting with me sometime. Tony and I need another hand on it anyway. Last time I got a bull it took us three days to bring him in."

Amadeo went into the kitchen to eat lunch. "If you want to look at the place," he said before he left, "get Vicky to show you around. Vicky, take him around. You're going back to school tomorrow, so you might as well enjoy yourself today."

"I'm not ever going back to school," Vicky said. "I'm going to work and help support you."

"I'll tell you when I need help," he said. "I don't mind trouble with game wardens, but truant officers are too much for me. If you won't go by yourself, I'll put you in a sack and carry you down there."

We put on our coats and went outside. It was a clear afternoon, not too cold for walking. Vicky pulled on a pair of black rubber boots, and Don Carlos followed us, sometimes wading through snow up to his belly.

Vicky said very little on the tour, but answered questions when I asked what something was. "That's the bean field," she'd say, or "that's the barn," or "watch your step, that's a ditch." Once she even said, pointing to a woolly-looking bay mare, "That's a horse." I don't think her heart was in her work.

"I know it's a horse," I said. "I could tell right off it was a horse."

"I thought you were from the city," she said.

"Look, if you don't want to show me around, tell me. I can go back to the store and wait for the bus. You don't have to entertain me."

"Isn't there anything you want to see?" she asked.

"I'd be very happy to see everything, but if it pains you to be a guide, you can forget about it. I can see your place some other time. If you want to be sore at somebody, be sore at my mother. I am."

"I don't know your mother. I don't remember her."

"Well, she's the one who's causing all the trouble. Not me."

She plodded along beside me solemnly, her rubber boots making deep prints in the snow. Don Carlos was investigating things under the snow, and plowing ragged, crazy furrows around us. Once he left us and bounded yelping through the snow to a cow which was placidly eating bale hay under a tree. He snapped at her hooves, barking, until she moved off. He ran her until she got close to another cow, circled them both, and ran back to us.

"What was that for?" I asked.

"He herds our stock for us in the warm months," Victoria said. "He's just keeping in practice. If we weren't walking together, he'd herd us. He hates to see animals scattered. People too."

"I thought he was more like a hunting dog."

122

"Oh, he hunts with Papa," she said. "He says Don Carlos is good for almost every kind of game. He went duck hunting one time, and did real well at it. Then Papa bought some ducks, not wild ducks but, you know, farm ducks. And it got Don Carlos all mixed up. Since the ducks were always around the yard with nobody shooting at them he knew he wasn't supposed to kill them, but he had to do something. So one morning last spring, when the ground was still soft, he took all the ducks and buried them."

"What do you mean, buried them?"

"Oh, he didn't hurt them. He dug little holes all over the yard and picked up the ducks in his mouth and put them in the holes. Then he covered them up with mud except for their heads. He did thirteen ducks that way, and was digging a hole for another one when Tony found him. We talked about it for a long time. Papa said Don Carlos was afraid the ducks might run away, and since he didn't know how to build a cage he put them in holes. He's a smart dog."

We were near one border of Amadeo's farm when I saw the little wooden building with a cross on the roof. It looked very old and weathered, with no windows and a chain and padlock on the door.

"Is that a church?" I asked.

"It's what we call a *morada*," she said. The Penitentes use them instead of regular churches."

"Is Amadeo a Penitente?" I asked. The Penitentes were a sort of outlaw branch of the Catholics who took everything very seriously, especially Good Friday. They'd pick a member of the church to play Jesus every year. He'd carry a cross while his friends all whipped him with rawhide and cactus and then they'd crucify him. In recent years they just tied him to a cross and left him all day in the sun. A hundred years ago they did the job right, with nails.

"No, he's not," she said. "He never has been."

"Then what's the *morada* for?"

"You promise you won't tell anybody?"

I said I promised, though it seemed a foolish thing. I didn't care what they used the building for. Victoria and

I walked to it and she took a key ring from her coat pocket, unsnapped the padlock and swung the door open.

The *morada* was sheltered on the north slope of a hill, and in the winter the sun never reached it directly. It was the perfect spot for a meat locker. Amadeo had three venison sides hanging from the rafters, and a wall was lined with shelves on which sat stone crocks, filled with jerky. On a wooden pole that stretched between the side walls were several dozen rabbit carcasses.

"Everybody around here hunts out of season," Victoria told me, "but they get caught. Papa says not even a game warden will go busting into somebody's private church."

"If anyone asks me," I said, "I'll tell them your father's a very religious man."

"I just didn't want you to think he was a Penitente," she said. "The Archbishop hates them. Papa's just a plain Catholic."

We walked back to the big house, and I said good-by to Amadeo and Excilda. "Why don't you and Victoria go to the movies sometime?" she said. "You don't have to marry her if you don't want to."

Victoria seemed cool to the idea, which I'd been about to suggest myself. "I have enough trouble," she said, "without having an Anglo boyfriend."

"You'll never get any kind of boyfriend with those manners," Excilda said. "You're not too big to spank, you know."

"Will you go to the movies with me, sometime?" I asked dutifully.

"Ask me some other time, when you really want to," she said.

Amadeo drove me back to the post office—hardware store, and the bus limped in a few minutes later. I gave the driver the rest of my ticket, and we started off toward the valley.

"I broke a fan belt just before I got to La Cima," he said. "I was afraid I'd have to spend the night up there. Damn, I hate it up in La Cima. I've been driving this bus for eight years, and I go there every day but Sundays, but those damn people stare at me like I was a

124

foreigner. They won't talk to me. They been living up there too long."

My mother was out of bed and dressed when I got home, and she was sober. "Jimbob's getting out of the hospital in a few days," she said. "Do I really have to tell him to leave? It will break his heart."

"That's up to you. I don't see much of him anyway, so I don't care. By the way, I didn't go to school today. I went up to Río Conejo and talked to the Montoyas."

"Are they coming back to work?" she asked. "It really wasn't a smart thing to do, fire them."

"Maybe. Not right away. We'll make out."

"I'll scramble some eggs," she said, and she did. They were edible. She read for a time while I washed dishes, and then went back to bed. I went to the cellar and chose two bottles, a Hermitage and a Beaujolais, and walked down to Romeo's studio with the wine in a paper bag. I heard voices through the door, but only after I'd knocked did I realize that a fight was going on inside. Romeo jerked open the door, his face still flushed from the argument, and said, "Look what you've done. Look!"

Shirley was striding around the room, waving her arms, calling Romeo a goddamn dago bastard. It was somewhat confused, but I got the idea that she didn't like to wear sandals, and wanted some new shoes and to get her hair done downtown.

"It's those thyroid pills," he said. "It's just like giving her benzedrine. She's been going on like this for a day and a half."

"Close that goddamn door, you stupid Guinea son of a bitch, I'm freezing my ass off."

"Come on in, Josh," he said.

"I'd better not," I said. "Here." I handed him the bottles. "This may help out. Maybe you ought to cut the dose down on her."

"No," he said. "I'll buy her a big bottle and send her back to San Francisco. She'll make out all right now."

"Shut that effing door!" Shirley yelled.

"Good night, Josh. Thank you for the wine."

"I'll see you later," I said.

14

JIMBOB BUEL LEFT the hospital at the end of the week, and came back to our house. He was shaky and weak, and went straight to bed. He'd done so much complaining when he was well that being sick left him nothing to say, so he lay quietly while Mother fed him toast and cocoa and canned chicken broth. It occurred to me that he was lonely; he was the only person I knew who never got any mail. The people he knew were probably afraid that if they wrote him he'd answer with a suggestion that he come and stay at their house for a while. I don't know what his record was as a guest; his visit to Sagrado was stretching into months.

Sometimes my mother or I read to him. So far as I knew, pneumonia didn't affect the eyes, but he said the strain of sitting up and moving his eyeballs back and forth was a little too exhausting. He had some sort of taste, but it wasn't mine. He liked fancy boys: James Branch Cabell and Lafcadio Hearn. I tried reading the war news to him: the First Army had taken Aachen, the Canadians had cleared out the Scheldt Estuary so we could use Antwerp as a port, the Russians were in East Prussia, we had won a big sea battle in Leyte Gulf. He said he didn't give the tiniest damn for the Scheldt Estuary, that it was all too coarse for his frail condition.

My mother said it might be better if I read something gentle to him, so I opened *The Wind in the Willows*, the gentlest book I know, suitable for invalids of all ages. He said the Water Rat and the Toad were too vomit-making. After that, I left the reading to my mother.

I had lots of school work to do anyway. The grounds at Helen De Crispin High School couldn't compare to the lush grass and hockey fields at Point Clear, but the instruction was first-rate. For one thing, nobody taking American History at De Crispin had any doubts about who won the Civil War. It was right there in the text-book.

The school even had a few traditions, and the one that set the standard was the Annual Indian Lore Lecture by Helen De Crispin herself, a rich Boston lady who'd moved west about the time of the Battle of the Little Big Horn. The Sagrado City Council gave the school her name because of a timely and generous donation she'd made.

When the architect designed the school back in the 1920s, he forgot to put in the washrooms, and the building was finished before anyone noticed the oversight. During the first term the students and teachers had to trot over and use the post-office facilities. Things got so crowded that the postmaster wouldn't let anyone in the bathroom unless he mailed a letter first.

The appropriation money was spent, but Mrs. De Crispin came through with a big bundle for construction of a separate building, full of toilets. It was such a decent gesture that the Council named the school for her, and the annex for the architect.

Romeo told me about her. When she moved west in the 1870s, leaving behind everything but her money, she took up Indians as a hobby. She lived with the Yankton Sioux in South Dakota for a spell, resided briefly with a Navajo band near Tuba City, Arizona, and eventually settled in Sagrado to be near the Pueblos. All the Indians were afraid of her. The Sioux felt she was personally responsible for the disappearance of the buffalo. Her Navajo visit coincided with an outbreak of Malta fever among the sheep. When she moved in with the Pueblos they were hit by a two-year drought, and their corn shriveled up. Now she lived in a big, gloomy house on

127

the outskirts of Sagrado, full of pottery, baskets, head-dresses and hunting fetishes.

Parker Holmes had been in her house once. He had baited his fox traps with some of the $3.50 vixen urine from Tennessee and caught Mrs. De Crispin's cocker spaniel. When he tried to return the dog she wouldn't let him in at first; she thought he was a Jicarilla Apache come to ravish her. He said she had a permanent cooking fire going in the middle of her living-room floor, and a hole cut through the roof to let out the smoke.

I walked down with Marcia to hear her lecture. Most of the students had turned out that evening, and there was a sprinkling of adults. We sat in front of two middle-aged Pueblo Indian men who talked quietly together in a mixture of English and Tewa, a language that sounds like someone choking on a fishbone. I don't know what they were doing there; maybe their lore was getting rusty.

Romeo was there. When I introduced him to Marcia he got very gallant and kissed her hand.

"What are you doing here?" I asked him.

"Helen is an old friend of mine," he said. "When I first came here, she was extremely kind to me, under the misapprehension that I was a Yavapai medicine man. She loaned me money and bought some of my pieces. Then I began to get bald, and she realized her error. Apparently Yavapais don't get bald."

"What a darling man," Marcia said when we returned to our seats. "I think I could have an experience with him. Yummy!"

Ratoncito came on stage and introduced the speaker. He was brief, for once.

She walked slowly from the wings, her arms folded across her chest. She wore an ankle-length squaw dress of deerskin, heavily beaded, and wrap-around moccasins. Her thin white hair was pulled back and tied with a red cloth from which one enormous eagle feather protruded like a scythe. Her cheeks and forehead were smeared with paint and she looked, generally, like Sitting Bull's grandmother.

Following her was a delicate-looking Indian boy about my age, dressed in a floppy apron than hung fore and aft, and staggering under a huge Sioux war bonnet. The effect of his costume was injured slightly by his shoes, a pair of white high-topped Keds which squeaked. He beat a small drum with a stick and pranced in a bouncy dance step, mumbling "Hey-yah, hey-yah," almost inaudibly.

Mrs. De Crispin raised her right hand solemnly and said "How!"

"This is my little friend Billy Birdwing," she went on, indicating the boy with the drum. "He's part Arapahoe and part Cheyenne, and he comes from far-off Oklahoma which, as you know, is a journey of many suns from here."

"I can make it in five hours in the pickup," an Indian behind me said.

When he was introduced, Billy Birdwing went into his mad little dance again and beat his drum frantically.

"Thank you, Billy," she said, and he stopped, looking sheepish.

"Many, many moons ago," she began, "which is the Indians' colorful way of saying 'a long time ago,' before the white man came with his evil and destructive ways bringing whiskey and gunpowder, the red man or Amerindian lived in total harmony with nature, feeding upon the mighty buffalo and the antelope. All was peace and tranquility, for to war against one's brother was to commit a sin against Gitchee Manitou or the Great Father. All Indian life was permeated with religion. Billy, will you say a little prayer for us?"

Billy set his drum down on the stage and walked forward, raising his arms. "Now I lay me down to sleep," he began, "I pray the Lord my soul to keep."

"That was very nice, Billy," she interrupted. "Can you give us an *Indian* prayer, please."

"Hey-yah, hey-yah," he chanted. He seemed lost without his drum, but essayed a few bounces in the tennis shoes.

"Indian dance is a form of prayer," Mrs. De Crispin went on. "Billy, do the eagle dance."

Billy spread his arms out to the side and performed the same step, throwing in a few hey-yahs.

"That's a dance that prays for eagles," she said ob-

129

scurely. "Once the Indians were a proud race, and the arrows in their quivers were many. They trapped the tender rabbit in their snares and hunted the wily buffalo."

"Oh, come on," one of the Indians behind us whispered. "I got a couple of Guernsey cows that are wilier than a goddamn buffalo."

"They stood proud and tall on their mesas and mountain tops and were One With Nature, strong and clean-limbed. Their women were comely and their children were fat. Peace reigned in their tepees, and they drank only fresh water from the clear streams. All Indians spoke with a straight tongue.

"When the evil white man came, he brought guns and ammunition and strange diseases. He brought the bitter medicine the Indians call Fire Water. Soon the buffalo were gone, and all the great warriors were betrayed by the Great White Father."

"Which one she mean?" one of the Pueblos asked.

"I don't know," the other said. "Probably Rutherford B. Hayes. Come on, let's get out of here." They stood up and walked stonily from the auditorium.

Mrs. De Crispin noticed the exodus, and paused until they left. "I am speaking of sacred things," she said, "of matters so holy that Indians don't want to hear it discussed. Isn't that right, Billy?"

"That's right, ma'am," Billy said. "Hey-yah, hey-yah."

"Today, after many cruel defeats and deceptions, the Red Man is a third-class citizen unless he goes the way of the white man. Billy Birdwing will tell you of the agonies this has caused him."

Billy Birdwing replaced her at the microphone, and wiped his nose with the back of his hand. "My Inyan name is Tse-hunk-ana-obobwi which means Boy With Wing Like a Bird, but the white man call me Billy Birdwing 'cause they can't say Tse-hunk-ana-obobwi."

"Disgraceful," Mrs. De Crispin murmured.

"They send me to the Disciples of Christ School and try to make me a Disciples of Christ. My father he's already go the white man's way. He got the John Deere

130

tractor franchise in Anadarko. But I don't want to go that way 'cause the white man speaks with a forked tongue. I want to go the Inyan way, in the path of my ancestors."

"Wonderful," Mrs. De Crispin said.

"So now I do a little dance for you call Deer Woman Dance. My friend Mrs. De Crismer she gonna do the dance with me, 'cause it takes two people to do this dance, a man and a woman. Mrs. De Crismer is a great friend of all Inyans."

Billy picked up his drum, and gave her the down beat. They both went into the hey-yah routine, and plodded around in a small circle. Mrs. De Crispin, dancing like an arthritic stork, got a bad kink in her leg and had to stop and rub it, but Billy bounced until he came to the end of the song. There was silence when the drum stopped until Ratoncito came back on the stage, clapping his hands hysterically to get the applause started.

"How you like?" Marcia asked me. "You got the old lore?"

Romeo met us on the auditorium steps and offered us a ride home in his truck. "What do you think?" he asked me. "Isn't she an odd old bird?"

"I was expecting something a little more scholarly," I said. "Maybe a fire-making demonstration with two dry twigs. I don't think she did her research."

"She's been making the same talk for twenty years," Marcia said. "I've heard it four times. Always with a different Indian boy, naturally. This one was the worst. Where does she get them?"

"I believe she travels yearly to Indian reservations and shops for them, like apples," Romeo said. "She has a lot of money, you know."

We drove through the snowy streets in silence for a while, and Romeo pulled up near the rectory. "Can we go to your studio?" Marcia asked him. "I'd like to meet your mistress."

Romeo was aghast. "My what?"

"Your mistress. I understand you keep a mistress, and I've never met a real one. It would be part of my education."

"Has this idiot been. . . ." He pointed to me.

131

"Oh, no. He didn't tell me anything. It's just one of those things you hear around, like 'So-and-so's going broke' and 'So-and-so's got a whale tattooed on his stomach' and things like that."

"Occasionally, only very occasionally," Romeo said, "a young woman comes to model for me. Sometimes these women have little money, and I allow them to stay at the studio. At present I am without a companion."

"What about Shirley?" I asked.

"The Thyroid Wonder should be back in the San Francisco Bay area by this time. And if she hasn't run out of pills she's doubtless down at Fisherman's Wharf calling everybody a Guinea bastard."

"I'd love to model for you, Mr. Bonino," Marcia said. "I have absolutely no modesty about my body."

"Get in your house, young lady, and pray for forgiveness. It's cruel to tempt an old, sick man. If your father had any decent human instincts he'd beat you to a pulp."

"Well, some day I'm going to get in with that wild artistic group. It's the only thing that makes this town different."

"The 'wild artistic group,' as you put it, has an average age of fifty-seven, and most of us have heart disease and bladder trouble. Go home. Out!"

I walked her to her door and said good night, while Romeo waited. "I'll see you in the morning," I said, "when the barking dogs arouse the sleeping tepee village and the smell of roasting coyote is in the air."

"My sisters will prepare me," she said. "I shall come to your wickiup in my white doeskin dress and lose my innocence on your buffalo robe."

"I will give you little ornaments to put in your hair, black as the crow's wing. I will give you red flannel and a looking-glass so that you may groom yourself."

"I'd also like to have a little spending money and a charge account at Wormser's," she said.

"Good night, Maiden Who Walks Like a Duck."

"Good night, Warrior Who Chickens Out at the Least Sign of Trouble."

"Hurry up, Josh, before I freeze," Romeo yelled.

We drove to his studio, and he offered to share one of

my father's bottles with me, to toast the departure of Shirley. "You were right," he said. "If I hadn't started her on the thyroid she'd have stayed around here for years and finally grown on me, like a fungus."

Wine is very heady at 7,000 feet, and I was woozy on the way home. I scraped some old snow off a wall and rubbed my face with it, and chewed on it, and then pulled off a piñon twig and gnawed on the needles, hoping it would act like coffee beans for alcohol breath. I could have saved myself the trouble; Mother and Jimbob were asleep when I came in, and all night I tasted turpentine.

15

IN DECEMBER it began to snow in earnest and the novelty slowly wore off. There would be an almost-warm day, with low impenetrable clouds, and in the night it would snow, and all the next day. East of the town, beyond the cordillera, the wind would blow blizzards and ranchers would find their cattle frozen, still standing huddled against a fence. But the mountains protected Sagrado from the winds, and the snow fell straight down. After a snow the sky would turn a thin blue, and an Alaskan cold would move in to stay for a week.

Jimbob Buel finally arose from his sickbed and returned to moping around the house and playing bridge with my mother's summer friends. She always referred to them as "the girls," and would say, "Joshua, please don't go downtown quite yet. The girls are coming and I'll need your help."

The girls arrived on Saturdays at noon. None was under sixty, and I was required to help them from their automobiles and hold them upright while they groped for their canes or crutches. One even carried a staff, a slim black pole six feet long with a gold top. The girls hobbled and limped into the house and lowered themselves carefully into chairs and made deep rumbling noises in their bellies. The six girls, with my mother and Jimbob, made up two tables for bridge. When each of the ancient liners was berthed, I would leave and walk somewhere: to Romeo's, to Steenie's, to Rumpp's, to the movies, sometimes to Chango's house for coffee with his parents, who had begun to call me *primito*, or little cousin. Occasionally I took hikes through the snowy foothills with Marcia, who felt that walking kept her hips from getting too wide. "There's nothing I can do with the basic structure of the pelvic girdle," she would say, "but the flab is definitely unnecessary. Race you up the next hill; last one to the top is a *gallina*."

With no formal word from Dad, Amadeo and Excilda remained in Río Conejo, using up the stored beans and the hanging venison for the children. I saw Amadeo in Sagrado one morning; he'd come into town to trade some of his illegal deer meat for flour, corn meal and sugar. It was something that went on all the time in winter, he told me, and the game wardens looked the other way if it was a question of survival, which it often was. He said that Victoria returned to school in Yunque, and had stopped feeling so noble. "My family's always been hard working," he said, "but thick in the head. Victoria's the first real smart one in a long time, and I don't want her to end up as a waitress in the Del Norte Café. You hear anything from Mr. Arnold yet?"

I said no, not a word, but that mail delivery was probably slow wherever he was. There was a picture in my mind, probably not accurate, about how the Navy got letters delivered: Somebody flew over the ship in a light plane and dropped a bag of mail on the deck. If it missed the ship, tough.

The cooking at home was terrible, and nobody seemed to mind but me. Jimbob tucked it away three times a day and just beamed at my mother, and said things like, "Miss Ann, this is surely the sort of nectar they dine on in Olympus." She'd discovered a commodity, one of the atrocities of war, consisting of pieces of ground-up cat mixed with oatmeal and pressed into the shape of a brick. You could fry it or bake it or boil it or eat it raw and it always tasted the same, like a deck shoe. Then she got very fancy and began slicing bananas over everything, sometimes heating them first in a sort of sweet cream sauce. When the spirit was on her, she'd put the creamed bananas over the brick, and wouldn't we have a feast!

I made a special trip to the El Chivo Bookstore and bought something the woman recommended by Fannie Farmer. It was to be a Christmas present for my mother, but I gave it to her early. *"Boston* Cooking School?" she said. "What do Yankees know about food?" Then she showed up old Fannie Farmer by cooking a real old time Italian dinner, letting the spaghetti boil for a couple of hours ("Long cooking brings out the flavor of spaghetti") until it turned into a gray lump with bubbles in it. Jimbob thought it was simply scrumptious, and said so.

I stayed away from home as much as possible, going there only to sleep and steal wine for Romeo. He told me the Châteauneuf-du-Pape and the Nuits-Saint-Georges were too rare and expensive, and suggested I pilfer only Beaujolais and Bardolino. "It's a fine point, I admit," he said, "but an important one. I'm going to have to face your father some time, and I don't want my guilt to lie too heavily."

Sometimes the house got too oppressive for sleeping, and I'd stay with Steenie for a night or two. Mrs. Stenopolous didn't mind; for a woman with only one child, she was the most harried mother I've ever seen. I think it came from having everything she planned—meals, parties, small chores, sleep—interrupted by frantic telephone calls from women in labor. She knew that no matter what she started she couldn't finish without the telephone ringing. "Hello," she'd say. "Yes, this is Mrs. Stenopolous. Well, he's just sitting down to . . . eight minutes apart, eh? Well, surely you can hold out until. . . . No, *I'm* not a doctor, but . . . Yes, I'll tell him." She'd hang up and walk into the dining room and raise one eyebrow at her husband. "That was Mrs. Gillespie. She's at the Emergency Room, having the world's first baby."

Dr. Stenopolous would take a last look at his dinner,

and leave. He was a thin, mild man, and never complained about the work which kept him hopping. He looked like a plumber going out to unplug a toilet; it was his wife who took the great mystery of birth to heart, and I think she loved her role as a martyred wife. "Joshua," she would say to me, "I've given this advice to my son, and I'll give it to you: Never marry an obstetrician. It's hell on earth."

"I wasn't even considering marrying an obstetrician," I said. "The thought never crossed my mind."

"Don't let it. If I ever hear that you're going to marry an obstetrician, I'll come running into the church and make a scene. No human should have to live with an obstetrician. Look. Look at that nice dinner getting cold on the table. *That's* what happens when you get involved with an obstetrician."

"Yes, but that's his dinner, not yours. Yours isn't getting cold."

"Don't argue with me, young man. I tell you, it's a miserable existence and I ought to know. If I knew when these damned babies were being conceived, I'd go from bedroom to bedroom pouring cold water on the couples. The birth rate would drop to nothing."

"Wouldn't that be kind of bad for business?"

"Oh, there's other specialties he could have followed. His best friend at medical school had some brains. He's a dermatologist. Nobody ever wakes him up at three in the morning to treat a hot case of boils. No, sir! I told him, I said, 'Bill go into ophthalmology. Go into eye, ear, nose and throat. Go into pathology. Anything.' But would he listen?"

"Nope," Steenie said. "Wouldn't listen."

"Right," said Mrs. Stenopolous. "Here, have some more *moussaka*. Thank God there's somebody who'll eat my cooking."

On the nights I stayed at Steenie's house he provided me with a bedroll, and I arranged it on the floor near his bed, which wasn't big enough for two. As part of his physical conditioning program, to make himself lean and hard for the Commandos, or the Musketeers, or whatever it was, he turned off the heat and opened all his windows at night. The bedroll, a Sears, Roebuck item designed for sultry nights in the tropics, would begin to become inadequate about two in the morning, and I'd flop around on the concrete-slab floor, and roll into a ball, seeking a warm spot, and finally wake Steenie.

"I'm freezing my tail off down here. I'm turning blue."

"Really cold down there, is it?"

"You wouldn't believe it, but there's an inch of frost on the bedroll. I think my toes are starting to rot."

"Well, if it's that cold. . . ." He'd whistle, and his dog Thunder, an eleven-year-old sheepdog-poodle mixture, would drag his frail old bones off the floor and jump into bed with Steenie. "Can't let my faithful hound get too cold," he'd say. "Man's best friend deserves better treatment than that. There you go, boy. Snuggle down there under the covers. Attaboy. Good old Thunder."

My mother didn't really approve of my staying with the Stenopolouses, because they weren't in my class. I finally pointed out that there wasn't anyone in Sagrado who measured up to her standards, and that I was trying to make friends with the best of a bad lot. It was that or go crazy for lack of companionship, I said.

"You *could* learn to play bridge," she suggested.

"Never," I said. "I just haven't got the head for it. I'll have to take my chances with the locals."

"I wish we were back in Mobile," she wailed.

A bulky envelope from Dad arrived one afternoon shortly before Christmas. In it was a letter for me, and what appeared to be a parchment scroll. I looked at it more closely; it was a parchment scroll. The letter said:

I have written to your mother and told her, clearly I hope, that Amadeo and Excilda are technically un-fireable except for cause. Cause consists of grand larceny or murdering a member of the family. They work for us at a stipulated salary, and have a contract to do so. The contract is no less binding because it is oral and not written.

If the Yunque River were navigable, I would steam up the channel right now in this ponderous bucket and knock a few heads together. As it isn't, I am forced to rely upon you and your mother to behave like rational people.

The document Amadeo requested is enclosed. I can't vouch

for its legality, but it's a damned fine piece of draftsmanship. A young Seaman First named Boudreau, a Negro who studied art at the University of Chicago, did the lettering and design, and even located the parchment, no mean feat on a destroyer escort. Needless to say, Boudreau is a steward aboard this vessel, having advanced to that post in six years from his former position as garbage collector. I feel he merits a somewhat higher responsibility in the Navy but, as the Skipper pointed out, he lacks several credits toward his M.A.

Don't worry too much about that business in Bastogne. I have it on excellent authority that it's a last-ditch act of desperation by Von Rundstedt. The Germans are getting short of fuel, a happy situation in which I hope I am playing some small part.

For God's sake keep things going evenly around there, and try being a prop instead of a burden, for a change. The psychologist at Point Clear told me that, in spite of the severe brain damage, you would be capable of simple tasks, like feeding yourself and locating the men's room.

By the way: Romeo Bonino is congenitally poverty-stricken and can't afford decent wine, of which he's extremely fond. I believe he ordinarily drinks something called Flor de Yunque, an insecticide produced in the valley. Please take him some bottles from the cellar (*not* the claret, please). Many of the smaller red Burgundies are going to turn into salad dressing if not drunk soon, and no one would enjoy them more than Romeo.

I give the war, in this theater, six more months, Von Rundstedt notwithstanding. My scheme to sail up the Rhine with a fleet of shrimp trawlers and overpower the enemy with the stench has been turned down by a near-sighted group of Academy people, and we shall have to continue the fight along more orthodox lines.

It is time for me to make a tour of the various officers of the deck. They are a generally inept bunch, particularly an Ensign named Taylor, who was anchor man in his Reserve class at Southern Illinois University. When he isn't spitting into the wind, he sees U-Boat periscopes in every clump of flotsam, and now holds the fleet record. Once he thought he saw one rising twenty yards off the beach at Cannes, but it turned out to be the foot of a skinny, eight-year-old French boy who was diving for periwinkles.

Carry on,
Dad

The parchment scroll was heavily decorated with loops

and curlicues in several colors, and the "K" was illuminated, like the letters in hand-written Bibles. It said:

Know all Men by these Presents, Greetings:
I, the undersigned Frances Arnold, holding a Commission as Lieutenant Commander in the State's legitimate Force of Arms (Nautical), and being engaged in Combat á outrance with the State's Enemy (A. Hitler, Commander in Chief), and therefore unable to discharge my several Duties as Head of Household in Corazón Sagrado without committing Desertion and bringing Disgrace upon my Head and Dishonor to my Family Name, do hereby appoint my Son, Joshua M. Arnold, aged seventeen years, my Agent and Attorney in Fact, and do further State that he may issue, give and pronounce Orders, Edicts, Commands, Directions and Ukases pertinent and relevant to the Operation of said Household and abutting Lands, providing he seeks Sage Counsel before so doing, and doesn't get too big for his Britches. Done the Eighteenth Day of December, A.D. 1944, aboard the Destroyer Escort USS JOHN T. MAYS, Captain Philip Baines, U.S.N., Commanding.

My mother got a letter from him in the same delivery. I don't know what it said; she never showed it to me. She came in later and said, "I've been thinking it over, and I can see I shouldn't have let the Montoyas go. I really can't run this house by myself, particularly with a guest here."

"Yes," I said. "About that guest. How much longer is he going to stay? I don't know anything about courtly manners, but I think his welcome's pretty well worn out."

"Oh, surely he can stay for Christmas. It would be awful to ask him to leave just before Christmas."

"Well, maybe you can find another bridge partner after New Year's. Jimbob goes, the sooner the better."

"He's a very lonely man, Joshua."

"I don't wonder. Do you think he'd still be hanging around if Dad were here? Do you think Dad would stand for him? Do you know what the talk is around school?"

"Talk? School? Do you mean that people are gossiping?"

"Look, Mother. This is a very small town. Everybody

knows what everybody else is doing. Mostly they don't care, but they know. I've been getting the needle since he got here. Your reputation is about shot."

She spaced her words out slowly. "That . . . is . . . the . . . most . . . disgusting . . . thing. . . ."

"Sure it's disgusting. How do people know that all you do is yell 'no trump' and 'vulnerable' at each other and sip a little sherry together? Don't forget: You think these people are low and coarse. Why should you be surprised that they think low, coarse thoughts?"

"That . . . is . . . ridiculous."

"Sure it is. So you fired the Montoyas, and there went the chaperones. And it was you who used to give me that stuff about avoiding the appearance of evil."

"The Montoyas will come back, won't they?" she asked, in a small and subdued voice. "You'll reach them for me, won't you? Maybe Excilda can roast a turkey or something. You know, I'll have to ask the girls about this. I wonder if they think I. . . . No, it just isn't possible."

"I'll talk to the Montoyas," I said. "And please keep Jimbob away from Amadeo. According to this, I can give the orders from here on." I handed her the scroll, and watched her while she read it thoughtfully.

"Your father is sometimes a very whimsical man," she said. "The war must be a great strain on him."

"He's holding up better than you are," I told her.

Then Jimbob began to whimper for a snack in his bedroom, a pitiable sound, and I walked downtown for a hamburger and to see a movie, "Arsenic and Old Lace." It gave me some interesting ideas for the disposal of Jimbob, but digging up a concrete cellar is rugged work.

I spent my whole lunch period the next day in a phone booth at Rumpp's Pharmacy, trying to reach Amadeo. The only telephone in Río Conejo is at the combination post office-opera house-alchemist's shop, and the girl who answered said to hang on, there'd be a truck passing pretty soon and she'd ask the driver to stop at the Montoyas' house and say there was a phone call. It took forty minutes for the message to be delivered and for Amadeo to drive to the store.

140

He said he'd received a letter from Dad, too, and that he and Excilda would be in Monday, and if Mr. Buel even so much as looked at him funny he'd hit him with whatever he had in his hand at the time, and he hoped it would be an axe.

Then I called Dad's Sagrado lawyer, a Mr. Gunther, who'd played bridge at the house a few times. I don't know why he needed a lawyer in Sagrado; the only time he came in handy was when Dad bought the place in the '30s, and somebody had to untangle all the problems about the title. Every piece of land around here had, at one time, belonged either to the Indians or to the King of Spain (and his title seemed a little shaky to me). If somebody bought as much as a square yard of *caliche* with a dead coyote buried in it, a lawyer had to trace the land's history back to 1634. First there would be the general, over-all grant from His Majesty, which might include a million square *varas* of what he called "New Spain," an area bordered roughly by the Mississippi, on the east, and the Pacific Ocean, on the west. Nobody knew exactly how big a *vara* was, but it was somewhere between a cubit and a league, its length depending on who the viceroy was at the time. Once the lawyer got that figured out, he began sorting through the families that had owned it and willed it to their children. The families were named Vigil or Espinosa, and wrote their wills in old-fashioned Spanish, in a spidery hand, with light purple ink. Then there would be histories of counterclaims, suits to "quiet title" which never seemed to work, liens by banks and insurance companies, abandonments, quit-claim deeds, reappraisals, tax sales and something called "eminent domain seizure for consideration." A good lawyer who paced himself could make a land sale last for ten years and send his kids to Princeton on the fees.

Gunther hadn't been allowed to spend more than six months on the deal when Dad bought the land and built the house, and it had always galled him. But when I talked to him, and said it was very important, he agreed to see me in his office after school.

I showed him the parchment scroll that Dad had sent

to me, and he read it—the way lawyers seem to read everything—very slowly and carefully, with a faint sneer, as if it had a mashed bug on it.

"This is a very singular instrument," he said when he'd finished. "I assume it's some sort of joke."

"No, sir, it's no joke," I said, and told him the details, leaving out the part about the sherry and Doctor Temple.

"How old are you, Joshua?" he asked. "Not more than seventeen, surely."

"Seventeen is right," I said. "Why?"

"At seventeen," he said, "you are what the law terms 'an infant.' Aside from the obvious things you're not allowed to do, such as vote and purchase beverage alcohol, you may not sign contracts, form or be an officer in a corporation, operate a motor vehicle without permission of parents or guardian, marry—marriage is a form of contract, of course—serve on a jury or hold public office."

"That's all okay with me," I said. "This thing just says that I can give orders around the house while my father's away."

He said "Hmmmm," and thought about it. "Has your mother been declared incompetent?"

"Well," I said. "I've as much as told her I thought she was incompetent."

"Not the same thing at all. It is a judge, usually on the advice of a psychiatrist, who declares a person incompetent. And then it is necessary for the same, or another, judge to issue a writ of emancipation in behalf of the minor. In other words, he makes you, for certain legal purposes, an adult. The degree of emancipation is generally limited."

"I don't want to try to go through all that," I said. "What I really wanted to know was, is this thing on the parchment scroll any good? I mean, can I act on it?"

"In my opinion as a practicing attorney, the document has value only as a curiosity. Legally, it doesn't hold water, and a court test would show that very quickly. However, assuming that is your father's signature at the bottom, and disregarding for the moment the amusing

142

archaic language, it does seem to express Mr. Arnold's will in certain matters relevant to the operation of your household. Although your father is absent, physically, from the situation, he may, as the head of your family, delegate certain responsibilities, I suppose. In ordinary, informal practice, of course, the mother is, uh, next in line of authority. I've known Ann Arnold for a good many years, and she's always seemed eminently competent to me. A very fine bridge player, for example, which generally implies a sound mind and cool judgment."

"I don't think Dad's saying she's incompetent. It's just that I know she doesn't particularly like giving orders to Amadeo and Excilda, and. . . ."

"Who are Amadeo and Excilda?"

"The Montoyas. I told you. They work for us. They've worked for us since I was a baby. Amadeo sort of does the heavy work and Excilda cooks and keeps the house clean. Mother doesn't like to give orders, or if she does she gives orders the wrong way and makes everyone sore. And then this guy Jimbob Buel I told you about, who's staying with us, he gives orders too. Amadeo can't stand him, and I don't blame him. What was happening was that Mother would say one thing and Jimbob would say something else, and sometimes they contradicted each other. Amadeo and Excilda got caught in the middle."

"And they resigned?"

"They got fired. Mother fired them one night when she was . . . when she was in a bad mood. Dad says nobody can fire them except for cause, and there wasn't any cause. They have about a dozen children, and not a lot of money."

"I'm sure that your concern for their welfare is commendable, but surely if your mother fired them. . . ."

"That's just it. She doesn't have any right to fire them, Dad says. He hired them, not Mother. And this parchment scroll says I can be the boss, sort of, as long as I seek—what is it?—Sage Counsel."

"Yes," said Mr. Gunther. "Sage Counsel. I assume he means the counsel of your mother."

"I don't think so. I believe he means the counsel of Amadeo and Excilda, since they're both pretty sage."

"But they are the employees. Surely the employer—or, in your case, the informally delegated agent of the employer—doesn't seek the advice of the employee before telling said employee what to do."

"That's the way it always worked. I mean, Amadeo would come to Dad and say, 'The limb on one of the apple trees needs propping or the weight of the apples will snap it off come October.' And Dad would say, 'Go ahead and prop it up.' That way, Dad gave the orders, but Amadeo told him what orders to give. As Amadeo told me once, those aren't *his* apple trees. He knows what he'd do if they *were* his apple trees, but since they aren't he has to ask for the orders before he does anything."

"I believe I see what you're getting at, but the whole affair is really out of my province. It seems to me that if your mother is willing to accept this, uh, eccentric document as the wishes of your father, and if she is further willing to abandon to you her position as head of the household *pro tem* (a Latin expression meaning for the time being, as I'm sure you know), then you have no problem."

"Good. That's what I wanted to know."

"If," he continued, "if on the other hand she does not wish to accede to the document, and chooses to ignore it as the playful product of a sarcastic mind, you are then back where you started. Legally, you have no rights, and your mother has all of them. It boils down to this: Is your father's word law around your house, or isn't it? Will your mother accede to his wishes or won't she? These are matters to be decided not by attorneys but by the parties involved."

"I think she'll do what he wants her to do," I said. "He's always had the responsibility; she's never liked it much."

"Then you have no problem. For your purposes, the document is adequate. I wonder . . . would you wait a few minutes while my secretary copies this, uh, thing? I'm lecturing at the University on Contracts next week, and I'd like to show the students a textbook example of what happens when a man not trained in the law attempts to write one."

"Sure," I said. "Go ahead. But I thought it was pretty good."

"I must admit that it's a work of art, but is it airtight? Is it sound? Ah, no. Contractually speaking it's as feeble an instrument as I've ever seen."

"Well, thank you, Mr. Gunther," I said. "How much do I owe you for your time and so on?"

"Nothing, my boy. Nothing. You've helped breathe life into next week's lecture."

So Amadeo and Excilda came back the following Monday, which was Christmas Day. Jimbob got out of the sack for dinner, and cooed over the roast lamb, not forgetting to whisper to my mother that of course it wasn't as good as it would have been if *she'd* cooked it. But his heart wasn't in the lie. I thought about telling him the truth: That it wasn't lamb at all, but roast kid, but decided it would be un-Christmaslike to make the poor fellow sick again. He'd lost weight with the pneumonia, and looked very fragile. I was allowed a small glass of red wine—a Mâcon, I believe—with my meal, after promising my mother I wouldn't get drunk on it. We all toasted each other: Jimbob, always a good man with a literary allusion, said, "God bless us, every one!" and then spoiled the effect somewhat by murmuring, "Thackeray." I asked Excilda if she'd come into the dining room and give us a Sagrado-style toast, and she raised her glass, fixed her eye on Jimbob, and said, with a big smile, *Más vale llegar a tiempo que ser invitado.* Then she translated it as something about health and wealth, and we applauded.

What it really meant was: "It's better to arrive in time for dinner than to be invited."

16

ON NEW YEAR'S EVE afternoon, a gray, cold day which showed no promise of turning into a gala night, Steenie and I picked up our celebration mates and walked them to the movies, a rerun of "The Thief of Bagdad," with Sabu and a giant genie whose name escaped me. It wasn't clear whose companion was whose; Marcia was one of them, and the other was Eleanor Pickens, a classmate who'd just won the National Honor Society pin because she had a trick memory for algebraic formulae. Marcia was to spend the night at her house, across the street from Steenie's. I was staying with Steenie, on the concrete floor of his bedroom. Eleanor's parents were in Denver, at a building contractors' convention, Steenie told me as we stood side by side in the men's room of the theater. We'd gone there together, partly for obvious reasons, and partly to escape the short subject, which featured a third-rate conga band—Bananas Lupo and his Island Bunch—shaking castanets in a daytime night club, with fifty extras sitting at little tables, smiling at each other and nodding their heads in time to the music. I suppose it's the way Hollywood makes junior directors start their careers. If they can put movement into a group of bored Cubans on a bandstand, they can go on to better things. The camera angles would change —a long shot of the whole ensemble, a medium shot from the left as the trumpet players jumped to their feet to blow a measure, then a close-up of the castanet man, shaking all over like a Model A truck and showing gold teeth. It was one of the few things that could drive me away from the screen, and it never missed.

"There's something in the air," Steenie said. "Know what it is?"

"Snow?" I asked. "It was clouding over pretty solid when we got here."

"It's love," he said. "Eleanor is an enthusiastic necker, and Marcia hates to be left out. No matter how we pair off, there's a promise of action."

When we returned to our seats, Marcia said we'd missed the best part. "There was a girl with a big plate of fruit on her head," she said, "who looked just like Carmen Miranda's uncle. She sang 'Shoo-Fly Pie' in Portuguese. Then there were three colored tap dancers wearing silk suits and two-toned shoes."

"I'll come down again tomorrow and catch it," Steenie said.

We ate egg rolls and spaghetti at the Chinese restaurant, which had a Japanese chef until the war, when he was interned. The new chef was a Greek. We passed up the minestrone subgum as too chancy, and the sweet-and-pungent spareribs wrapped in grape leaves as too exotic. With all the bars closed—it was Sunday—Sagrado was going to have to have a peaceful New Year's Eve.

After a chilly walk to Eleanor's house, we built a fire and grumbled while the girls made hot chocolate. "They're just putting off the hour of reckoning," Steenie said. "I shall not be denied."

"Yes, you shall," Marcia said, coming into the living room with a tray and looking very housewifey. "Eleanor and I have been talking it over. We'll dance, play Monopoly or tell ghost stories, but no kissing except at midnight."

"We're bigger and stronger than you are," Steenie said. "We'll take you by force. Right, Tiger?"

"Right," I said. "You might as well submit peacefully."

"Drink your cocoa before it gets cold," Eleanor said. "I'll get the Monopoly set."

"I've got half a mind to break off negotiations right now," Steenie said. "I can play Monopoly when I'm eighty or ninety. Right now the sap is running."

Eleanor got three houses on Park Place very quickly, and Marcia erected a fine, modern hotel on the Boardwalk. Steenie and I were wiped out by eleven.

"I don't seem to have much instinct for real estate," I said. "I think I'm more the artistic type."

"You owe me exactly two thousand dollars," Marcia said. "I don't think mortgaging Baltic Avenue is going to do you much good. Fish or cut bait."

"Let's sit on the couch and watch the fire," Steenie suggested. "I don't suppose you have a bottle of champagne, do you, Eleanor?"

"Daddy's liquor is all locked up in the sideboard," she said. "Would you like some ginger ale?"

"In the sideboard, eh? Eleanor, you've just said a very indiscreet thing."

The lock was childishly inadequate, and by scarring the finish just a little with a pocket knife Steenie unearthed a nearly-full bottle of Gilbey's gin. "This looks like very good stuff," he said. "My father uses it as an anesthetic in difficult labor." He peered into the sideboard again. "Hmm. Johnny Walker. I think that's some kind of bourbon, or sherry. It probably mixes very well with the gin."

"Leave that alone," Eleanor pleaded. "Daddy's been saving it all through the war."

"Hoarding is unpatriotic and chicken," he said. "Hey, what's this in the unlabeled bottle?" He removed a flask full of a colorless liquid. "Has your old man been moonshining? Naughty, naughty." He unscrewed the top and took a small swig. "That's the real stuff," he said, shuddering.

"That's chafing-dish fluid," Eleanor said.

"And it's pretty *rotten* chafing-dish fluid. I'll stick with the gin and sherry."

"I don't know what I'll say if Daddy finds out."

"He'll never know. I'll just take a little off the top. He's

148

not the kind of skinflint that measures levels, is he?" He gulped some of the Johnny Walker from the bottle, chasing it with a little gin. "So *that's* what a martini tastes like," he said wonderingly. "Josh, why don't you join me? I think I can find a clean glass somewhere."

"No, thanks," I said. "I'm a wine snob."

"Come *on*. Come *on*. It's just like Sal Hepatica for the smile of health. It's a medical fact: No one your age has ever contracted cirrhosis of the liver. The healthy tissues of youth just slough the alcohol away, and absorb the vitamin A."

"All right," I said. "Let me have some of the Scotch. I'll get some ice."

"Scotch? Which one is Scotch?"

"The Johnny Walker," I said.

"That's Scotch? I didn't know you made martinis with Scotch. Live and learn."

"You're both a couple of pigs," Marcia said. "You're ruining our New Year's Eve."

"Daddy'll know," Eleanor wailed. "I just know he'll know."

"My father will make full res . . . restitution to your father," Steenie assured her. "Soon as the war's over. Oooh, looky! A whole 'nother bottle of Gilbey's gin." He pronounced it Jilbey's. "Looks just like water. He'll never, never know, unless you squeal. All the world hates a tattletale."

I drank two glasses of the Scotch, which was horrible-tasting, and filled the bottle back to its original level with tap water. It looked a little paler afterwards, but I thought it would pass inspection. Steenie stayed with the gin. At midnight we heard the cathedral bells announce the New Year, and looked for the girls, but they had locked themselves in Eleanor's bedroom. We opened Mrs. Pickens's secretary desk, wrote "Happy New Year, with love and XXXXXXX from Steenie and Josh, January 1, 1945" on a sheet of her expensive-looking stationery, and slipped it under the door. We congratulated ourselves by having a drink; I changed to gin. Steenie said that my switching to gin was a genuine sacrifice, and that only a great gentleman and friend would have done it. I agreed. One of the girls knocked on the inside of the bedroom door.

"I b'lieve we have message," Steenie said.

"I'll retrieve message," I promised. A vast silent earthquake had tilted Eleanor's house thirty degrees, making it necessary for me to brace myself against a corridor wall on the way to the bedroom. The same sheet of paper was pushed under the door, folded once. As I bent to pick it up the earthquake tilted the house another ten degrees, causing me to lose my balance and fall. I got up and banged the side of my fist on their door. "Earthcake!"

"What?" It was Marcia. Poor, sweet Marcia. She was going to be trapped in the room, falling timbers, flames. We had to save her. Had to save Eleanor, too. "Gout. Housafallen!"

"Go jump in a kite," she said. Didn't care what happened. Wanted to stay in the room, die with her friend. Die with Eleanor. That's what friends are for. I went back into the living room and showed the note to Steenie. "Whaz say?" he asked.

"Very impornt letter." I opened it and tried to read it, but the letters kept sliding diagonally toward the edge of the paper. Earthquake was doing that. "Don't know. Written with mov'ble ink."

" 'Mposs'ble. No such thing. Here, have more Jilbey's. Sharpen up th' vision. Lem' see." I gave the letter to him, leaned too far forward, and fell into the fireplace, where piñon was crackling.

"Gout fireplace," Steenie said. "Geh burn. Thirda gree. Haf' do skin graf. Paaaiiiinful."

"Read letter."

"Saysen I quote: 'Gode hell. Sign Marcia Neleanor.' "

"Earthcake's gun gettm. Don' care. Have nother Jilbey."

We left Eleanor's house some time later, and walked carefully across the street to Steenie's. All the houses on the street were still standing. "Jus' little tremor," I said. "On'y earth coo-ake unner El'nor's house." Steenie paused by a tree and threw up on it. "Good for tree," he said. "Organic matter. Good fer'lizer. Sick. Egg rollzen spaghetti."

In Steenie's room, I sat on the floor on the bedroll and undressed. Steenie sat on the edge of his bed and looked at his right foot. "Foun' out somethin'," he muttered. "Jilbey's makes feet swell up."

"How y'know?"

"Couldn't get m'galosh on m' foot, hardly. Hadda walk over with on'y one galosh on. Geh pneumonia. Now can' get it off."

"I'll help pull," I said. His galosh was stuck very tightly, and for five minutes he pushed at it while I pulled. When it came off, we saw that there was another galosh under it.

"Y'put two galoshes on one foot," I said. "Thass why stuck."

Steenie's face screwed up, and he broke into tears. "Thass beautiful explanation," he said. "The mos' perfect explanation I ever heard. It makes everything so clear. I mean . . . I mean . . . answers lota questions. Plan y'whole life on a thing like that." He wiped his eyes on his sleeve, and undressed. "G'night, Josh. Gah bless you."

"Gah bless you, too, Steenie. Where's light?"

"Onna wall." I crawled carefully to the wall, stood up and turned out the light. The earthquake had slowed down, but the bedroll continued to toss until I slept.

17

EXCILDA INVITED ME to have Christmas dinner with her family in Conejo five days later. Christmas on December 25 is considered a Protestant heresy in the mountains; the people hold their own on January 6, which is what we call Twelfth Night in Mobile. We didn't do anything about it there; we just called it Twelfth Night and let it go at that.

Since the Montoyas were more or less back in the chips, there were lots of people for dinner, and Excilda served the meal in shifts, starting at noon. She'd been working on the dinner for three days, cooking at night when she returned from Sagrado, and it was a feast that made an Anglo Christmas dinner look like starvation rations on Devil's Island. There were two *lechoncillos*—that's suckling pig, stuffed with apples and onions and corn meal—and three *guajalotes asados,* which were turkeys surrounded by red chiles and buried in a pit filled with hot rocks for a day or so. That was just for starters, of course. I was sitting next to Victoria at the big table, talking English to her and trying to make conversation in Spanish with an uncle, or a fifth cousin, who had no teeth, when I got a bad case of hiccups and had to go out on the *portal* to hold my breath and stand on my head. Don Carlos was out there, too, eating what appeared to be an elk, or dinosaur, thighbone. When I stood on my head he walked over and licked my face, and I started laughing and fell over, with my hiccups gone. It's complicated, but it's a hiccup cure I'll recommend to anyone.

I went back inside and finished dinner, forcing myself to eat more slowly and decorously. It wasn't an outstanding performance on my part; I could only get down two *empanadas* before the fog closed in, then retired to the big room to lie on the floor and gasp. Victoria sat on the old sofa nearby and looked down at me. "You need some exercise," she said. "You want to walk around?"

"Sorry, I can't move," I told her. "I think I've injured myself."

"You just ate too much," she said. "Come on. Let's go for a walk."

Victoria pulled on my hand while two of her younger brothers pushed from behind, and together they wrestled me onto my feet. They had to hold me while I put my snow boots on; I couldn't seem to bend forward without staggering.

Amadeo came out of the dining room, patting his stomach. "Where you going?" he asked.

"For a walk," Victoria answered. "Josh ate too much."

"You want some exercise, why don't you chop some wood?"

"Aw, Papa, he doesn't want to chop any wood. Nobody chops wood on Christmas."

"Go on, then. Walk. Have a good time."

Don Carlos came with us again, carrying the elephant bone balanced in his jaws. I carried the wrapped package I'd brought to Conejo with me; it was too big to put in my coat pocket, so I carried it under my arm. Victoria was too polite to ask about it. We walked up the road until we could see the next village, Amorcita, from a high point. The little town, almost covered by snow, seemed to be on fire. Thick gray smoke was rising from every house.

"They're burning their *luminarias*," she told me. "They have a sort of parade every Christmas, in the evening, and everybody lights a bonfire in front of his house. They do it in La Cima, too."

"What's it for?"

"I don't know. Some kind of old custom. Papa told me they used to do it in Conejo and the other towns but they stopped. You want to go up to La Cima and see it tonight? It's pretty."

"You mean walk?"

"No, Papa can drive us, or maybe he'll let you take the truck. The road's okay. Just don't get out of the truck. They're kind of mean up there."

When the wind began to blow harder, we went into an old log barn near the road, and sat on some hay bales. Don Carlos, still gnawing on his dinner, guarded the door.

"I have a present for you," I said. "Merry Christmas." I handed her the package, which had been getting heavy during the walk. She could carry it down.

"I noticed you were carrying something," she said. "Can I open it?"

"Of course. Wait a minute. You *can* read Spanish, can't you?"

"Sure I can read Spanish. What did you think?"

"Okay," I said. "Then Merry Christmas."

The woman at El Chivo Bookstore had had a difficult time finding a Spanish edition of *Don Quixote*. Her regular book-buying channels offered her a variety of translations, but I said it had to be in Spanish, or never mind. She finally got it through the University, and it was a college edition, with a glossary in the back for the out-of-date words. I had written "For the Fair Dulcinea" on the end papers, and signed myself "Don Josué del Corazón Sagrado."

Victoria removed the book from the wrapping paper, weighed it in her hands, read the title, flipped through some pages, and read the inscription.

"Hijo!" she said. "What is it?"

"What do you mean, 'What is it?' It's a book. It's *Don Quixote.*"

"For me?"

"Sure, for you. Keepsies."

"To read?"

"If you want to. That was the idea."

"Oh. We already had it in school. About the windmills."

"I'll bet you didn't have the whole book. Look." I riffled through it. "Nine hundred and forty-three pages. In two parts. There's a lot of other stuff beside the windmills in it."

"How come it's in Spanish? The part I read was in English. We have this book down at school, called *Broadening Your Horizons*. It's got a lot of stories and poetry in it. All in English."

"The man who wrote it," I said, "wrote it in Spanish. He *was* Spanish. They have it translated into a lot of different languages for people who don't know how to read Spanish. But this is the original, just the way Cervantes wrote it."

"Is it hard?"

"It's long," I said. "I wouldn't say it was hard. It rocks along pretty well, especially in the first part."

"I promise to read some every night until I get it finished," she said, "no matter how hard it is."

"I didn't mean it to be work," I told her. "I wanted you to like it. It was supposed to be fun."

"Thank you for the lovely present," she said, as if she were reading the sentence from an unfamiliar script.

"You're welcome."

"Who's this Dulcinea in the front? That's not my name."

"I know it's not," I said. "That was supposed to be fun, too. Dulcinea's the girl in the book, the one Don Quixote fights all his battles for. She's beautiful."

Victoria put her hands on my shoulders and kissed me on the cheek. "You're the first person who ever gave me a present, except for my family," she said. I put my arms around her and kissed her on the lips, and pulled her back onto some loose hay. Don Carlos left his bone and padded over to us, growling.

"Go away, boy," I said. His growl became more urgent, and he put his muzzle next to my ear, to be sure I heard him.

"Good boy," Victoria said, sitting up. "You love me, don't you?" Don Carlos licked her hand and wagged his tail. He loved her all right. "We'd better get home," she said, "before it gets dark. How's your stomach?"

"Much better, thanks," I said. We stood up and brushed the hay off. Victoria picked up her *Don Quixote* and Don Carlos retrieved his bone. When Victoria got married, I hoped the dog wouldn't go on the honeymoon.

Amadeo drove us to La Cima at sunset. It's only fourteen miles or so from Conejo, but it's a tricky drive on a narrow road, and it climbs three thousand feet. In Amorcita, the village Victoria and I had seen from a distance on our walk, the main street was lined with small bonfires, and a group of children were singing in front of someone's house; but there were also some gaudy cardboard Santa Clauses hanging from wires stretched high across the street. It was one of those mixtures that doesn't quite come off.

The snow lay more deeply along the road as we climbed out of Amorcita, and the piñons disappeared, giving way to tall pines and spruce. The cold became sharper, and we were all thankful for the pickup's heater, which roared and made conversation difficult. The stars were very bright. It was easy to see the white, steep country.

"It's pretty up here," I yelled at Amadeo, leaning across Victoria to do so.

"Yeah," he answered. "It's a tough son of a bitch to drive, too."

"Do you get up here often?"

"No," he said. "Not too much. These La Cima people are funny. They don't like strangers to come up here much."

"You're not a stranger."

"Yes I am. They figure if you don't come from La Cima, you're a stranger."

"They talk funny," Victoria said.

"Yeah, they talk Old Spanish," said Amadeo. "It's different. They use a lot of old words. There was a man, a language teacher from the University, came up here a few years ago. Said he was writing a book or something. He rented an old house and talked to the *alcalde* and said he wanted to . . . uh. . . ."

"Interview," Victoria said.

"Yeah, interview people and see how they talked. Then he'd write it down in one of his books. They stole all his tires the first day, and the next day somebody stuck a rag in his gas tank and burned up his car. There aren't any telephones up there, so he couldn't call the sheriff. And every time he came out of the house he was living in, somebody would throw a rock at him. One of the rocks broke his glasses, so he couldn't see good."

"What about the police?"

"The cops don't go up there unless they have to, and they don't like to do it. If somebody gets killed, the people like to handle it themselves. Sometimes the man that did the killing gets killed too, and sometimes he doesn't. They figure it's none of the cops' business."

"What about the professor, from the University?"

"Oh, they didn't kill him. They finally busted into his house and burned all his papers and books. They took all his money, too, and left him just enough for bus fare back to Sagrado. He raised a lot of hell, but there wasn't anybody could do anything. There it is."

We had pulled up onto a stretch of level plateau after a hard climb. Ahead of us, across a steep gorge, was La Cima, perched like an eagle's nest on a bluff, the white peaks shining behind it. A thousand tiny fires made the village glow, and the wind from the mountains brought the sweet smell of pine and piñon smoke to us.

"It's beautiful," I said, and it was. Two hundred years seemed to disappear, and we were back in the days of the viceroys and the Apaches. Only the truck's motor, and the roar of the heater, kept us in the twentieth century. I couldn't tell immediately what it was that made the village look so antique, and Amadeo helped me.

"There's no electricity there," he said. "They use fires and kerosene lamps. They don't want electricity."

He put the truck in low and we started down the valley, the road twisting and bending. At the bottom was a frozen stream crossed by a wooden bridge, and then a Highway Department sign: "Village Limit, La Cima, Pop. 406, Alt. 10,789." Beneath the lettering someone had scrawled *"Chinga todos,"* by way of welcome.

We made it up the last hill to La Cima, slipping and skidding on the snowy road. Amadeo said the state snowplow didn't cover the last half-mile to the top, because when it arrived somebody always stole a piece of gear from it. It sounded like a good place to spend a vacation.

Like the other mountain villages, La Cima had just one street. It curved along the top of a narrow ridge, faced on both sides by thick-looking houses built of heavy logs with mud chinking. Many of them seemed to have no windows at all; others had hide stretched tightly over small square holes, the hide oiled to let light through. Apparently the only outsider the La Cima citizens had allowed to stay for a while was a galvanized tin sales-man. All the roofs were of corrugated metal, pitched steeply like those on Swiss chalets, shining dully in the firelight. The snow had fallen deeply and heavily here, and had slid off the roofs and piled high between the houses.

The level summit of the ridge was no more than a hundred feet wide, enough for the road and the front rooms of the houses. Then the land dropped off sharply, and I could see that a house one level in front was two or three levels high in back, the rear portions braced and buttressed against gravity by lodge poles and boulders. The dark houses seemed to belly up against the slope, like animals standing on their hind legs to feed on whatever came along the road.

Most of the adult population of La Cima stood or leaned against the houses on our left as we drove to the center of the village and parked. It was very cold. The men and women wore dark blankets over their shoulders, holding them closed with their hands in front. They were watching the scene on the other side of the street, a little drama which moved toward us from house to house.

Thirty or forty children, many of them carrying burning sticks for torches, swarmed and eddied down the narrow street, chanting something in a tune that seemed to have only three or four notes, none of them recognizable as music. With them was a couple: an old man with a short, dirty white beard, who walked with the aid of a cane, and a handsome young woman, dressed lightly for the weather in a print dress. The woman was enormously pregnant—I'd have said fourteen months along, if it were possible—and pushed her belly before her like a wheelbarrow full of melons. The old man supported one of her elbows, a young boy the other. She was wearing, as her only concession to the weather, a floppy pair of hiking boots, with the laces undone and hanging loose. As the group approached, I could see that some of the children were leading a burro.

"Even a Protestant ought to be able to get the idea," Victoria said.

The children halted before a house and began to sing again. I couldn't make out the words, but Amadeo murmured a rough translation for me:

158

"The night is very cold
We have traveled a long way
The woman needs to lie down
Her feet are bleeding.
With her is an old man
He walks with difficulty
Please open your door
And give us shelter and food."

When the children finished the song, the couple walked heavily to the door and the old man rapped on it with his cane. It opened immediately, and a woman came out shouting and cursing rapidly in the strange Spanish. Then she threw a pan of water on the pregnant woman and slammed the door.

"She said, 'There's no room here and stop tracking up my yard,' " Amadeo translated. "That's leaving out the bad language."

They moved to another house and repeated the song. This time a man and woman came out, and while the woman yelled and cursed, the man kicked the burro, who brayed in pain.

We were parked at the side of the road, near La Cima's only filling station, dark and shuttered, with one hand-crank gas pump. When the children and couple approached it, Amadeo started the pickup and backed into a snow-filled alley at one side of the station, making sure that his truck got in no one's way. The group collected near the pumps, the pregnant woman shivering in her wet dress. The observers across the road slowly detached themselves from walls and walked toward us, each man carrying a piece of wood or a tree branch. One by one, the men knelt in the open space in front of the filling station and placed his wood on the ground, beginning with a rectangle and building it higher until it was a cubical pile. The old man with the cane picked up a pail and slowly cranked gasoline into it, then carefully walked to the pile of wood and soaked it. The children tossed their burning torches, and the fire whoofed up, bringing with it a strong smell of gas, which slowly receded as the wood caught. No one paid any attention to us or the pickup, which I found comforting.

The fire lit hundreds of dark, shining faces, all expressionless except the children's, which had rapt, excited looks. Two or three of the men, huddled together near the blaze, began to play tiny flutes, short, homemade instruments with just a few finger holes, and the crowd started singing. I recognized it dimly; I'd heard the choir in Lacey's Catholic church in Mobile singing the same thing, but I couldn't remember the name of it. It had a different tone here in La Cima; it sounded Oriental, or Arabic, and the words were in Spanish instead of Latin.

"Weird, huh?" Victoria said, and her father shushed her.

The crowd, which circled the bonfire, parted at one side, and four large men came into the ring, pulling fiercely on lengths of chain. They pulled and stumbled and sweated in the firelight, and into the circle they dragged a black bear, a big one. The singing stopped, and a murmur went up from the people. The only words I could catch were *"Oso santo."*

"What's this all about?" I whispered to Amadeo.

"I don't know," he said. "I'm a Catholic. Just don't get out of the truck."

"Don't worry," I said. "I'm not about to."

The bear was snuffling and swinging its head from side to side, as the four men pulled at the chains attached to its wide leather collar. Parker had told me that black bears weren't particularly dangerous, unless they fell on you or if you got cute with their cubs. They ate berries and honey, and had never developed a taste for people as had browns and grizzlies, now happily extinct in the area. This one looked big and dangerous to me, though. It had heavy shoulders much higher than its rump, 3-inch-long claws, and a look of impatience that was turning into downright irritation. I wondered whether it was kept in a cage for the annual show, or if the people of La Cima trapped a new one every year, and was about to ask when the pregnant woman stepped carefully into the circle of firelight.

Now, beside her thin wet dress and boots, she wore a pair of canvas work gloves—for bite protection, I guessed—and a crown made of wreathed evergreens. It

160

was a ridiculous costume, but something about her, her huge belly, perhaps, or her serene expression, kept it from being funny. She approached the tethered bear with no sign of fear, walked around the men who were holding the animal and, raising her wet dress almost to her hips, clumsily straddled the bear's wide back.

The crowd was silent, the men struggled noiselessly with their chains, and the woman on the bear stroked its thick neck and whispered to it, leaning forward on its shoulder hump. Amadeo was watching intently, with a faint look of disapproval. Victoria was hiding her eyes. There was no sound except the sharp cracking of the fire and the bear's panting.

There was no singing now. All the faces in the densely ranged crowd were turned toward the woman and the bear, watchful, intent; all but one face, which was puzzled and seemed slightly horrified. A dark, pretty face.

"Hey," I said to Victoria, "I know that girl." Without thinking I opened the truck door and stepped down. Amadeo grabbed for me, and said, "Jesus Christ!"

I had trotted partly around the circle when my mind, numbed as usual by the low temperature, told me where I was and what I was doing. By then, I had already called "Viola!" and it was too late.

She pulled her eyes away from the bear and looked at me, with confusion and then recognition. I was only a few feet away, and I saw that she was terrified. She put her hand over her face, turned and started to run toward the shadows across the road. Someone pushed me, and then another, and I fell on my knees in the road. Then people were kicking me. I rolled over on my back, and saw a ring of angry faces and a lot of boots. Some faces came close to mine and spat.

Two men grasped my ankles and dragged me roughly back to the truck, where Amadeo and Victoria were standing with pale, frightened faces. The men dropped my feet, and one of them shoved Amadeo against the truck door. "Get him outa here," he said in English. "Get the hell outa here right now."

We got in and slammed the doors, and Amadeo drove slowly and carefully around the ring of people. Some of them watched us leave, but most had turned back to the woman, who still rode the bear and talked to him. My ribs hurt when I reached for a handkerchief to wipe the melted snow and spittle from my face. Victoria had begun to cry.

"You all right?" Amadeo said.

"Yeah, I'm all right. I'm sorry."

"Boy, you could have gotten us all killed back there, you know that?"

"I know. I'm really sorry."

"What made you jump out of the truck like that? I told you to stay inside."

"I saw somebody I knew, a girl I go to school with in Sagrado. I wasn't thinking when I got out."

"You think anything's broken? They were kicking you pretty hard when they had you down."

"My ribs are sore. I don't think they broke any. They're rough up there, aren't they?"

"That's what I've been telling you," Amadeo said.

Victoria had stopped crying by the time we drove into Amorcita, and we held hands the rest of the way to Conejo, our linked hands on the seat between us so that Amadeo couldn't see.

I slept that night in the Montoyas' living room in a bedroll, near the fireplace. Excilda made me take off my shirt so that she could see the damage. She agreed that nothing was broken, but bruises were starting to show and she rubbed them with horse liniment, which stung sharply and had a powerful, pungent smell. She and Victoria told me I was very brave, but Amadeo kept insisting that I was only stupid, which was nearer the truth.

When the household got settled down, and the dozen kids packed off in the warren of bedrooms, I lay looking into the firelight, nursing my sore ribs, and wondering what the hell Viola Lopez was doing at the Christmas bear-riding ceremony in La Cima. She had always been the most devout girl at school, a future nun, engaged to Jesus, as I understood it. Well, I'd ask Chango about it Monday.

It was near midnight when I got quietly out of the

bedroll and pushed open the door to Victoria's room. There was enough light through a window to see her, sleeping on her side, her thick black hair on the pillow. It was light enough, too, to see Don Carlos lying beside her slippers, his head raised, looking at me calmly. I backed out of the room and closed the door softly. "Here, boy," I whispered, "here's your nice hamburger with the nice strychnine in it. Yum yum." Then I got back into the bedroll, and went to sleep on the side that hurt less.

18

CHANGO SAID: "Viola? Amigo, you're crazy."

"Chango, I'm telling you it was Viola. I couldn't have mistaken her. It wasn't just the face, it was . . . you know." I cupped my hands in front, and waited for him to hit me, but he only nodded.

"Sometimes at night she goes over to the convent," he said. "It's for some kind of instruction. She wants to take orders after she gets out of school, and the nuns are teaching her stuff."

"She was in La Cima about eight o'clock Saturday night," I repeated. "Standing with a crowd of people around a fire, watching some sort of business with a bear. I don't know. Maybe it's a kind of instruction, but I didn't see any priest with her."

"She was staying with a friend Saturday night," he said.

"Don't take my word for it. Ask her."

"I'll talk to her tonight. She stayed home today," he said.

We were in Social Studies class that afternoon, soaking up those little-known facts about the Lame Duck Amendment, when we heard the yelling in the corridor, and Black John Cloyd came roaring in with Ratoncito yapping at his heels. Cloyd had his shotgun and he was still limping somewhat, although his cast was off.

"If you'll please come to my office," the principal was saying, "I'm sure we can. . . ."

"Shut up, you little jay fart," Cloyd said. "You ask them kids or by Jesus I'll ask 'em with this." He brandished the gun.

Ratoncito fiddled with his little bow tie and cleared his throat. "Boys and girls," he began, and then stopped and turned red. "I can't just ask them like this," he said to Cloyd. "I'm sure there must be. . . ."

"Then I'll ask 'em," Cloyd said. "Git!" He pointed the shotgun at Ratoncito, who turned pale and left the room. Mrs. Loughran was still standing at the blackboard, the chalk in her hand, arrested and apparently hypnotized by the scene. She had just written "Ratified February 6, 1933."

Cloyd was wearing the same black hat I'd seen when Parker and I had gone to pick up the girls. I'd heard that his suit had been thrown out of court, and that he wasn't going to get a nickel for his back, and no more than expenses for the leg, which had probably helped to put him in a sour humor.

"Alrighty," he said. "I want all the girls over on that side of the room—" he pointed to the side with the windows—"and all the boys over to the other side. Lively, goddamn it!"

It was like a spelling bee as we shuffled to our directed posts, boys against the girls. As usual, Marcia thought the whole thing was exciting, and her eyes danced. Steenie and I stood together near the wall, and he whispered, "Go take his gun away, Josh. Use the hold I taught you, the arm-breaker."

"You do it," I suggested. "I haven't got it down yet."

"Next feller that talks is gonna git his ass blowed off," Cloyd said conversationally.

Bucky Swenson detached himself from the row of boys and faced Mr. Cloyd, pale but brave, the picture of virtue. "Surely you are aware, sir," he started, but Cloyd pulled down on him and said, "I'd as lief it was your ass as somebody's else." Swenson stood there a second or

164

two longer, to show he was not afraid, and stepped back into line.

"Alrighty," Cloyd said again. "Somebody's been diddling my two girls, and I want to know who. I figure it's one of you fellers took their advantage. I want him to answer up smart, so I can blow his head off." Mrs. Loughran dropped her piece of chalk, but there was no other sound.

"Both of 'em," he said, "both of 'em is pumped up like a nickel balloon."

He surveyed the line of boys with his eyes and the muzzle of his shotgun. "Both of 'em," he repeated. "Three months gone and startin' to pooch out. There's a whole bunch of you fellers I've seen out to my house, sniffing around like a pack of hounds. You, whatsyername, the skinny feller." He pointed the gun at Parker.

"No, sir," Parker answered up. "Not me. All I ever did was take Venery Ann to the movies. Isn't that right, Josh?"

"That's right, Park," I said, grateful that he had brought me to Cloyd's attention. "Just the movies."

"And you," Cloyd said to me.

"Just the movies." I said again. " 'Sergeant York.' "

"What?"

" 'Sergeant York.' You know, about this guy from Tennessee or Kentucky somewhere that believed in the Bible and didn't want to kill anybody and was going to be a conscientious objector only they drafted him and he used to get into arguments with this officer. . . ." I knew I was rattling on like a baboon, but I couldn't stop. The gun was pointed at me. ". . . about whether God wanted you to kill people if it was a good cause and York said 'No' but they finally talked him into going to France and put him in this infantry company and. . . ."

"Goddamn it, shut up!" Cloyd yelled. "Jesus Bird Christ, ain't there nobody around here to give me a straight answer?" He limped quickly to the door and jerked it open. Four or five teachers stood outside, bent over as if to hear better. They straightened up when they saw him.

"Git outa here!" They scattered down the hall, and

Cloyd turned back to us. Mrs. Loughran had taken the opportunity to crawl under her desk.

"Mr. Cloyd?" It was Marcia, naturally, always ready to join in anything that wasn't her business. "Have you tried asking the girls?"

Cloyd looked at her truculently. "What'd you say?"

"Did you ask the girls who the . . . who was responsible? It might be a better idea than going around scaring people."

"Oh, I asked 'em, but do you think they'd tell me, their own daddy? No ma'am, not them little whores." Several of the girls started at this, being more afraid of the word than they were of the shotgun, as far as I could tell. "You know what they told me? They told me they didn't know. How you like *them* berries? Don't that beat all?"

"Probably true," Steenie whispered to me.

The door opened again, and Ratoncito came back in with the sheriff. Chamaco was wearing his official hat and badge. His pistol, in a tooled leather holster, was strapped low on his thigh in the manner of Wild Bill Hickok. Ratoncito pointed dramatically at Cloyd, and said, "There's your man, Sheriff," which seemed unneccessary. Cloyd was obviously too old to be a student, and he was the only person in the room carrying a gun.

"Hello there, Mr. Cloyd," Chamaco said easily. "You got some trouble?"

"Goddamn little mouse-turd boys won't answer up," Cloyd said. "I wasn't really gonna shoot any; just wanted to stir 'em up."

"I'm sure of that, Mr. Cloyd," Chamaco said. "Why don't you let them get back to their estudies now? I think you got them estirred up enough. How about we all go down to the office and talk about it?"

"Goddamn little humphoppers," Cloyd said, losing steam and lowering the shotgun. "It was one of 'em, I'm sure of it. Maybe two of 'em. Ought to speak out like a man and take their medicine."

"You're sure right about that, Mr. Cloyd," Chamaco said. "Yessir, you're right there."

"Damn right," said Cloyd.

166

"Let's leave 'em alone now for a while, Mr. Cloyd."

"Sure, this bunch of little pissants ain't worth my time. They ought to all have their ass blowed off, but it ain't worth my ammunition." Cloyd broke his shotgun and extracted the shells, putting them in his coat pocket. Then, as Chamaco led the way out to the corridor, he grabbed Ratoncito's tie and pulled him up to his toes. "It wasn't you, was it Shorty?" Ratoncito said, "Guh guh guh" and began to turn red again. "Naw, it sure wasn't you," said Cloyd, releasing him, then catching him as he started to sag and pushing him out the door.

We left our places near the wall and went back to our desks. Some of the girls—not Marcia, of course—were embarrassed and crying, and wouldn't meet our glances. Marcia went to help Mrs. Loughran, who was having difficulty getting out from under the kneehole of her desk. When she was extricated, she went off to the room marked Faculty Women.

"My," Marcia said, "wasn't that breath-taking! Were you scared, Steenie?"

"I remained cool and clear-headed at all times," Steenie said. "It would take more than a twelve-gauge side-by-side to ruffle my calm."

"Then how come there's sweat all over your face?"

"Well, it *is* a warm day."

"It was about eighteen above when I came in this morning," she pointed out.

"I admit it. I feared for Josh's life. Boy, you came within a centimeter of violent death at the hands of an irate father."

"You know Josh had nothing to do with it."

"Maybe, but he looked guilty. Did you ever see guilt written so clearly on a human face? And did you hear him raving about that movie? He was gibbering in terror."

"I'll bet the old brute did it himself," Marcia said. "He looks like he wouldn't be above incest. Filthy old man."

"I'm sure you're wrong about that," Steenie said. "I have a candidate for it, but I don't want to slander him. He's bigger and stronger than I am."

"By the way," Marcia said, "did you see the way

Chamaco handled that man? It was masterful. I'll never yell at him again."

"I was hoping he'd drop him with a thirty-eight to the left eyeball," I said, "on the order of the Lone Ranger. I was ready for shooting. I even had a place all picked out to hide: behind Steenie."

"Don't underrate Chamaco," Steenie said. "I admit he's an idiot, but he doesn't go shooting people unless he has to. In fact, the first time he's drawn his pistol for years was the time he shot the elk down at the bank. He'd have tried to reason with it if it had understood Spanish."

Mrs. Loughran came back into the buzzing room and pleaded for order. "We were discussing the Lame Duck Amendment, Mrs. Loughran," Steenie told her. "You brought out some very interesting points on the subject, particularly the issue of presidential death or disability."

"One more word, William Stenopolous," she said. "Just one more word."

Chango caught me when the lunch bell rang at noon. "Hey, man," he said, "I don't like to bother you, and if you got something else to do forget I asked you, but could you come home with me? I think I ought to at least ask Viola about what you said."

"It doesn't matter," I said. "I probably mistook her for somebody else. It was dark up there."

"Come on, man. Please."

Viola was helping her mother get lunch ready for the family when Chango and I walked in. Mrs. Lopez said she'd be happy if I'd stay for lunch, and I said I appreciated it, which was true. They were having *sopa de menudo*. Viola had a purple mouse under her left eye, and looked generally very un-nunnish.

After lunch, we went into Chango's room, Viola protesting that she had to do the dishes, and Chango insisting. He'd changed the décor a little. The old magazine photograph of Vincent "Mad Dog" Coll was gone from the wall over his dresser, and he'd replaced it with portraits of Pope Pius XII and General Eisenhower.

"Where'd you get the black eye?" he began.

"I told you where," she said.

"Where?" I asked her.

"None of your business."

"Tell him," Chango said.

"I fell off the sidewalk by the chancery, on the ice. It was slippery, and I wasn't looking where I was going. I was thinking about Saint Teresa. Father McIlhenny said she was a great mystic, just like Sister Polycarp."

"I can telephone Father McIlhenny right now," Chango said, "and ask him if you were there Saturday night."

"Don't do that," she said quickly. "He's out of town. He . . . he went to Phoenix, Arizona, to open a new church. Our Lady of the Ocotillos."

"He was on the Plaza at quarter to eight this morning, having a snowball fight with one of the brothers."

"He was going to leave at ten o'clock, he told me."

"Did somebody hit you in the eye? Punch you?"

"Of course not. Listen, I have to go wash dishes. I don't have to sit here."

"Josh said he saw you up in La Cima Saturday night."

"He's crazy." She looked at me. "Why did you tell him that? I couldn't have been in La Cima. I've never even *been* to La Cima."

"I guess it was somebody else," I said. "It sure looked like you, though."

"What was the girl you saw wearing?" Chango asked me.

"I don't know. A coat, a long coat, black or dark blue. With a scarf over her head. It was cold up there."

"Viola has an overcoat."

"Lots of people have overcoats," she said. "Anybody around here who doesn't have an overcoat is crazy."

"All of a sudden everybody's crazy," said Chango. "You want me to tell Papa?"

"There isn't anything to tell Papa," she said. "I didn't go anywhere. I was at the chancery. You stop being such a damn *jodido*."

"You hear what my sister calls me?" Chango said. "That's some nun she's gonna be. Next thing she'll be telling me *'toma la verga.'* "

"I was probably wrong," I said. "Anyway, I don't want to get anybody in trouble. We're friends, huh, Viola?"

169

"Not any more, you bastard."

"Oh, you're gonna make a fine nun," said Chango.

Viola left us and returned to the dishes. Chango lay back on his bed and put his hands behind his head. "You're right," he said. "She's lying. She never lied before, so she doesn't have any practice at it."

"I was pretty sure it was Viola I saw up there."

"You know," he went on, "all those people off in La Cima have been kicked out of the church. Every once in a while the priest gives a sermon about them. They don't have a priest any more. They made him leave about five years ago because they said he was interfering with their religion. I know that sounds funny, but that's what they said. So they've all been excommunicated, and they're all going to hell."

"That's rough on them," I said.

"They don't care. They're a mean bunch of guys up there. That's why I can't figure what Viola's doing with them. Man, she's a good Catholic. She's the best Catholic I ever saw most of the time. She likes Mass better than the movies."

"Maybe she was just trying to find out how the other half lives," I suggested.

"She's not even supposed to go there. Nobody's supposed to watch that stuff they do up there. One of the priests said they were witches, they put spells on people."

"Nobody put a spell on me," I said. "They just kicked the crap out of me."

"Did Viola watch that?"

"No. When she saw me, she ran off somewhere. She wasn't around for the fun."

"Man, I don't know what to do about it. If I tell the folks they probably won't believe me. I already have a sixteen-year record as a no-good bum, and Viola's kind of the family favorite. I mean, all these years she'd bring a bird home and fix its wing, and I'd be out kicking dogs."

Mrs. Lopez called us to say it was time to get back to school. As we left, Chango said something to Viola in rapid Spanish, and she dropped a dish. As her mother bent to help pick up the pieces, Viola gave us the finger in a professional manner. She seemed to be picking up most of Chango's old, bad habits.

Ratoncito called an all-male 10th, 11th and 12th Grade assembly that afternoon and, as Marcia put it, his balls were in an uproar, an expression she'd evidently picked up in her father's Episcopal Bible Class. The Mouse wasn't the most stable member of the faculty at best; he generally felt that the students weren't respectful enough of him, and his voice tended to squeak when he was under tension, which was most of the time.

"I heard him chewing out Mrs. Loughran at noon," Marcia said, "as if it were all her fault that Mr. Cloyd came into her room in the first place. He's probably chewed out everybody but Cloyd. I think he's afraid he'll get picked up by his tie again."

"I hope he doesn't give us a lecture on morality," Steenie said. "I don't want to start laughing and get thrown out of assembly."

"I think you guys are getting movies," she said. "They're setting up a projector in the auditorium. I *wish* they'd let the girls see it. We all have to go out in the snow and play field hockey this afternoon."

"That's understandable," Steenie said. "They believe that violent exercise will slow you down in the passion department. I could tell them it doesn't work, but I'd hate to destroy their childlike faith."

"We're already getting a reputation as the horniest school in the state. I hear boys are coming from as far away as Denver to try the goodies," Marcia said. "They're going to start chartering special busses now, probably."

"This kind of thing has happened before, then," I said.

"Oh, sure," Marcia answered. "Every once in a while a girl disappears from school and her family leaves town and the rumors start going around. But this is the first time we've had all this action, as far as I know, with shotguns and all."

"The Cloyd girls were a special case," Steenie said. "They were a couple of walking scandals. It was just a matter of time before somebody rang the bell. Of course, both at one time is pretty crude. It wouldn't surprise me if it was on the same night in the same car."

"In a car?" I asked.

"Where else? They'll do anything for a ride in a car. One of them told me that whenever their old man moves he gets a beat-up truck and puts his wife and dog in the cab, with the girls riding in back. That's why a genuine automobile looks so good to them."

"Steenie, I want you to give me all the details on your movie this afternoon," Marcia said. "Don't spare me a thing."

"You mean, you want a complete anatomic report, with every pustule?"

"Is that what it's going to be? A Syphilis Special?"

"Sure," Steenie said, "just like a Commando training film. Ratoncito's going to try to scare us into virtue."

"Well, I'm glad he's finally getting around to spreading some facts around here. Remember that sex hygiene movie a couple of years ago? About the Mother Egg and the Father Seed?"

"Yeah, and those endless pictures of salmon moving up the Columbia River with leers on their faces."

"I'll never forget it," Marcia said. "I wasn't so worried about boys, but I was afraid to go swimming for six months."

"I want you and the other girls to play your hearts out on the hockey field today," he said. "I want you to come in too pooped to think dirty thoughts. If that doesn't work on you strumpets, we're going to the Manual Arts building and turn out a few dozen chastity belts on the lathe. As I understand it, you're all a bunch of unclean vessels."

At the assembly that afternoon, Ratoncito gave it to us as straight as he could, in spite of the coarse laughter that kept bubbling out of his audience.

"Now you all know the Facts of Life," he began, "because as a regular part of the curriculum we show a film on . . . uh . . . reproduction and . . . uh . . . sex. This information is supposed to prepare you for the state of marriage which comes later—*much* later—when your schooling is finished.

"However, it has come to my attention that . . . uh . . .

172

a few students have been . . . uh . . . anticipating the marriage ceremony and have actually been . . . uh . . . engaging in—I know this will shock you, but I'm going to say it—sex practices. Yes, sex practices! It's too revolting to think about, but it's the truth."

"What does he expect from a bunch of horny adolescents?" Steenie whispered. "Madrigal singing?"

"The administrator of St. Boniface Hospital has kindly lent us a film which they use in nurse training. I must warn you that this is a very . . . uh . . . *graphic* film, and it was only when I assured him of the urgency of the problem that he let the school borrow it. It is an adult film for professional medical people, and I don't want any laughing or giggling out of you.

"Before we show the film, Dr. Arthur Temple, one of the leading psychiatrists in the West, has a few words to say to you about the . . . uh . . . dangers of . . . uh . . . this sort of thing from the mental standpoint. Dr. Temple, are you . . . uh. . . ."

The doctor, who had been sitting in the front row, climbed the steps to the stage and stood in front of the microphone peering at us owlishly through his horn-rims.

"Hello, boys and girls," he said to the all-male audience. "I say girls because some of you, whether you know it yet or not, have a preponderance of female emotional characteristics and will someday be, if you have not already become, homosexuals. Or, as you would say, fruits. This is nothing to worry about. This is perfectly normal and, according to some statistics which I have developed, at least thirty-four per cent of you . . . ."

"I think Ratoncito got the wrong boy for this lecture," Steenie said to me.

". . . to orgasm by various means, including. . . ."

"He's trying out one of his books on us," Steenie went on. "He used to get them published in Europe by the same company that puts out stuff like 'The Sailor in the Sultan's Harem.' "

". . . intercrural as opposed to oral. . . ."

"My God, he's giving directions up there."

"But that is all quite beside the point in the present circumstances, which, as Mr. Alexander has explained to

173

me, involve experimental heterosexual contact resulting in pregnancy. I would like first to point out that sexual experimentation is perfectly normal and healthy. It is in fact beneficial. There is little doubt that many of the present ills that afflict the world, including the present war, which has made it impossible for European firms to publish significant psychiatric textbooks, spring from the repression of normal sexual activity.

"The illicit pregnancies that have come to our attention, however unfortunate they may be for the young women who had the bad luck to be born in a restrictive culture, are obviously the result of furtive and doubtless unskilled behavior. The acts were probably performed hastily and in secret, with feelings of nervousness beforehand and guilt afterwards. As any reputable physician will tell you, these are the most damaging circumstances possible. The immediate and inevitable results, aside from unwanted pregnancy, are neurotic fears of punishment by authority and revulsion for man's most emotionally rewarding experience."

From where we sat, Steenie and I could see Ratoncito in the wings, red in the face again, making wild gestures at Dr. Temple, who ignored him. None of the Mouse's assemblies seemed to go the way he liked.

"It is criminal, yes it is *criminal*, to place social barricades across the adolescent's path to sexual happiness. From the day he is born, perhaps even *in utero*, the human is a sexually oriented animal, and any attempt to instill fear or hesitation in his natural drives is the work of a sadist. This regrettable incident would never have happened if the students had been properly instructed in sexual techniques and the use of contraceptive devices."

Ratoncito, his frantic gestures at the speaker proving useless, bounced onto the stage from the wings, holding his hands above his head and applauding. "Thank you, thank you, Dr. Temple. Thank you *very* much."

"But I haven't. . . ."

"Yes, thank you so much for taking time out from your busy schedule to address the student body. I'm sure we all appreciate it, don't we, boys?"

We all clapped, and someone yelled, "Yea, Temple!"

174

Dr. Temple was looking over the tops of his glasses at Ratoncito. "But I've only just. . . ."

"Just let me get the microphone out of the way," Ratoncito said, "and we'll start the film. Lights. Lights!"

Dr. Temple and Ratoncito struggled briefly over possession of the microphone as the lights went down, and they were silhouetted dramatically against the screen when the movie started. We could see their shadows clearly against the title: "Classic Luetic Symptoms, Series 13, U. S. Public Health Service." As the musical score began—it was played by a string orchestra, and seemed pretty romantic considering the subject—the two men moved to the side of the stage to continue their battle.

There was some hooting during the first few minutes, which featured a doctor pointing to a wall chart indicating that syphilis was increasing right along with B-17 production, if not faster, and some interesting photographs of *Treponema pallidum* dancing on a microscope slide. The jeering died down shortly after the moviemakers got into the clinical end of it. I could hear someone throwing up in another part of the assembly room, but there wasn't a real epidemic of it. One guy—I never did find out who—yelled that the picture on the screen compared favorably to his own symptoms, but he was shouted down. It was all unpleasant, but no surprise after reading Dr. Stenopolous's books on the subject.

After an interminable passage showing pathology slides of things like spleens and aortas, with the narration in Latin and Greek, the film-makers cut to a small room in a Health Service hospital somewhere, the camera hidden behind a two-way mirror. The narrator said the man about to come in for interview had tabes dorsalis and general paresis. The doctor sitting at the desk had camera fright, although the narration didn't mention it.

The patient—he was referred to as the subject—came in and walked somewhat jerkily to a chair, not knowing he was on camera—a pretty cruel trick, if you ask me. I'd have sued for invasion of privacy.

"Hello, John," said the doctor, smiling big for the camera. "How are you feeling this morning?"

John sat down warily, licked his lips and ran the heel of his hand over his thin hair. "Hunner' per cent, doctor. I feel hunner' per cent."

"Now, John," said the doctor unctuously, "I'm going to ask you a few questions. Is that all right?"

"Hunh?"

"How's your coordination, John?"

John ran his hand through his hair again. "Coordination hunner' per cent."

"Are your reflexes good?"

"Reflexes hunner' per cent."

"Here's pencil and paper. Will you write your name for me?"

"Write your name hunner' per cent," John said, not taking the pencil. "Hunner' per cent."

"Very good, John," the doctor said. "How much are four and four?"

John rubbed his hair. "Four and four?"

"Take your time, John," the doctor said soothingly. "Four and four."

"Reflexes hunner' per cent, Doctor," John said, giving the doctor a big prideful grin and stroking his head. "Ludwig van Beethoven."

"What?"

"Ludwig van Beethoven," John repeated. "Seventeen seventy to eighteen twenty-seven." He paused to consider. "Hunner' per cent."

"Thank you, John," the doctor said. "That will be all."

John arose with the help of his cane and heel-walked to the door, moving like a badly handled marionette.

"Good-by, John," the doctor said.

"Four and four is eight," John said. "Four and four is eight. Arithmetic hunner' per cent." He stuck his tongue out at the doctor and departed.

The film slid downhill after the scene between John and the doctor, and ended back at the venereal disease chart which showed syphilis to be increasing as fast as the population of India. There was a plea for compulsory Wassermann tests and the music, "The Battle Hymn of the Republic," swelled to a climax as the movie ended and the lights came on.

Ratoncito had apparently got rid of Dr. Temple. The program closed with a brief coda by the principal on the obvious, graphically presented evils of what he called "bad sex behavior" and a hint that spirochetes were everywhere around us, waiting to pounce.

"I don't know about that," Steenie said as we walked back to the last class. "You might get crab lice from the Cloyds, or ringworm, but I think that's all."

The girls had worked up a sweat at snow hockey, despite the cold, and came clumping back rosy and fragrant. "Anybody who doesn't get pneumonia from this is just lucky," Marcia said. "How was the movie? Lots of chancres?"

"Movie?" Steenie said, rubbing his hair with the heel of his hand. "Movie? Hunner' per cent."

"Right," I said. "Ludwig van Beethoven. Four and four is eight. Hunner' per cent."

"You're a couple of imbeciles," Marcia said. "I knew you wouldn't tell me."

"The Healthmobile's coming tomorrow," Steenie said. "All hands get a Wassermann test. Meanwhile, don't use the toilets."

Marcia deepened her voice in imitation of Mr. Cloyd. "Next feller that talks is gonna git his ass blowed off."

"Did you know that Marcia was the only girl who ever got kicked out of the Brownies with a Bad Conduct Discharge?" Steenie asked. "She was teaching the other Brownies the words to 'Roll Me Over in the Clover' at the Campfire Sing and Weenie Roast."

"For a virgin, I have the worst reputation in town," she said. "I might as well offer myself to the basketball team."

"Start with Swenson," Steenie said. "He'd look cute with tabes dorsalis. As a matter of fact, he might have it already. I see his game's been off recently."

"Chango's got him all tensed up," I said. "He's still all full of good sportsmanship, like an Englishman at a cricket match. When Bucky tries for a free throw, Chango's always there yelling, 'You can do it, Bucky. You can do it, fella.' Makes him flinch."

177

"Do you still insist you saw Viola Lopez at that orgy in La Cima?" Marcia asked.

"I saw her, all right. Chango and I worked on her a little bit, but she won't admit it. Chango knows she's lying."

"Maybe she'll tell me," she said. "People always tell me their secrets for some reason."

"Not because you're discreet, certainly," said Steenie. "You've got the biggest mouth in town. Tell Marcia something today, and tomorrow Tokyo Rose is yelling about it."

"I'm very discreet," she said. "I can carry a secret to my grave. For instance, I never told anyone about the time in fourth grade when you got to giggling over that note I sent you and wet your pants."

"Not until now, you didn't," he said. "Telephone, telegraph or tell Marcia."

"You've been reading that World War I joke book again, haven't you?"

"Josh, do they have any girls like her in Mobile?"

"No," I said. "They're all ladies down there. A little stupid, but ladies."

"Next feller that talks is gonna git his ass blowed off," Marcia said.

"Do you realize," he said, "that in a few years this girl is going to start breeding? The mind boggles."

19

I'LL HAVE TO ADMIT that Jimbob tried. When he had recovered completely from pneumonia—and it was one of the longest convalescences on record—he began writing letters to everyone he knew, begging for shelter. I mailed some of the letters for him; that long, deadly hundred-yard hike down to the mailbox on the corner just wore him to a nubbin. He seemed to know people all over the country. Most of them were in Virginia, or around Atlanta, Mobile or New Orleans, but he tried Phoenix and Seattle and Cleveland and Boston. He'd go anywhere for a free flop, three squares and an opportunity to be rude to the cook.

After dinner one evening I sat with him and Mother in the living room while they sipped a little sherry—they were sipping it now; the stock was getting low—and he went over his mail.

"Well, fancy that," he said. "The Appersons are divorced and Millie's living in a two-room apartment. Not room enough to swing a cat, she says here."

"You wouldn't like it in Chicago anyway," my mother said. "Cold and dirty."

"I guess you're right, Miss Ann. Well, let's see what Peter and Fliss Cathcart have to say. Hmmm. My gracious! Peter says Fliss is a major in the Women's Auxiliary Army Corps and he's growing a Victory garden. She always was a little mannish, I thought. Says the house is full of English refugee children, and I'm welcome to come if I don't mind sharing a bedroom with three little boys from Manchester. No thank you."

"And Atlanta's so tacky, anyway," my mother said. "All that vulgar Coca-Cola money."

"Now here's one from Buster and Dot Bemis. I don't think you know them; they're from Quincy, Mass. But nice. Both of them born near Charleston."

"Kin to Larry Bemis?" she asked. "I used to go with him when I was at school."

"I declare, Miss Ann, you know everybody worth knowing. I'm sure he must be related. No, must *have been* related. Buster's airplane got shot down over Hamburg, Dot says."

"Maybe you could go to Quincy and comfort the widow," I put in.

"You get more and more dreadful as you get older, Joshua. If I wasn't so frail I might just take you in hand. Your daddy would thank me for it."

"Sorry," I said, before my mother could tell me to apologize. "I withdraw the suggestion."

Jimbob read some more letters aloud. The war had

naturally touched everyone he knew. People were divorced, dead, unsettled, living in strange cities, living different, narrower lives. Each letter came as a surprise to him: the war was an ill-mannered oaf that disturbed his friends and made it harder for him to mooch. All the gentle, well-run establishments had gone through convulsion and turmoil; the guest rooms were closed off, or rented to servicemen; the butlers and gardeners were riveting in shipyards, navigating bombers or swabbing bilge. The whole business was simply too barbaric for words.

"Now here's a possibility," he said. "The Hackenschmidts. I know you've never met them, Miss Ann. They're from Wisconsin Rapids, Wisconsin. I met them in Alexandria, somehow. Clothes, I think. Women's clothes. They're *dying* to see me. Those are her . . . what's her name? Oh, yes. Opal. Heavens! . . . those are Opal's very words. 'Bernie and I are dying to see you again, Mr. Buel.' Bernie! She says, 'It's a pity and a shame you missed the Menomenee Cranberry Harvest Festival, but we're having the Tri-Cities Birchbark Canoe Voyageurs' Race in March, as soon as the ice melts.' The *ice* melts! Stars above!"

"It sounds like a real opportunity to me," I said. "It's a genuine invitation, with no hidden clauses."

"What do you suppose the Tri-Cities are?"

"I've read all about them," I said, "in Geography. Wisconsin Rapids, Nekoosa and Port Edwards. They make paper or something. Full of Scandinavians."

"It's heartbreaking that the Hackenschmidts should be the only ones. I simply can't picture myself in the Tri-Cities. I can tell you just what it's like. Tall timber and people wearing plaid caps and earmuffs. Probably no opera whatsoever."

"Unlike Richmond," I said, "which as everyone knows sends its cast-off tenors to the Met."

"You really are a vile little boy," he said. "Miss Ann, is giving sulphur and molasses still allowed?"

"I'll drink any quantity you can force down me, Mr. Buel," I said, standing up. "I'm ready whenever you are."

"Now stop that, Joshua," my mother said. "Sit down and behave yourself. The war's been particularly hard on Jimbob. His wonderful way of life has just crumbled around his ears."

"You mean, while Dad's out there on a rusty destroyer escort with Germans shooting torpedoes at it, you're weeping about. . . ."

"Now, that's enough!"

Jimbob gave me a wintry smile, the adult equivalent of "Nyaah, nyaah, so there," and went back to his letters. The enthusiastic invitation from Wisconsin Rapids was the only good news he got; nobody else would have him. Thereafter, whenever I brought up the subject of Jimbob finding a home somewhere else, I got a wet-eyed look from Mother.

Sagrado brightens up in the summer, when the tourists and the summer residents come, but the winter there is dead. In the fourth year of the war there was almost no gasoline, and the streets were empty. The plows piled the snow onto the sidewalks—where there were sidewalks; Sagrado didn't have many—and everyone wore boots and stomped through it, packing it down. January and February were one long sixty-day month. Nothing happened. There wasn't even a good fire, although Steenie and I made elaborate plans to burn down Baca's wood yard. We gave it up because we had no getaway car.

The Cloyd girls dropped out of school, and went back to their father's cabin in the *cienega*. Mr. Cloyd lost his insurance suit on a technicality, the paper said. He'd been jaywalking when struck. The girls finally told who was responsible for their condition. It was Bucky Swenson, all right. He'd picked them up in his father's car on his way home from Sunday evening Bible class. Mr. Cloyd turned up at the Swenson's house with his shotgun, but Bucky had joined the Army the day before. Steenie, Marcia and I tried to think of a suitable outrage to celebrate the event, and eventually decided on a six-dollar loving cup, splitting the cost three ways. We had "Father of the Year—Buckminster Swenson" engraved on it at Manx's Jewelry Store, and slipped it into the trophy case alongside Bucky's other awards for basketball, football and track. Ratoncito didn't see it until the president of the school board pointed it out to him. We had another assembly, and an inconclusive lecture on good sportsmanship.

Parker's little sister, Betsy, caught chicken pox and gave it to Parker, who gave it to everyone else. I caught it, too, and passed it happily on to Jimbob, who was sick as a dog for three weeks. It was really the high point of the winter, but it didn't kill him.

Amadeo, grinning like a boy, brought Victoria into Sagrado one Sunday morning in early March. She waved a letter at me, said, "Look look" and kissed me. It was from the Dean of Admissions at the University; she had a scholarship, full tuition, renewable yearly if her grades were high enough.

"What are you kissing me for?" I asked her. "Not that I mind it."

"It was *Don Quixote*," she said. "I wrote a book review for English—Mrs. Saiz said pick any book we wanted—and I wrote one on *Don Quixote*. Then she sent it to the University without even telling me and said, 'If you don't give Victoria Montoya a scholarship I'll quit teaching high school and be a barmaid.' "

"That must have been some book review," I said. "How long was it?"

"Oh, forty pages or so. It was just the usual junk."

If Yunque High was anything like De Crispin, the usual junk was something like:

TREASURE ISLAND
by
Robert Louis Stevenson

My book review is on "Treasure Island" by Robert Louis Stevenson, which is about this boy named Jim Hawkins who goes out with a bunch of English people named Dr. Livesy and Squire Trelawney to find this treasure, and there's this pirate with them he has a wooden leg named Long John Silver. And Jim hides in this apple barrel and hears the pirates say there going to take the treasure, and they get to the island. I didn't get to finish the whole book because we had only three weeks, but it's a very good book and very exciting. I liked it very much.

I took her into the living room and introduced her to Mother.

"You were just a little girl the last time I saw you, Victoria," she said. "Haven't you gotten pretty!"

"Vicky just won a scholarship," I said. "Smartest girl in the valley; got a head on her like Albert Einstein."

"A scholarship to which school, dear?"

"The University," Victoria said.

"Joshua is going to Harvard." This was a line I'd been getting since the fourth grade. I don't think Harvard knew about it. "That's a wonderful university in Boston."

"I'll believe it when I see it. Come on, Vicky, let's go see a movie. They have one in town that's only two years old."

We saw "Yankee Doodle Dandy" and decided that James Cagney was the greatest American since Tom Paine and Chief Crazy Horse. Vicky told me that Don Carlos had tried to bury a turkey, but the ground was frozen too hard for him to dig. Having agreed about Cagney, we agreed also that Don Carlos was an exceptionally fine dog. I didn't mention that I'd wanted to poison him once.

"You like to hear things like that?" she asked me as we walked through the snow on our way to the house. "You like getting little social notes from the farm? It must seem pretty tame, here in the big city."

"That kind of talk is going to win you no sympathy. All of us city boys long for the countryside. You know; we have that brittle sophistication, cocktail parties every day at school, after Gym. We never look at the tall buildings the way you rubes do; why, I pass Wormser's Dry Goods every day, and never even notice that it's two stories high. But inside, in here, where the heart lies, we long for simple, pastoral pleasures: dogs who bury turkeys and girls who write forty-page essays on Cervantes."

"Río Conejo's a pretty small place," she said. "On Saturday night we all go down to the store and listen to the dogs bark."

"Before the war," I said, "a friend of mine named Steenie told me he used to come down to the Plaza at night and read license plates to see what states the cars came from. One night in August he saw cars from eleven states. It was a big night for him, and he never forgot it."

"Now you're making fun of me."

"Well, why not? You're talking like a dope. Conejo's big enough to get a scholarship from." The sentence didn't sound right. "You know what I mean."

"What's it like in Mobile, Alabama, where you come from?"

"Wet. Hot, except in the winter, when it's nasty. Full of dopes. The only good part is the ocean."

"I've never seen an ocean," she said. "Is it blue?"

"It's the color of the sky, blue, gray or black. Sometimes when it's shallow and running over sand, it's green." I stopped walking, and faced her. "Victoria, what the hell did you say about *Don Quixote* to get a scholarship? I wouldn't mind getting one myself. With my grades, I'll be lucky to get into the University of Alabama, and all you need there is a couple of sworn statements that you're white."

"I just said it was a sad book, instead of a funny book. I mean, it had funny parts in it, but it was mainly sad. I said I thought Mr. Cervantes started out to be funny and changed his mind as he went along. It's the best book I ever read."

We walked up Camino Tuerto, toward the house at the top surrounded by spruce, poplars and fruit trees, all heavy and white with recent snow. The land around the house was always tidy and well cared for; paths were neatly shoveled in winter to the bird-feeding stations and the outbuildings. Amadeo worked hard on it, like a farmer instead of a gardener, and gave it the same careful, knowledgeable attention that he gave his own land in Conejo. We could see warm light through the windows of the house, smoke rising from three of the corner fireplaces. The warmth and good care that shone through the house was Excilda's. It had always been snug and comforting to be the boss's son; even better than that feeling, however, were the people who forgot it, or didn't bring it up, or knocked it out of me with a word, a whap on the behind and a knuckle in the eye. I was never less

184

the boss's son than with Victoria; to her, I think, I was an amiable imbecile with neither brains nor dignity.

"You have the biggest place in Sagrado, you know that?" she asked as we turned up the driveway. "My father says you have almost nine acres up here, right in the town."

"That's what I hear," I said. "It's a big responsibility, too. Don't think being a duke is all fun and games. I have to ride out on the estate every day, beat the serfs, deliver babies in the spring, send around baskets of food at Christmas, collect taxes—I tell you, there's lots of work involved. Sometimes I wish I were one of the common people. Just sit around the cabin laughing and scratching."

"I can see where that might get tiresome," Victoria said. "Do you ever have any trouble with the serfs? Any revolts?"

"They wouldn't dare. When I ride out, there's a full retinue of men-at-arms with me, just aching for trouble. First guy that doesn't tip his hat, one of the troops cleaves him from crown to fork. We use a mace on the children under four."

"Where were your men-at-arms that night up in La Cima? Was it their day off?"

"Now that's an interesting question," I said. "To be quite frank, that episode took place off the estate. The First Law of Primogeniture, sometimes called Salique Law or Napoleonic Code, says if you bring armed troops onto another duke's property, you have to pay Chain Mail Tax or be guilty of Aggravated Tort. It's all there in the Magna Carta. Look it up."

"You were a great-looking duke, down there in the snow with people spitting on you."

"Even dukes have their off moments. Here we are at the castle. If you give the password, they'll lower the portcullis for us. Tonight it's 'Arnold and St. George.' "

"Why don't we just go in?" she said. "It's cold out here."

"You can't just walk into a castle. You have to go through the routine."

"My feet are getting numb."

"It's people like you who make it hard to duke," I said, opening the door. "Are you staying for dinner?"

"Am I invited?"

"I think dukes command rather than invite. I'll have the varlet set another place."

"That's my mother you're talking about," she said.

"That's right," I said. "Sorry. Dukes don't have very good manners."

Mother and Jimbob were pretty decent about having the cook's daughter as a dinner guest. Of course, it was wartime, and prewar rules were suspended. Victoria answered up politely to all questions, even the stupid ones, and Jimbob had trouble keeping his eyes off her. She *was* pretty, no doubt about it. When Jimbob and my mother began to talk about their families—it was a social disease they both had, irritating, but not catching—Victoria listened attentively and said the right things: "Isn't that interesting!" and "My, my!" and "I hadn't known *that* before!" and "Imagine!" There had been Devereaux on hand to help Oglethorpe settle Georgia ("You know where Georgia is, don't you, dear?") and a Buel had operated an early commercial venture at Jamestown. "In sixteen-seven, if you can imagine it," Jimbob said. "Quite a while ago."

"Has your family been in America long, dear?" my mother asked her condescendingly.

"Not too long, Mrs. Arnold," Victoria answered. "By America do you mean what's now Mexico or what's now the United States?"

"Well, I suppose I mean here. Around Sagrado."

"I'll have to figure it out in my head," Victoria said. She closed an eye and mumbled something like, "Eight from fifteen, seven, borrow one," and announced, "Three hundred and forty-seven. No, forty-six. They came in August."

"Let's see," Jimbob said, looking slightly depressed. "That would be. . . ."

"Fifteen ninety-eight," she said. "Of course, this part of the country was all part of Spain then. They were just colonists. They had a king."

"Well, naturally," Jimbob said, seeming relieved.

"Nothing like Jamestown," I said, "which started out a hundred per cent American."

"I thought Jamestown was an English colony," Victoria said, "with a king."

Jimbob was becoming agitated. "But the point is," he said, waggling a finger, "the point is that this is an English-speaking country. That was the colonization that took, so to speak. The English-speaking, Jamestown colony determined the culture and language of the United States. Am I right?"

"Sí, claro," Victoria said. *"Usted tiene razón."*

"No cabe duda," I said.

"Let's all have some more chicken," said my mother, "and talk about something else."

"And don't forget the Spanish Armada," Jimbob put in.

"No, sir. I certainly won't," Victoria said.

"You know where Virginia is, don't you, dear?" I said to her.

We had some more chicken, which Excilda had cooked in herbs and wine, leaving out the chiles in deference to Jimbob, who was still recovering from chicken pox.

"You remember that girl we saw in La Cima on Old Christmas?" Victoria said suddenly.

"Oh, yes," my mother said. "Joshua told me about Old Christmas. He said it was delightful."

"Delightful?" Victoria said. "He almost got. . . ."

I kicked her under the table. "I got into the spirit of things," I said quickly. "There was plenty of carefree dancing in the streets, fireworks, Santa Clauses—very colorful. I wanted to go caroling, but Amadeo and Victoria said it would be better if I didn't. I didn't belong to the Chamber of Commerce, or something like that."

"Joshua has loved Christmas ever since he was a little boy," my mother told Victoria. "Even now the season makes his eyes fill with tears."

"I noticed that," Victoria said. "Anyway, that girl you saw there in the crowd around the. . . ."

"Around the carol singers, yes, I remember. What about her?"

"Which girl?" my mother asked.

"A girl from school. What about her, Victoria?"

"Was it that nice Amanda Sue Cloyd? You know, Joshua, I was so hoping you'd ask her to dinner."

"No, Amanda Sue went back to Texas," I said. "The whole family had to go. They struck oil on the pasture and the cows started to get sticky. As she explained it, it's bad ranching to have your oil and your cattle on the same range. The oil gets in the meat or something. Victoria, when did you see her?"

"Oh, it was about a week ago," she said. "The folks hadn't come back from Sagrado yet, and Tony and I heard a noise on the road near the house. The girl was out there with a boy, and they were trying to fix a flat in the dark. Tony went in and brought a flashlight so they could see. That's all. It was the same girl."

"What did the boy look like?"

"Spanish," she said. "He kept his face out of the light, as if he didn't want anyone to recognize him. He just looked like one of those La Cima *pachuquitos*. A lot of hair and sideburns."

"Maybe Viola's doing a little social work before she takes the veil," I said. "I guess you have to know life before you can renounce it."

My mother broke in. "I do wish you would speak English at the table, Joshua. It's unfair to leave us out of the conversation. What is a pachakeeto?"

"It's sort of the local version of a Dead End Kid. You know: broken homes, underprivileged, petty crime, standing around the pool hall whistling at girls, stealing apples off the vegetable cart."

"Killing people," Victoria said.

"Killing people. The usual things."

"I'll bet that some of your best friends are pachakeetos," Jimbob said. "You always were an infracaninophile."

"I'm willing to admit it, Mr. Buel," I said. "That's a word I've never come across in the world's great literature."

"It means 'underdog-lover,' " he said. "You ought to read more."

"I just can't seem to focus on those little bitty letters. For instance, there's this book I've been working on since Thanksgiving. I think it's a pretty good yarn, but reading it makes my head hurt. There's a boy named Dick and a girl named Jane, and they keep doing something with a ball. Every once in a while, a dog called Spot runs in barking and breaks up the action. The book doesn't say what sort of dog Spot is, but he looks like a *bouvier des Flandres* with maybe a touch of whippet."

"I think I've read that one," Victoria said. "Aren't there some people named Father and Mother in it, too?"

"Don't tell me how it comes out. I want to plow through this baby myself."

"You're really becoming unspeakable," Jimbob said.

"We have a dinner guest, Mr. Buel. Could you save the compliments for later? I get embarrassed."

"You should be embarrassed," my mother said, "behaving like this in front of this nice girl. You're making dinner very unpleasant."

"I thought this was a nice, quiet dinner," Victoria said. "At my house there are usually fourteen people at the table, all yelling at each other, and a dog begging tortillas. No, this is very pleasant, and I thank you for asking me." I decided right then that the following Monday I'd go down to the El Chivo Bookstore and buy Victoria a copy of the complete plays of Lope de Vega. She had the best natural manners I'd ever seen; it was too bad she couldn't get into Harvard.

Victoria and I helped Excilda with the dishes after dinner; my mother and Jimbob had an engagement to play bridge at the house of one of the girls, the one with the whiskers and the bad hip. Our car was up on blocks in the garage, so Amadeo drove them there in the pickup. That had been Dad's idea; Amadeo used our gas coupons because of the commuting.

"That girl," Victoria said. "What's her name? The one at La Cima."

"Viola Lopez. Her brother's an ex-*pachuco*, now trying out for sainthood. Viola says she's going to be a nun, but I don't know. I believe that she's discovered boys."

"She's not a bad-looking girl. I don't know why she has

189

to go clear to La Cima to find a boyfriend. And I know she could do better than the one I saw her with. He had that *macho* look; you know: 'Don't mess around with me 'cause I'm tough.' And ugly. Looked like somebody had chewed off his ear."

The next morning, when I'd told Chango about it, he said his mother and father had worked on Viola long enough to get her to admit she wasn't seeing Father McIlhenny at the chancery, but it was all she'd told them. "She wouldn't say where she was," he said. "She said she took long walks and thought about Saint Teresa and had mystical experiences."

"Well, that's the story," I said. "From somebody who doesn't even know her."

"She really said the guy's ear was funny?"

"She said chewed off."

"I guess we better tell Chamaco," he said. "He doesn't like to go up to La Cima, but it's in Cabezón County and it's his territory."

"You want me to call him?" I asked.

"I'll call him," Chango said. "It's my sister."

When Chango and Viola went home to lunch, Chamaco met them there, Chango told me that afternoon. He said Chamaco wasn't too rough on her—the parents were both present—but he broke her up in a few minutes.

A few days after Tarzan had put Chango in the hospital, Viola found out where he was hiding. She asked an old fighting honcho of his, who wanted the police to find Tarzan but was too chicken to tell them himself.

Tarzan had built a little shelter out of rumpsprung sofas and broken-legged kitchen tables at the dump north of Sagrado. It hadn't occurred to him to bring food, and in a short time he would have been hungry enough to start eating dead horse. Viola simply hiked out to the dump and found him there, huddled under a red-and-green davenport. She came, she said, to forgive him, and brought her rosary with her. The idea was for them to pray together; his soul had been cast adrift, and she wanted to bring him back.

Viola and Tarzan Velarde spent three chilly afternoons

under the davenport in the city dump saying Hail Marys. She brought him bean sandwiches and water, and looked for a better place to hide her prize. She felt, she told Chamaco, that it would be good practice for a future nun.

Tarzan moved into the storeroom of the old Armory building, a warm, secure hiding place which Viola cased for him. The National Guard hadn't been in it since 1941, when they were suddenly mobilized and shipped to the Philippines, where the Army felt their knowledge of Spanish would help them. (It hadn't; they were all dead, or in prison camps learning Japanese.) Tarzan scrounged blankets and a serviceable cot; Viola kept bringing food to him after he'd broken open some K-Rations and found them inedible. She prayed very hard, she said, and Tarzan prayed with her. Sometimes she went there at night for more prayers, and she told Tarzan about St. Teresa of Avila, St. Francis of Assisi and St. Phillip of Neri. She told him everything that Sister Polycarp had said about being a nun. Tarzan listened to her carefully for several weeks, nodding his head at the right times, asking her intelligent questions, relearning all the Catholic prayers of his childhood, putting on weight from the food she brought, which was heavy on starches, and turning into a proper student.

And then one night in November he left the Armory storeroom and broke into the Bottle 'n' Corkscrew Liquor Store, making off with two gallon bottles of La Voragine Sweet Vino. He drank one gallon that night, and was well into the second one when Viola arrived the next evening with a covered bowl of tripe stew. She set the bowl down on the olive drab footlocker which they used as a table, and then noticed Tarzan's eyes and the bottles. She tried to run, but he caught her ankle, tripping her, and did something to her that no amount of prayer would ever fix.

Ruined as she was—she had no doubt that ruined was the right word, and never questioned it—there was little for her to do but continue her life of ruination. The same thing happened almost every time she went to the Armory. She began to enjoy it, to look forward to it, the natural consequence of ruin, which gives you a different outlook, making evil things seem good and good things evil. When the weather got so cold that Tarzan began to shiver all night in the empty Armory, Viola gave him eleven dollars and he bought a bus ticket to La Cima, where, as might be expected, he had relatives. She bought a false mustache for him at Woolworth's, trimming it down so that it didn't look too ridiculous, and a felt cowboy hat and wool scarf at Wormser's. He wore the hat low over his right ear and, with the scarf and mustache, was unrecognizable.

He had no trouble in La Cima. He lived with a cousin who was literate and consequently wanted for forgery. Tarzan had the best credentials possible for La Cima: He was being sought for assault with a deadly weapon.

Viola told the story to the sheriff and her parents with a great deal of tears, Chango said. She'd continued to see Tarzan, but not as often. The cousin he lived with worked in Sagrado, drove in and back several times a week and gave her rides in his truck. She knew her story about instruction with Father McIlhenny wouldn't hold up forever, but she didn't care; she was a sinner, this was sin, and she wanted to do it right. Her plans were all made, she said. She was going to take a bus to El Paso and be a prostitute, there being no other path, unless it became necessary for her to go to jail for harboring a criminal. She was quite prepared for that, too.

Chamaco quieted her down and soothed the parents as much as he could, hesitantly suggesting that they take her to a doctor and get a blood test done. "He told me he'd be surprised as hell if Tarzan didn't have seven different kinds of the clap," Chango said. "You know, you'd think she'd know better."

"How do you mean?"

"Ever since I was eleven or twelve she's been praying for me: 'God, please make Maximiliano a good boy,' and that sort of stuff. She sent priests to see me. Once she fasted four days a week for a whole year, and walked barefoot out to the Guadalupe chapel in Texcoco carrying two buckets full of ten-penny nails. None of it worked. I just went on being a prick."

"I thought your desperado days were over," I said.

"Yeah, but she didn't have anything to do with it. I was gonna stop anyway. I was getting tired of Chamaco and his boys coming after me every time somebody stuck an icepick in a tire or wrote something on a wall. It got so when Chamaco didn't have anything to do he'd find me and throw me around some. He may not look it, with that belly, but he's strong. He said he'd never killed a juvenile, but he was gonna come around on my eighteenth birthday and blow a hole in me with a three-fifty-seven Magnum."

"Well, he didn't," I said.

"No, and Viola thinks it's all because of the praying. She told us it worked so well with me that she tried it on Tarzan, and it would have worked with him, too, if he hadn't got drunk that night."

"What's Chamaco going to do about him?" I asked. "If he's holed in up there in La Cima they'll need an armored division to get him out."

"I guess he's got something figured. He hasn't been looking for Tarzan all winter because he thought he was dead. Now he's real sore."

Steenie and I went to the sheriff's office after school to be deputized. We knew how it worked in the movies: You take an oath and the sheriff tosses you a badge, telling the clerk to put you on the payroll. Chamaco didn't seem happy with the idea.

"I know some foolproof come-along holds, Sheriff," Steenie told him. "You won't even need handcuffs for him. All I have to do if he gets rough is put a little pressure on and his elbow snaps."

"Jesus," said Chamaco.

"I can identify him," I said. "I got a real close look at him one day. It wouldn't be any trouble for me to pick him out of a crowd. And I know how to handle a revolver and an automatic."

"You boys are real bloodthirsty, huh?" Chamaco said.

"No, sir," said Steenie. "We just want to see justice done. I mean, if you take all of your regular deputies up there, who's going to mind the store in Sagrado? There'll be a crime wave while you're gone."

193

"If you're worried about the responsibility," I said, "I'll sign a paper."

"Let Arnold carry a gun," Steenie said. "I won't need any weapons at all. My Commando training will pay off."

"And you want me to deputize you?"

"Wouldn't that be better?" I asked. "I suppose we could make a citizen's arrest, or whatever they call it, but it would look more official with the badges. I'll just call my mother and tell her. . . ."

"Let me tell you something," Chamaco said. "Before you say one word let me tell you something."

"If you're going to say it's dangerous," Steenie began, "we already know that."

"SHUT UP!" Chamaco stood up and put on his cowboy hat. Then he went to the door and yelled, "Alfonso, come in here." A small, wiry deputy came in, chewing a toothpick. "Yes, sir, Sheriff," he said.

"Alfonso, this is Choshua M. Arnole, white male American, age seventeen. That one is William Estenopolous, white male American, age seventeen. No identifying marks or escars on him; Arnole's got a little round escar on his head. They're a couple of esquirts."

"Yes, sir," Alfonso said.

"It was Arnole found out where Velarde is."

"Yes, sir."

"Him and his buddy want me to make a couple deputies out of them and help me pick him up."

"That right?"

"That one's a Commando or something. This one's a gun-eslinger. They're real dangerous."

"Yes, sir."

"I'm going up there now and get Velarde. You keep these two esquirts here for an hour, then let 'em go home."

"You can't do this," Steenie said. "My father's a. . . ."

"I know," Chamaco said. "Your father's a taxpayer. So's yours," he said to me. "Well, they're gonna get their money's worth today. Alfonso's gonna make sure neither one of you gets killed, and when you go home your

194

mommies are gonna be glad to see you healthy and give you a big dinner and tock you in."

"Are you going to La Cima alone?" I asked. "Hadn't you better take some help?"

"Arnole," Chamaco said, "going to La Cima is the only excitement I get around here. I've been sheriff for twenty-three years, and the only thing I do almost is take care of esquirts. In twenty-three years there's only been three killings in Sagrado. Two of them were second degree—knife-fights in the cantinas—and the other one was man-eslaughter. So there's nothing to do. All I get is esquirts. The esquirts break windows and eslash tires and escare gorls and throw rocks at dogs and write dorty words on the walls. That isn't police work, that's truant-officer work. The magistrate just sends 'em home. Sometimes I get so tired of sitting around that I go out and direct traffic. Sometimes I sit and pray that a Boy Escout gets lost up in the Cordillera so I can organize a search party and get a little riding and hiking time in. And about once a year there's trouble in La Cima that's bad enough for the police to come in, and that's the times I wait for. When I go to La Cima people espit on my car and throw rocks at me. One time somebody even shot at me with a deer rifle, and broke my windshield. It's the only thing that keeps me thinking I'm a law-enforcement officer and not a social worker. And you two esquirts want to take my fun and exercise away from me. If you really want to do me a favor, go out and rob a bank or assassinate the mayor."

"I never looked at it that way, Sheriff," Steenie said. "Good luck up there."

"You esquirts want the county to buy you an ice-cream cone while you're here? It's a little service we give."

"No, thanks," I said.

"Can I call my mouthpiece?" Steenie asked. "This is a bum rap."

"Alfonso, let 'em go at four-twenty," Chamaco said, and left.

We stayed at the sheriff's office for an hour, reading the Wanted posters and fingerprinting each other. Steenie found a copy of the Criminal Code, and we tried to figure out what Tarzan might be wanted for. By stretching what we knew, we finally decided on Assault with a Deadly Weapon, Attempted Murder (First), Statutory Rape, Trespassing on Government Property, Burglary, Breaking and Entering, Possession of Liquor by a Minor, a possible charge of Draft-Dodging and Operating a Vehicle without a License. Unless he were asleep when Chamaco arrived, we guessed that he would add Resisting Arrest to the list.

At home, that night, I kept the radio turned on for news of the events in La Cima, but everything was about the war. The local radio station didn't have any news department anyway, and the reporters on *The Conquistador* either hadn't heard about Tarzan, or had lost interest in him. In Europe the countryside was thawing and we were beginning to move again, with The Bulge straightened out. The Germans had blown up all the bridges across the Rhine except one, and we had put some infantry across it. I guessed that a Nazi engineering officer was standing at attention in front of a field marshal saying, "But . . . but . . . but. . . ." You can't win 'em all, Corporal Hitler. *Jawohl*. But there was nothing about Tarzan until the paper came out the next afternoon.

Chamaco could have used some help. Not help from me and Steenie, maybe, but some. We heard what happened the next day. He took a county automobile into La Cima, turned it around and parked it heading downhill, and walked to the cousin's house. Tarzan didn't try to run; according to the report he was lying on a cot, whittling on a piece of wood with his *hojita*, when Chamaco opened the door and said, "Come on, Tarzan." Velarde came outside with him, to the single road that runs through the town, and as they started to walk toward the police car, with most of the population watching quietly, Tarzan spun around and slashed Chamaco with a knife. He had aimed for the eyes but missed, and opened a long half-moon cut across his forehead, from eyebrow to eyebrow. A great flap of flesh fell over Chamaco's eyes, and blood poured over his face and jacket. He said in a tired, bored voice, "Oh, goddamn it," stepped back and pushed the flap of forehead up with his left hand, waited until his vision cleared, and shot Tarzan in the right shoulder, at approximately the point where a duck-shooter rests the butt of his shotgun. Tarzan sat down and screamed and Chamaco stood there and watched him, holding his head together with his free hand and bleeding. Nobody came to help him or Tarzan. Nobody moved, and the tableau remained static for five or ten minutes. It was obvious, after a while, that Tarzan wasn't going anywhere, and Chamaco tried to find someone who would drive his police car back to Sagrado. The people he asked swore they didn't know how to drive. There was no help at all. And then the blue bus came rattling and jiggling into La Cima, several hours late because of gasket trouble. Chamaco and the bus driver loaded Tarzan aboard, and they made it back to town by sunset with Tarzan screaming whenever the bus hit a bump.

20

SPRING CAME and retreated several times during March and April. Robins moved in and then froze; showers turned to hail, followed by snow. *The Conquistador* did a picture page—"Sagrado Spring Fever"—with all the springtime clichés: Little boys playing marbles, early lilac blooms, free-running streams, the first sandlot base-ball game of the year. When the photographs were print-ed, two days after they were taken, there was a foot of new snow on the ground, the lilacs had turned black and nobody could find second base. Sagrado was at the right latitude for spring, but the altitude was wrong.

There were other timely and interesting stories in the newspaper. An Associated Press dispatch from Mule-shoe, Texas, ran under the headline "Former Sagrado Man Injured," and told of a John Cloyd who'd been struck down by a milk truck in Muleshoe, and was now recovering slowly from a wrenched back. We were happy to hear that he was back in business; he'd need the money to support his grandchildren. An Army public-information office release, in a later edition, reported that Pvt. Buckminster Swenson, former athletic great at De Crispin High School, had been named Recruit of the Month at Camp Chaffee, Arkansas, and had fired Marksman at the rifle range. "I knew we judged him unfairly," Steenie noted. "He's got all the makings of a corporal."

In April, a neighbor discovered the body of Mrs. De Crispin in her big, gloomy house. The coroner said it was a heart attack, not uncommon in a woman of her age—it was only eighty-seven, we learned—and he reported that she went out peacefully. None of us believed that; when she was found, lying on the pillows around her living-room cooking fire, she was holding a decorated Comanche lance, a genuine collector's item, to which were attached three old Kiowa scalps in good condition. Everyone in school was let out early for her funeral. Her will called for an Indian ceremony, but the Pueblo people around Sagrado, who had always thought of her as bad luck, wouldn't cooperate. Marcia's father read the service, the standard passage from the *Book of Common Prayer,* and an eloquent abridgment of Chief Joseph's speech of surrender to General Howard and Colonel Miles at the Bear Paw. "Hear me, my chiefs. I have fought; but from where the sun now stands, I will fight no more, forever." We thought of it as a decent and touching gesture, Episcopal in spirit if not in content, as Marcia described it later, tearfully.

Romeo Bonino came to the funeral, too, and admitted great sadness at the loss of his early patroness. "She might have supported me for years if I'd had just a little Indian blood," he said. "On the other hand, where would art be today if Michelangelo had been a Comanche? These things must balance out, somehow."

With Romeo was his new model, a large, smiling redhead named Gwendolyn, who, he told us, had been a cherished figure in all the ateliers on Royal Street in New Orleans before the high water content in the Louisiana air began to give her the constant sensation of drowning. "We've got her pretty well dried out now, haven't we, Gwendolyn?"

"Yes, dawlin'," she said, squeezing his arm.

"Say 'superb,' " he said.

"Supabe."

"Say 'bird.' "

"Bade."

"Now there's an accent I can live with," he said. "And God, can she cook! What was that thing you did last night?"

"That wasn't anything but *gumbo aux herbes,* sugah," she said. "That's chahld's play. Wait'll Ah cook you a *doberge.*"

"Ever hear anything like that in your life, Josh?" he asked me. "Soft and sweet like honey. Josh, when are you coming over for dinner?"

"You call me when she cooks red beans and rice," I said, "and I'll bring a bottle of claret, no matter what Dad says."

Gwendolyn began to complain of the cold—a lot of people from the South, I've noticed, tend to start freezing when the temperature drops below 85 degrees—and Romeo escorted her from graveside to his waiting truck outside the cemetery.

"I think that one might turn out to be permanent," I said. "That Creole cooking may just do it."

"She didn't have a brassiere on," Marcia said. "Did you notice?"

"You mean she's a brazen hussy?" Steenie suggested.

"Well, it's just plain lewd. And at a funeral, too."

"It's too bad she didn't come in her modeling costume," I said, "wearing nothing but a fixed stare. I think you're still put out that Romeo wouldn't let you model for him."

"Great sculpture requires a bosom," Steenie said. "Look at Venus de Milo."

"Look at all those big Dutch farm girls by Rubens," I suggested.

"You look at them," Marcia said, pouting. "All those glands get you in trouble when you're about forty."

The cemetery was on a low hill north of the town, with a fine view for the corpses, if they were interested, of the Cordillera and the valley. Patches of snow still lay in the shadows, and the mountaintops were pure white. In the valley, trees were starting to green, but they were bare in Sagrado. It was such a pretty town, even in the last of winter, the soft tans and grays seeming to grow naturally from the earth. Nothing soared, nothing stuck out. Even the school, clearly visible from the hill we stood on, was partly obscured by leafless trees, and gave the foreign-looking town a comforting, American note, like a Nebraska railroad depot.

"How many people in Sagrado?" I asked Steenie as we walked slowly down from the cemetery.

"I don't know," he said. "Seven or eight thousand. My father said it hasn't grown much since he's been here, that's since nineteen twenty-five. He was the second Anglo doctor in Sagrado, he told me once. He couldn't get used to being called an Anglo; said it was an insult to a Greek. Something to do with politics. The population was almost all Spanish, then. Both Senators were Spanish; the kids in school were still having a bad time with English."

"It'll get bigger after the war," Marcia said. "You watch. All those guys will come home and want to change things. They'll pave all the streets."

"God, I hope not," I said. "I love it just the way it is. In a place like this, you feel you can. . . ."

"Hide," she said. "I know. Hide from a war, hide from cities, hide from people scrambling around, hide from little brick houses with front porches, hide from rich people who sling their money around like a baseball bat. Oh!" She touched my arm. "I don't mean you. Your father's not like that. He used to come here because he liked to get away from Mobile in the summer. You know, my father used to play chess with yours. Mr. Arnold would come to the rectory sometimes and play, or they'd walk down to the Plaza and sit on a bench and play there."

"I know," I said. "He always told me he was going to come here for good when he retired. He was going to do what Ulysses did, he said—walk inland with an oar on

200

his shoulder, and settle in a place where nobody knew what the oar was for."

On Zebulon Pike Street we watched an old man with a string of burros pass by slowly and fragrantly. Each burro carried an impossible load of piñon wood, cut into fireplace lengths, and the old man talked to them softly in Spanish, threatening them gently with excommunication and mutilation.

"His son's probably working in a plant in Phoenix," Steenie said, "and I'll bet his grandson's in the Army. When the war's over, they're not going to be interested in the wood business any more. Pretty soon there aren't going to be any more burros, except in zoos, and everybody in Sagrado's going to have central heating. They're going to tear down all the adobe houses and put up new plastic models. First guy they hear speaking Spanish, they're going to take away his membership in the Rotary Club, and make him turn in his Moose tooth, or whatever it is."

We bought a copy of *The Conquistador* on the Plaza, before we separated. The Russians were on the outskirts of Berlin; there was no word on Hitler. "He's probably up there on a mountain peak in Birches Garden, or whatever they call it, making a speech to the mountain goats," Steenie mused.

"When they catch him," Marcia said, "they ought to turn him over to the chief rabbi and let him perform a big public circumcision, using the top off a sardine can. I think the rabbi ought to get real drunk first, so his hand shakes."

"Well, the war hasn't changed everything," I said. "You're still the sweet little girl you always were. I'm surprised the dogs don't bark at you. They always bark at Frankenstein's monster and the Mummy."

"I just wish President Roosevelt were still around to see it, that's all," she said. His death had hit all of us hard, two weeks earlier, and we were still trying to get used to the sound of "Jesus H. Truman Christ," which didn't seem to have the right ring to it. "Why don't you two lunks join something, and make me proud of you?

You're both old enough. If the Germans are shot, there's still the Japanese."

"I've got this low back pain," Steenie said, "in the region of the sacrum, which has been bothering me for years. I threw it out in Commando training, I think. There's nothing for me in the Army. I'm 4-F."

"Not me," I said. "I'm joining up. The Coast Guard. Shallow-draft boats for me; something a torpedo will go *under*, not into. Of course, I'd like to get a B.A., and maybe a little work toward my Ph.D., before I enlist. There's no place for the unskilled in the modern Coast Guard."

"As soon as the war in Europe is over, I'm going to give myself to the first man in uniform I see," Marcia said. "It'll be my personal contribution to the war effort, a generous, Christian act."

"You'd better put on a few inches up here," Steenie cautioned her. "Those guys in France and Italy might have gotten a little choosy."

"A lot of them are going to come back with some interesting diseases," I told her. I stroked my hair back with the heel of my hand. "Hunner' per cent. Ludwig van Beethoven."

"They can cure that now," Steenie said. "My father told me all about it; some sort of distilled bread mold. Takes three days."

"Have they got a cure for Creeping Crud or Singapore Foot yet? I hear that's pretty common, too. Ninety-three point six per cent of all corporals between eighteen and forty-two have it, I read somewhere. Your fingernails turn to cellophane, and these green lumps break out all over your. . . ."

"Can't scare me," Marcia said.

Steenie left us, and I walked Marcia home. It was pleasant to walk with the snow melted, and we held hands and scuffed our shoes on the clay sidewalks, doing a lot of pointed inhaling to sniff the first scents of spring, which were largely imaginary.

"I'm going to Barnard, I think," she said as we reached the rectory. "My mother went there. I'm scared to death. I'm so stupid, and it'll break my poor father."

"You'll do fine," I said. "You've already got a head start on the New York girls in categories like blunt talk and dirty words."

"Are you really going to Harvard? I don't think anybody from De Crispin has ever gone to Harvard."

"That's always been a pitiful little dream of my mother's," I said. "It's more likely that I'll go to the University of Alabama. It's more my speed. They have forty fraternity houses and one classroom, where they teach the History of the Confederacy. They have a good record, though. They haven't been guilty of education since eighteen thirty-one."

"Well, where do you *want* to go? Don't you care?"

"Barnard's part of Columbia, isn't it?"

"That's right."

"I want to go to Columbia."

Marcia puckered up like a little girl, and kissed me on the cheek. "Herbie Abernathy," she said, "I think you're the nicest boy on our whole block." Then she ran inside.

Amadeo met me at the door when I got home, and gripped me on the arm. "Come in, boy," he said. "Come in. We got bad news." Excilda was screaming and crying in the kitchen. Jimbob was on the telephone, yelling over a bad connection. My mother was in the living room, sitting stiffly, unnaturally, in a soft chair, her hands covering her ears, her eyes closed. The telegram, that goddamn telegram that turns up in all the war movies, was lying on the coffee table.

Dr. Temple gave her a shot of something a few hours later, and when she slumped over we carried her to bed. "Come to see me in a day or two," he said to me. "There's something the matter here, I think." I told Amadeo and Excilda to go home; there was nothing they could do. When they had left, Jimbob came to me and put his hand, in manly fashion, on my shoulder, and said, "I lost my father, too. I know how you feel."

"One favor," I said. "Just one favor. Please." I found a five and a one in my billfold, and gave it to him. "Spend tonight at La Posta Hotel, will you? If this isn't enough, you can charge it to Dad's account."

I telephoned Marcia and Steenie, and told them.

Then, making sure that my mother was still asleep, I walked down to Romeo's, and told him, too. He hugged me, and said, "Oh, shit. Always the best. Every goddamn time." Gwendolyn gave me a cup of coffee, and I walked home again.

When she awakened, late the next afternoon, my mother put her hands over her ears again and didn't move. I discovered she hadn't bothered to get up to go to the bathroom, so I called Dr. Temple again. I signed something he gave to me, and he and a nurse helped her to an ambulance. "This is a very strange arrangement," he said. "Please come to my office in a few days. Call me at any time. Don't worry about Tsigmoont; he's not answering the telephone any more." Mr. Gunther came; I showed him what I'd signed, and he said it was all right. Just temporary. Paolo Bertucci telephoned from Mobile.

"God, Josh. God, I'm sorry. Jesus, why did it have to be him?"

"I don't know, Mr. Bertucci. It just was."

"Everything's all right down here at the plant. We're closed today, in . . . memory. Goddammit. The war's almost *over*, for Christ's sake. What was it, do you know?"

"The telegram said a mine. It didn't say where."

"Goddamn filthy bastards. Jesus, I hope it was a German mine, not an Italian mine. I'm going to change my goddamn name." He told me some more about the plant. "Lawyers all over the goddamn place," he went on. "Little guys from the War Production Board scurrying around, looking worried. Hell, we're not going to miss a beat. Listen, who the hell is James R. Buel?"

"He's, ah, a family friend. Why?"

"The guy called me yesterday. Said he was calling from your house out there. Is that right?"

"Yes, he's staying here."

"Well, he told me about your father. Then he started asking me a lot of dumb questions about money. Aren't you and your mother getting the check every month?"

"Yes, sir, as far as I know. Five hundred a month, isn't that it?"

"Yeah, well, this idiot seemed like he was awful worried it was going to stop. I mean, why the hell should it stop? And what the hell does he care? I was so goddamn upset by what he told me, about Frank, I don't know what the hell I said to him. I think I told him to go screw himself. Was that all right?"

"Yes, sir. That would have been the right thing to say."

"Yeah, well. Okay. Look, are you and your mother coming down? I don't know what Frank's will says, but you're probably joint owners of a shipyard. I mean, I can run the son of a bitch all right, but we got to have a board meeting pretty soon."

"Mother's in the hospital, Mr. Bertucci. She took the news very hard. Why don't you just go ahead and have the board meeting without us?"

"Your mother. Christ almighty! I'm sorry, Josh. Well, hell, I'll just go ahead and be acting president like before until the lawyers tell me what to do. You take care of yourself, for Christ's sake. This goddamn war."

"Mr. Bertucci, can you send me some money?"

"Some money? Hell, yes. I'm up to my ass in things I can do. How much do you need?"

"I don't know. There's some things I might have to do, and I'll need some money. How about . . ." I mentioned the biggest amount I could think of. ". . . two thousand dollars?"

"I'll get a check off to you. Stay loose up there, Josh. Jesus, I'm so sorry."

I didn't go back to school. They sent me a note, saying I wouldn't graduate with the Class of 1945, and I sent the School Board a note saying I was sorry. Mr. Gunther telephoned me the next day, and said, "I got your note, Joshua. I'm president of the School Board."

"I didn't know that," I said. "I'm still sorry."

"We discussed it this morning. You have excellent grades, and in the opinion of the faculty you have exercised a beneficial moral influence on the student body."

"I think they're talking about somebody else."

"Be that as it may," he continued, "we'll award the diploma anyway. One of your teachers was at the meet-

205

ing, and spoke *very* forcefully in your behalf. A Mrs. Loughran. I, ah, did the same, I may as well admit. Could you come to my office? Right now?"

Jimbob Buel was in the office when I got there; he hadn't been back to the house since the night we got the telegram. He looked fit, the son of a bitch.

"Mr. Buel," Gunther began, "has made what I consider to be an extremely arresting offer. An offer, I may say, that is fraught with. . . ."

"Your mother's very sick, Joshua." Jimbob said. "Broken up. She's going to need care. She's a very sensitive little lady, your mother."

"Mr. Buel seems to be correct. I've talked to Dr. Temple at some length. She appears to be quite ill, a sort of breakdown, caused no doubt by grief and worry."

"No doubt," Jimbob said.

"Mr. Buel, who has, he assures me, your best interest in mind, has suggested that he be named your guardian since your mother is, for all practical purposes, not available at the present time to act in a parental capacity."

I glanced over at Jimbob. He looked composed and elegant in his old Virginia tweeds, and his expression would have been almost pious if he hadn't been licking his lips.

"Do I *have* to have a guardian?"

"No," Gunther said. "No, you don't. There hasn't been probate of your father's will yet—I spoke to his attorney in Mobile this morning before the School Board meeting —but as of now, you are the only member of the family with any capacity for executive action. You are . . . seventeen?"

"Yes, sir. I'll be eighteen next month."

"Do you remember our previous talk, about the document your father sent you? I discussed emancipation."

"I remember."

"We can arrange for a partial emancipation with no trouble whatsoever. You will lose your minority status in certain matters, and there will be no need for a guardian. The court and I can guide you with respect to legal questions."

206

"That boy needs an adult hand," Jimbob said. "I'd be ashamed to face his dear mother if I allowed . . . Mr. Gunther, as an intimate friend of Francis and Ann Arnold, as their oldest friend. . . ."

"My father hated your guts, Mr. Buel. No, that isn't true. He thought you were some kind of butterfly. I think he even felt sorry for you. You've been mooching off him for almost a year, now. Why don't you go see those people in Wisconsin and mooch off them for a while?"

"That's a lie. That's nothing but a hideous and childish lie. Mr. Gunther, I implore you. To think. To think of letting the future of an important Southern shipyard get into the hands of a boy!"

"Ah," said Mr. Gunther. "Ah, yes. The shipyard. I'm so glad you brought that up. What's it worth, do you suppose, Mr. Buel?"

Jimbob didn't hesitate. "Why, I'm sure that shipyard could liquidate right now for three million seven."

"Joshua," Gunther said. "I have the necessary papers right here, and Judge Chavez said he'd be in chambers until three. Of course, you still won't be able to vote, or consume beverage alcohol, but. . . ."

As we walked across the street to the courthouse, he said, "You know, your father once told me I was a pompous horse's ass. Well, perhaps I am, but I still know how to have fun, and this has been fun. Who is that man, really?"

"He's a friend of the family's. He really is. I've known him all my life."

"I'll never understand the South," Mr. Gunther said.

21

AMALIE LEDOUX TOOK the train to Albuquerque and the bus to Sagrado. She had all the papers ready; I signed them with my new emancipated signature, and immediately things seemed a lot less complicated.

"I'll get you a good price for it, Josh," she said, "but I don't see how you and Ann can bear to part with that old house."

"Amalie, there's nothing in that old house I like except a bathtub with gold lion's feet."

She went to the hospital to see my mother and cried a little when she came back. "She doesn't seem quite *right*, if you know what I mean, but she's sure not as bad as I thought. One thing she said was now that the war's over in Europe, Frank ought to be coming home pretty soon. I didn't know *what* to say to that, so I just kept my mouth shut for a change. Then she looked at me and said, 'No he isn't either, and who do I think I'm kidding?'"

"That's the sort of thing that makes Dr. Temple pleased with himself. He calls it 're-establishing contact with external data' or something. You know, it was her idea to sell the Mobile house and stay here. She said Mobile was too damp and dreary. If that isn't clear thinking, I don't know what is."

Amalie fixed herself a bourbon and poked around the house. She found it hard to believe it was made of mud.

"I guarantee it's mud," I said. "If you built one of these in Mobile it would melt in two weeks."

When she finished her drink, she said, "Show me around. I've never been in the West before. And the air! So clear!"

"Put on your walking shoes," I advised her. "Bring a jacket. We have a special tour for flatlanders and swamp rats."

Amadeo loaned me his pickup, and I drove her to the place Romeo Bonino had showed me. It was a cool, sweet-smelling afternoon. A spring rain had released all the spicy fragrances the ground had held during the winter, and the thin air was like perfume. "There it is," I said, when I stopped the truck. "Teta Peak, the thirteen thousand, three hundred and forty-second highest mountain in the world."

She rocked back slightly on her heels and looked up at it. "Mountains make me dizzy," she said. "That one looks just like a. . . ."

"Yes," I said quickly. "It does, a little."

"What does 'Teta Peak' mean? It sounds so romantic."

"It means, ah, Bosom Mountain."

"It means 'Titty Peak,' and you know it. Your father told me about it once. What are you trying to do? Shield me from the vulgar world?"

She wasn't a very good climber—I hadn't been, either, when I first got to Sagrado—but she was game, and we made it to Romeo's sculpture grove. The great heads excited her. "They're magical," she said. "It's something God would do."

"I think that remark would make Romeo feel very humble," I said. "He says he does it to beautify Nature; Nature disappoints him sometimes, so he fixes it up. He says it's the poor man's Mount Rushmore."

"They're so lifelike. Who are they?"

We wandered from head to head, and tried to identify them. "Romeo carves heads of people he admires, he says. No charge. Here's Leon Trotsky. He pointed him out to me one time."

"Is your friend a Communist?"

"No, I don't think so. He's got a head of Robert Taft

up here too, somewhere. That's Marian Anderson. There's President Roosevelt. Garibaldi's further up. Winston Churchill, Dante, Jefferson Davis."

"Imagine!"

"Haile Selassie over there. The guy with the nose is Artur Schnabel, he said. A piano player. Joe Louis. Socrates—he had to guess at that one. Humphrey Bogart. I don't know who this one . . . oh, my God."

A fresh stone, with no streaks of dirt from the melted snow, the neck deep in the spongy ground, stood under a spruce. It was my father's head, the stone eyes staring out over the broken landscape toward the cordillera.

"That's Frank!" Amalie said. "That's Frank Arnold!"

"I know. It's a new one. He must have rolled it up here alone, just a few days ago." My eyes filled with tears; there was nothing I could do to stop them. "Isn't that a hell of a thing?"

Later, we sat together on the hillside and watched the colors change on the cordillera foothills as the sun turned the world pink and purple.

"I loved your father," she said. "I don't mean just love like a good friend. I mean I'd have hopped into bed with him if he'd just winked at me. I was crazy about him."

"Amalie, please don't talk like that."

"No, I will. I want to tell you. He knew I loved him, and he could have made me feel like a two-dollar, sateen-dress, Bourbon Street whore if he'd laughed at me, but he never did. Nothing ever happened. He just went on being nice and protective to your mother. Protective. That's what used to make me so mad. Her daddy kept her wrapped up in tissue paper like a Wedgwood egg cup until she got married, and Frank went right on caring for the heirloom. One of these days you men are going to realize that underneath the crinoline and the dotted swiss and the lacy pantaloons and the delicate talk, Southern women are tough as a bunch of gawdamn railroad spikes. Well, the tissue paper's off your mama now, and don't try to tell me she broke. She just chipped. She'll be all right. The women are tougher than the men. If you don't believe me, look at Jimbob. Where is he, by the way?"

"He went up to Wisconsin to see some people named Hackenschmidt," I said. "His welcome finally wore out. The man that works for us drove him down to Albuquerque to put him on the train. He said he looked four hundred years old."

She brushed the pine needles off her behind, and we started down the slope. "Little Courtney Ann Conway's getting married to that numbskull Gagnier boy next month," she said. "I hope you're not too broken up."

I tried to remember what Corky looked like. Small, with honey hair and blue eyes. Brown eyes?

Mr. Gunther finally ran out of things for me to sign, and let me take the morning off to graduate from high school. Steenie's low back pain had mysteriously disappeared on his eighteenth birthday, and the Draft Board took note of it officially. "I demanded a rehearing," he said. "I insisted on Habeas Corpus. It was like talking to a brick wall."

"That's great talk for an ex-Commando," Marcia told him. "I knew you were chicken, ever since you refused to get inside that dead horse, the way Josh did."

"I can always malinger," he said. "I'll bet I can malinger better than any guy in the Army. I can talk the language all right. 'Sergeant, I wonder if I could be excused from latrine duty this morning. I think I'm coming down with erysipelas.' "

"You come back with a medal, William Stenopolous, or I'll tell everybody about the time you wet your pants."

Chango enlisted. Parker was drafted. I was deferred because I was a shipyard owner, or something like that. I telephoned Bertucci, just to make sure that the yard could get by without me. "We'll struggle along," he said. "I mean, you're a good kid, and technically you're my boss, but what in the goddamn hell do you know about building boats, when you come right down to it, for Christ's sake?"

A sailor named Boudreau came to the house one afternoon in early June, almost the first Negro I'd seen since I came to Sagrado. He said he was on his way from Portsmouth to San Diego, and thought he'd stop by to pay his respects.

I dug the illuminated manuscript out of a file and showed it to him. "Did you do this?" I asked him.

"Yes, sir," he said. "I did it for Commander Arnold. We both got a big kick out of it."

"Come on in and have some coffee," I said. I had a hard time getting him to sit down with me. He kept thinking "Mobile, Alabama," and looking around for a burning cross. "Why don't you forget that," I said. "Out here, we're just a couple of Anglos."

He told me the ship had hit the mine at night, about fifty miles off the coast of Portugal. It went down by the bows in ten minutes, with sixty per cent of the ship's company. "It was fast, man. It was really fast. Nobody was expecting anything like that. There wasn't any mine field 'way out there. The Navy figures one of them broke loose and drifted. Just a piece of luck."

After a long argument, he agreed to stay for dinner, and Excilda made rabbit stew with corn and chile in it. We had a glass of brandy afterwards, and he spent the night. He was calmer in the morning, but still glanced around nervously until Amadeo and I put him on the bus. At the post office, the Navy recruiting chief said two years was the minimum, so I took the two years.

It was going to be a green summer in Sagrado. The rains had been good, not heavy but frequent, and the valley would be lush by August. The war was over, or half of it was, and there was something satisfying about moving west with the rest of the troops.

Marcia came down just before the bus pulled out. She was red-eyed from studying; somehow she'd got the idea that Barnard had impossibly high academic standards, and she was spending the summer with her books. She came into the bus, ignoring the whistles from the other recruits, and kissed me good-by.

"When can you be back here? The very earliest."

"I don't know. Boot camp's about two months. I think they let you have a week off after that."

"You come back here, then. You get back here in two months, and I'll keep my eyes closed until then."

"What do you mean?"

"You're going to be the first man in uniform I see,"

she said, "and you better not come back with any 'hunner' per cent.'" She put her mouth to my ear, and deepened her voice. "Or you'll get your ass blowed off."

The bus sped south and left the plateau for the desert. The driver told us we could open the windows and get a breeze, if we thought we were men enough. The boy next to me struggled with the catch while I pushed, and we managed to raise it a few inches.

"Thanks," I said. We shook hands. "I'm Arnold, Joshua M." We had already found out the Navy preferred the names backward.

"Romero, Eladio P."

"Are you from Sagrado?"

He turned in the seat and pointed to the receding cordillera with his chin. "Río Conejo."

We rode in silence for a while. "San Diego," he said. "That's on the ocean, *verdad?*"

"Right on the ocean."

"I never seen the ocean. I never even been out of the county before. What's it look like?"

I said: "It's the color of the sky."

Bestselling

Classics

Here's a selection of the finest in literature from Pocket Books.